The Lost Letter

—

A LOVE STORY

Donnie Stevens

The Lost Letter

© 2013

Donnie Stevens

ISBN: 978-1-936553-27-3

This book is a work of fiction.
Names, characters and incidents are products
of the author's imagination. Any similarity to actual
people and/or events is purely coincidental.

Warwick House Publishers
720 Court Street
Lynchburg, Virginia 24504

Dedicated to my son, Justin, and his bride, Jennifer.
Thank you for the many special moments
and smiles you bring into my life.

PROLOGUE

There are no valid statistics on the volume of mail lost by the US Postal Service each year. They do, however, have mail recovery centers set up in Atlanta, Saint Paul and San Francisco to facilitate the challenge of trying to sort the millions of pieces of mail sent to them each year, called dead mail, and get it delivered to its designated recipients. A lot of lost mail is simply put in wrong boxes or people move and leave no forwarding address or incorrect addresses are given.

Often in the news we hear about unusual or untimely mail delivery. In 2010 a letter mailed 100 years ago from the maiden voyage of the *Titanic* was found. The letter, written by a young doctor to his mother, had been mailed from Cobh, known as Queensbury, the last port the *Titanic* visited before continuing its journey on the ill-fated voyage. The doctor didn't survive but his 100-year-old letter did.

Lost love letters have always intrigued me. A glimpse at someone's heartfelt letter written to a significant other, decades ago, captures my imagination and leaves me longing to know the outcome. Did the undelivered letter make a noteworthy difference? Could it have changed someone's life if it had been received?

Occasionally, we are privileged to learn how lost love letter stories unfold. A couple living in Brooklyn Center, Minnesota, recently received a letter sixty years late. It was the proposal letter sent by a US Army serviceman to his sweetheart. He had married her anyway while on military leave.

In 1993, a young French girl and British boy attending school together in England sparked a romance that lasted for six years but ended when a letter was misplaced. After finding the letter ten years later behind a fireplace mantle, they made contact and their reunion led to marriage.

And then there's the story of a lady I'll call Trudy, whom I met through a longtime friend in Lynchburg, Virginia. Hearing of my interest in lost letters, Trudy shared with me the letter she received in May of 2010. The envelope was postmarked August 15, 1975. After reading it, I knew there was a tale longing to be told. With her permission, this is her letter's story.

CHAPTER 1
August 1975

Seventeen-year-old Richard Vanderveer sat on a cot in a homeless shelter in Utrecht, Netherlands. With his elbows on his knees, his hands clasped and head bowed, he had nowhere to go and no one to turn to as he sought how to get his life together.

Two days earlier, gripped in his despair, he had packed all the clothes he could in a duffel bag, left school, and thumbed a ride to the train station in Groningen to buy a ticket to somewhere. Where, he didn't yet know.

He finally chose Utrecht because it seemed the place farthest away, or maybe it was the last destination listed on the ticket board. For eleven hours he stared through the dusty, smoke-stained window watching nothing, listening to train wheels squeal while ignoring the chatter of passengers who got on and off the train at numerous stops along the way. He was angry and hurt, and all he wanted to do was get away and hide where no one could find him.

With only the worn, leather duffel bag holding the few clothes he had packed, a writing tablet, and a photograph of a girl taken weeks earlier in a photo booth in a Woolworth's Department Store in Buena Vista, Virginia, he had but one thing on his mind. And that was how to get back to the States to the girl who had captured his heart.

His life as it had been was finished. Richard was determined to show the whole world, including his father, that he was his own man. He could make his own decisions and choose his own destiny. He would work hard, day and night, and save every guilder until he could afford to travel back to the States to be with her.

Meanwhile, he needed to let her know what had happened, where he was and how to get in touch with him. Desperate to hear her voice, he knew her words would make everything all right. He reached into the duffel bag, found his writing tablet and pen and moved over to the cot under the one light bulb in the dimly lit room of the shelter. He stared at the photo and thought of Trudy for a long while. Then he began pouring out his hurt and anguish on the page, knowing she would understand and call to comfort him.

After reading what he had written, Richard folded the sheet of paper, hoping Trudy would read into his intentions and call as soon as she got the letter. Would she trust his decision to leave home and work until he could save enough money to come back to the States to be with her? He had to get his message to Trudy and let her know what was going on or she would worry. No one knew where he was or how to get in touch with him and he had no intention of letting anyone else know.

Walking from the shelter house porch, he strolled down *Gaplaveide Straat* to the *Postkantoor* inside the *Markplein*. He asked the *postmeester* the fastest way to mail his letter. The man behind the counter suggested *luchtpost*. Richard purchased a *witte*-envelope bordered with red and blue stripes. He stuffed the letter inside, licked and folded the flap, then pressed the seal tightly. Carefully and clearly, he wrote Trudy's name and address on the envelope, wanting to make sure it would be delivered correctly. From his shirt pocket he pulled out a strip of glittering hearts he had picked up at the floral shop where he had just gotten a job, and pasted one on the back flap of the envelope. Richard gave his letter to the *postmeester* and paid with a guilder. He watched him stamp the word *luchtpost* and date, August 15, 1975, on it. He asked how long his letter would travel before reaching Fayetteville, North Carolina. "Maybe five days at most," the man told him.

That evening a mailbag tagged *luchtpost* was picked up in Utrecht. Overnight it was hauled to the Amsterdam post office. The next morning the mail was sorted and Richard's letter was added to a bag of mail marked *United States Mail*. At noon on August 16th, the bag was sent to the Amsterdam Airport and put on a KLM flight to London. After it arrived in London, it was transferred and scheduled to a Pan Am flight leaving for JFK Airport in New York the next morning.

The bag arrived at JFK mid-afternoon on the 17th and was sent through customs for inspection and then to the airport post office at 250 N. Boundary Road in Jamaica, New York. There it was sorted and regrouped with mail bound for Fayetteville, North Carolina, then sent back to the airport terminal and scheduled on a nighttime Piedmont Airlines flight. It arrived later that night in Fayetteville. The next morning it was loaded on a postal truck with other bags of mail and hauled to the post office at 5400 Ramsey Street in Fayetteville. Once the mail was sorted, instructions were noted it needed to be forwarded to an address in Lynchburg, Virginia. On the morning of August 19th, it finally arrived by Piedmont Airlines in Lynchburg, and was sent to the post office on Odd Fellows Road. The bag of mail was dumped on a counter and sorted and then put in post office boxes or grouped in route trays to be delivered by carriers. The mail would be delivered that day, except for the one envelope that had fallen, unnoticed, into a crack behind the sorting counter.

Seventeen-year-old Trudy raced to the front porch when she saw the mail carrier walking away. Today, every day, always at this same time, she watched and waited for him. Having moved to Lynchburg two weeks ago, she was disheartened and hurting and had no friends to confide in. She longed to hear from the boy she loved. Two weeks earlier, before leaving Fayetteville, she had written a five-page letter to Richard, pouring out her heartfelt emotions about the trauma that had suddenly shattered her life. Would this day be the one she had so anxiously awaited, knowing Richard's handwritten words would console her and inform her as to how he was going to make everything all right? She held her breath while reaching into the mailbox.

Pulling the mail from the box, she saw a couple of cards for her mother and a letter forwarded from Fayetteville. Her heart soared with hope but immediately faltered when she realized the letter she had mailed to Richard was returned to her, the words UNABLE TO DELIVER—RETURN TO SENDER stamped in red ink on the envelope.

CHAPTER 2
May 2010

Glancing at the microwave clock after eating her usual breakfast of Go Lean cereal, wheat toast with homemade strawberry jam and coffee, Trudy was relieved to see that it was just 6:30. She had enough time for her two-mile morning walk before going to work, but this time she chose the treadmill in the garage to avoid the high humidity outside.

Clipping on her iPod and fitting the earpiece, Trudy stepped onto the treadmill and set the speed at 3.0, at an incline of 2 and began walking. This morning the music from her favorite seventies downloads did little to soothe her.

Recently, troubling thoughts burdened her, day and night, making sleep impossible. She'd lain awake, staring at the ceiling, trying to figure out what to do about her broken marriage. At a time in their life when she and Kenny should be enjoying the fruits of their labor and living the dream like most middle-aged couples do, they found themselves separated, going on fifteen months. Kenny had been in Iraq for a year and would return home in two weeks. She was just as uncertain about what to do now as she had been when he left a year ago.

Maybe she expected too much, and perhaps it was normal for a marriage to go stale after twenty-four years. Or maybe she needed to accept the fact that yesterday was gone and relationships change as people get older and she just needed to make the most of what life had dealt her.

Whatever the reason, she had ignored the warning signs that were now so obvious. Conversations with Kenny were less frequent and had turned quieter, suggestions often became debates, and disagreements escalated more frequently into arguments. When Trudy did sit down with Kenneth and talk to him seriously about them, he listened, but in no time they were back into the same old rut. She figured this was how people lived after a quarter century of marriage.

When her mother noticed that something was wrong, she questioned Trudy, asking if she and Kenny were having problems. At first Trudy gave her short answers trying to ignore the inevitable. Eventually, Trudy sat down and had a mother-daughter talk. Trudy told her how bad things had gotten. Her mother listened but only advised Trudy to remember what had made her fall in love with Kenneth in the first place.

Maybe their marriage counselor was right. They simply needed to listen to each other and take time to do more together. When they both still had their full-time jobs, she as a teacher and Kenneth a Virginia State Trooper, they had always found time for sharing, especially while their daughter, April, lived at home. Four years ago, April left for college and Trudy started working endless hours with the FEW (Further Education for Women) Foundation, a non-profit organization she helped charter to support girls in obtaining scholarships for college. At the time Kenneth had been preparing for retirement and was training hundreds of extra hours to get certified to set up emergency responder units in community volunteer fire and rescue departments. Both were passionate about the career opportunities they hoped to pursue full-time once they retired. They supported each other's efforts wholeheartedly.

Shortly after retiring, Trudy was promoted to president of the FEW Foundation, and Kenneth became a partner in an emergency responder training business he helped create. They had accomplished their retirement career goals, but found themselves more engrossed with their new career choices than with each other. Trudy's schedule demanded her to be in an office all day or on the road somewhere at night, promoting the Foundation to clubs and businesses to garner their support. Kenneth's training schedule often kept him out late at night. He traveled a lot on weekends to train out-of-area volunteer responders.

Trudy didn't notice something was wrong when the romance in their lives started to dwindle. They no longer planned long weekend excursions together for intimate time as they used to. Their lovemaking became less frequent and it was no longer playful and passionate.

Trudy wasn't sure how or when their closeness started crumbling. Spending time together became a chore because they just couldn't get their schedules to cooperate. Eventually, Kenneth started complaining about her working too much, while she complained to him about not taking time for them to do anything together. Nevertheless, she admitted to herself that she was just as guilty of finding excuses as he was.

Long ago were the weekends she'd sat in a boat on Smith Mountain Lake at midnight, wrapped in a blanket, drinking coffee from a thermos to stay warm while Kenny fished. She didn't miss a chance to be with him because she felt it was important. And Kenneth used to never miss a chance to go with her on a weekend excursion when she had to attend educational seminars for her new career accreditation. While she worked, Kenneth was in charge of finding a special place for them to dine at night. He often discovered romantic, dimly lit restaurants tucked away in the city. She loved his surprises.

Feeling energized, Trudy moved the speed up faster on the treadmill.

Maybe it was the nitpicking or nagging that Kenny accused her of. Or the complaints and sarcastic remarks he let slip that had eroded their tolerance for each other. One evening after she'd prepared a rare, full-course dinner, Kenny came home three hours late without calling. She had gotten mad and was dumping it when he walked through the door. He claimed he had told her he'd be late. She scolded him for being inconsiderate and not valuing her time and efforts. Their conversation had turned cynical and harsh. A few minutes later they were in a full-fledged argument until Trudy threw a handful of plates on the floor, breaking all of them and screaming how miserable he made her. When Kenneth started to get the broom and dustpan to help clean up, she told him to leave her alone, she didn't need his help, and she was better off without him. He stared at her silently with anger or hurt, she wasn't sure which, but when he stormed out, she thought about what she had said and collapsed to the floor, sobbing.

After a week of ignoring each other and sleeping in separate bedrooms, they sat down to talk. They agreed they both wanted and needed a time out.

The separation was almost too easy. They agreed to temporarily live separately until they could figure out what they wanted. Friends suggested they each hire an attorney while separating. When the agreements were written up, they were nearly identical. Her attorney advised her that she was being overly generous.

Watching Kenny quietly pack and load his pickup to leave was a shock Trudy hadn't anticipated. She almost caved in to her panic to stop him and plead with him to stay. But knowing he was hurting and as disappointed as she was at how badly their marriage had deteriorated, she knew he needed time to make up his own mind or their efforts to reconcile would be fruitless. After he finished loading his belongings to leave, Trudy stood on the porch watching.

He glanced at her. "If you need anything, call."

She searched for words to say—anything that would give them hope and ease the churning in her stomach. She settled on, "I will." Watching him drive away after twenty-four years of marriage was devastating.

The first two months she tried to ignore her insecure feelings. When she did see Kenneth, he still wore his wedding band. She did the same. She became encouraged when he suggested they try marriage counseling two months later. It seemed to be working and they started having civil conversations again. At the urging of their counselor, they planned date nights without any expectations.

Two weeks later, Kenneth unexpectedly announced he'd been assigned for a year to Iraq to train Iraqi policemen. She tried to talk him out of it, but he refused. He explained that being unsure of where their separation might lead, and wanting to get away from the turmoil and emptiness encompassing his life, he had signed up immediately after they separated. Two weeks later, while they were in the midst of mending their relationship, he left. She found herself irritably wondering why he had even bothered to suggest counseling, knowing he'd be leaving soon.

Without noticing, Trudy bumped up the speed on the treadmill again, remembering her last night with Kenny a year ago.

—

Trudy joined Kenneth on the back porch with a glass of Merlot and handed him a beer. They'd had dinner at Outback Steakhouse with her mother, April, and her boyfriend, Matthew. She had gone with him to his apartment to help him pack the few things he needed for his trip and to empty his apartment since it wouldn't be needed while he was gone. Trudy had urged him to bring all of his clothes back home to store. They could have some time by themselves before he left.

She watched him sipping his beer as he stood leaning against a porch column, staring out into the night. She couldn't help but notice how handsome he looked with his crew cut, dressed in a pair of army fatigues and black boots. He had lost a lot of his excess weight since they'd separated three months earlier and looked almost as lean as he did when they first met.

Trudy leaned against the porch column opposite him, thinking about how quiet he had been all evening. "Are you having reservations about what you're about to do?" she asked.

"No, not really." He avoided eye contact. "I've actually been thinking about doing this for the last couple of years."

"Why didn't you tell me?"

"I figured it would be just something else we would disagree about and..." He let the words trail off.

Trudy held her breath, wondering if they were going to start arguing again.

"I shouldn't have put it that way. Sorry."

"Apology accepted." The last thing she wanted to do was fight with him before he left for Iraq.

Kenneth looked into the darkness and exhaled heavily. "I'm going to miss my evenings on the porch this summer."

"I'm going to miss our evenings on the porch, too," Trudy replied, watching him closely to see if he picked up on her subtle change following his comment. But he seemed not to have noticed. She gazed out into the yard. "Maybe before you get home I'll add some shrubbery and flowers to give the back lawn a face-lift. It would be nice to have some color back here when we're entertaining or dining."

"You were always good with plants."

"Something I learned as a teenager working on a plant farm."

Kenneth sipped his beer and cleared his throat. "You know, it seems like only yesterday you and I sat out here on nights like this planning for retirement. We were going to buy that lake house we always talked about. We wondered who and when April would marry so we could have grandkids to spoil."

"She hasn't said anything to me yet, but I think Matthew may be the one."

"There's something real and innocent about young love."

"Yes, there is." Trudy sipped her wine.

Kenneth stepped away from the column and turned toward Trudy. He paused before speaking. "Trudy, I know the last couple of years haven't been good for us, but they don't compare with the hell I've gone through the last three months since we separated."

"They've been tough for me, too."

"We both need to figure out whether or not we want this marriage to work so we can get on with our lives."

"I think we've made progress since going to counseling."

"I suppose that's helped. But now we're going to be separated for a year. Whether that will be good or bad, who knows? But we need to make up our minds by the time I get back home."

"What do you want to happen?"

Glancing down, Kenneth stared at his bottle and then looked up at Trudy, "I would like to know there's a new beginning waiting for us when I get back."

"A new beginning. I like that."

"Maybe we just need to take our counselor's advice and look forward and not back."

"Yes, I think that could work," Trudy agreed.

They stood silent for a moment waiting for the other to say something.

Finally, Kenneth shifted around and looked at his near empty bottle of beer. "My timing couldn't be worse, could it?"

Trudy wasn't sure what to say. He seemed restless, and she wanted to calm him. "You want another beer?"

"No, I've got to leave in a minute." He downed his last swallow.

"Are you worried about going?"

"No. I just know I'm leaving at a bad time."

Trudy knew the answer but asked anyway. "What's really bothering you, Kenny?"

"Trudy, what do you want me to say?" he shouted, his face contorted in anger. "That I've screwed up again. I had no idea two months ago when I signed up for this we would be trying to put our marriage back together. There's nothing I can do about it now."

"Nobody's screwed up, Kenny. It's all right. I understand why you're going." But Trudy could tell her gentle words were having little effect. "I'll be here when you return."

He wiped his face with his hand. "I'm sorry. I just wish it were different for us. Now, before and…while I'm away."

"Nothing's going to happen while you're away. When you get back we're going to sit down and talk about us and work this out. I just want you to promise me something."

He frowned at her.

"Promise me you'll take care of yourself…and come home to me."

Judging by his expression, she could tell her words surprised him. Appearing unable to speak, he nodded yes.

"Will you write and let me know how you're doing?"

"Yeah, sure." He nodded and glanced at his watch. "I have to check in at the armory at eleven. If I'm going to make it in time, I need to leave."

Trudy set her glass and his bottle on the table. They walked in silence around the house to his Dodge pickup truck. He turned to her and without saying a word, reached for her hands. His thumb massaged her fingers until it caressed her wedding band. He glanced at it then turned his gaze back to Trudy.

He finally spoke. "Thanks for not giving up on us."

"Some things are worth waiting and working for."

"Yeah, I suppose they are." He loosened his grip.

Trudy held firm and wouldn't let go. He searched her eyes then leaned over and kissed her lightly. Once their kiss ended, Trudy found herself wrapped in his arms. Neither spoke a word as their embrace lingered, his body warming her against the spring night that had suddenly chilled.

Finally, they separated and Trudy stepped back, her hands falling into his. She stared into his eyes, searching for words and settled on, "I wish we had more time."

"Maybe when I get back we can make up for it."

"I would like that."

Trudy squeezed his hands and whispered, "I love you, Kenneth Quinn." Whenever she called him by his full first name, she knew Kenny took her seriously.

"I love you, too," he echoed as her fingers slid from his palms.

It had been months since she had heard those words, and they reminded her of what they'd had before. She stood watching him drive away, knowing he was hurting. *Please, God. Bring him home. I could never forgive myself if something happens to him. Not like this.*

⌒

The letters Kenny wrote during his year away gave Trudy hope. He wrote about what he missed, her home cooking and teasing April. Sometimes his letters simply informed her about what he was doing with his army brigade. Once he wrote an in-depth letter reminding her of the goal they had set for themselves years ago, to buy a house on the lake. He mentioned the tax-free money he earned in Iraq could make the down payment on a lake house they'd so often talked about before retirement. He always signed his letters, *Love, Kenny.*

Trudy unconsciously bumped the speed up a couple more notches and picked up her stride.

The year apart had eased her emotional trauma. Trudy no longer felt insecure but comfortable having her own space. Convincing her mother to live with her, since she lived alone, was fun because they were best friends anyway. April also moved back home after finishing college. Trudy got used to having only women in the house. She liked the freedom to go and come and do what she pleased without having to plan around someone else's schedule.

Now, Kenneth would be home in less than two weeks. They had to work out their differences one way or another. They couldn't continue living in doubt, especially for April's sake. Maybe they should continue the counseling they'd started before he left or maybe they were beyond that. She cared for Kenneth but the memories of their fierce arguments haunted her. And the fifteen months apart had taken their toll. Could they reconcile and change or would they be setting themselves up for a harder fall next time? For certain, she had to have her mind made up in a couple of weeks.

Trudy glanced at the mile indicator and realized she had walked the two miles faster than she anticipated. She had unconsciously bumped the speed up to 4.5 and practically jogged most of the time. She wiped the perspiration from her brow and went outside to cool off in the clear morning air. Remembering she hadn't picked up the mail the previous day, she strolled down to the mailbox to get it and the newspaper. Thumbing through the mail on her way back to the house, she found a utility bill and a couple of advertisements. A yellow card from the US Postal Service caught her attention. It read, *Please come by Lynchburg City Post Office at Odd Fellows Road and pick up lost-and-found mail.* It was made out to Trudy Meyers, her maiden name, but had her mother's address on it. The notice had been forwarded to her address since her mother had arranged for all her mail to be delivered to Trudy's address. Thinking it must be another solicitation for donations from the college she'd attended thirty-four years ago, Trudy ignored it and dropped it into her handbag on the way inside to shower.

CHAPTER 3

Trudy fumbled in her purse for her keys and cell phone as she hurried across the parking lot to her car. Gripping the satchel filled with work-related material on her shoulder, she opened the door, slid into the seat of her black Acura TL, and threw her bag to the back seat. After securing her seatbelt, she called April.

Out of habit, she glanced in the rearview mirror and ran her fingers through her recently layered, bob-cut, blonde hair. Her mind raced through all she needed to take care of for Kenneth's surprise homecoming party and April and Matthew's engagement party just two weeks away. Realizing she was late to meet April, she cranked the car and sped toward the parking lot exit.

"Mom, where are you?" April inquired.

"Hello, Sweetie. I just got out of the Foundation meeting. I purposely started it at 8:30 this morning so I could leave here by ten-thirty and have plenty of time to meet you."

"What happened?"

"It's the same old thing. Mrs. Winkler questioned everything I said or asked for as though I'm not capable of making any decisions without the board's approval. We actually got into a debate over my suggestion to renovate the reception area and foyer where Jennifer works."

"Why is she always second-guessing you?"

"She retired and went to work for the Foundation full-time when I did. But because she was a supervisor in the school system, and I was a teacher, she feels she's better qualified to lead and be the president." Trudy continued to talk as she pulled onto the highway. "It's her way of taking on a more authoritative role or something, I guess. Who knows?"

"But the board unanimously made the decision to appoint you as president. After all, you worked with them for years as a volunteer and helped charter the Foundation. They know what you're capable of doing."

"I know. If it weren't for my love of working with the students, I wouldn't put up with it." After glancing in her mirror, she moved into the fast lane. "Are you already at Isabella's?"

"Yes. I'm at the boutique now."

"Did Mother come with you?"

"Yes, and Jan came by the house to give me more ideas for hors d'oeuvres for my party. She rode over with us so she could see the wedding gown I've chosen."

"That's great. Maybe she can have lunch with us. Has everyone seen the dress?"

"They're bringing it out now. Mom, it's beautiful!" she squealed.

Trudy smiled, imagining the look on April's face.

"Why don't you go ahead and put it on. I'll be there in less than ten minutes and I can see my daughter as a bride-to-be."

"I will. Drive carefully. Love you, Mom."

"I love you, too. I can't wait to see you in the dress. I know it's going to make me cry."

"Mom, you promised not to get emotional on me."

"I know, I know. But you're still my little girl even if you are twenty-two years old." She smiled at the thought. "Go put on the dress, Princess. I'll be there in a few minutes." *If there's any one thing Kenny and I have in common, it's love for our daughter.*

Trudy parked as close as she could to Isabella's Boutique and hastily walked up the sidewalk to the front entrance. Her platform heels almost made her trip on the uneven rock sidewalk, so she stopped and kicked them off. She never liked wearing heels and wondered why she bothered to wear them. When she bent over to pick them up, the fresh scent of lilies made her pause. She stood and inhaled the fragrance. The odor took her back to the times when she was a teenager and she and her mother would visit her mother's sister and brother-in-law in the Shenandoah Valley. Those memories quickly faded as thoughts of pain and rejection replaced them. Carrying her heels, she quickly made her entrance into Isabella's.

She glanced around the room to see if she could spot April, her mother or Jan. All she saw was an assortment of mannequins dressed in white bridal gowns covered with plastic and poised as if waiting for pictures to be taken. The right-side wall was well stocked with pastel-colored scarves, veils, and shoes. To her left were several racks of colorful tuxedos, vests, bow ties, and hats for men.

"Back here, Trudy!" Jan shouted, waving a hand to get her attention.

Trudy slipped on her heels and walked toward the fitting area.

Jan had become her closest and best friend when Trudy tutored Sheila, Jan's daughter, through advanced biology classes she needed for a pharmaceutical degree at Lynchburg College. Having similar interests, they eventually bonded over casual luncheons, and often found themselves volunteering to work for some of the same charitable organizations. Trudy and Kenneth had sometimes socialized over dinner with Jan and her husband, Malcolm, who was a practicing attorney with one of Lynchburg's elite law firms.

Three years ago Jan's life was shattered when Malcolm told her he didn't love her anymore and wanted out of their marriage. Jan frantically tried everything to convince him differently, but he refused to change his mind. Their differences eventually became a drawn-out fight over property and money.

Having allowed Malcolm to handle their finances, Jan was surprised to discover they had very little money saved in any of their joint accounts. She figured he must have squirreled most of their assets out of sight well before he left. As an attorney himself, Malcolm had unlimited legal representation.

After several court appearances, Jan realized that she would be left with nothing if she kept up the battle.

Eventually the truth came out as to why he wanted a divorce—Malcolm married his legal assistant as soon as their divorce became final six months later. Soon after that he purchased a $400,000 house.

Jan had a complete meltdown. Since she had not worked much during their twenty-three years of marriage, her insecurity caused her to withdraw from her friends and social activities.

Determined to help her friend mend her broken spirit, Trudy sat Jan down one day and convinced her to get a real estate broker's license. She had a hunch Jan would do well because she was an excellent communicator and had a great sense of humor.

Trudy tutored her through the courses. Once she was licensed, Jan proved Trudy right. In no time she was flourishing financially and bought a prime property that sat high on a knoll overlooking the James River in the city of Lynchburg.

Thankful for what Trudy had done for her during her time of crisis, Jan considered Trudy as close as family.

At the back of Isabella's, Trudy joined Jan sitting on a plush sofa at the entrance of a half-moon room. She wore an indigo top that hung loosely over her white jeans. Floor-to-ceiling wall mirrors brightened the area, where brides-to-be could get a 180-degree view while standing on a platform.

"Your hair looks great," Jan complimented Trudy. "Since you've cut it shorter, the natural blonde highlights really stand out, and I love that layered look."

"I let Lona talk me into it. It feels great." She slid her fingers through her hair, fluffing it out. "But I know everyone will think I'm trying to look younger and assume I'm going through a midlife crisis."

"Isn't every over-fifty woman, whether we admit it or not?" Jan laughed.

"I don't know if Kenny will like it. He's never seen me with short hair."

"After being away for a year, and now seeing how good you look, he's going to realize you're the best thing since cornbread. He'll fall in love with you again and again."

"Maybe," Trudy agreed, feeling uncomfortable broaching the subject. Glancing around, she asked, "Where's April and Mom?"

"April's in the fitting room trying on her gown," Jan pointed. "Your mother went back with her. They should be out any moment."

"Hello, Mrs. Quinn."

Mrs. Ferguson, the boutique owner, walked over. She was a petite woman with black, curly hair and wore a black skirt and white blouse. She carried herself with an air of sophistication and professionalism. "Your daughter made a wonderful choice for her dress. She looks absolutely stunning in it."

Trudy smiled. "I'm still trying to come to terms that she's all grown up and getting married."

"Well, you need to put it in perspective now," Mrs. Ferguson reminded her. "You're not losing your daughter but gaining a son."

"And knowing April," Jan interjected, "you'll have lots of grandchildren to claim one day."

Trudy giggled at the thought.

"This is my best friend, Jan," Trudy said to Mrs. Ferguson as an afterthought. "She's helping me with the food at April's engagement and Kenny's surprise homecoming party."

"You must be a wonderful friend," Mrs. Ferguson nodded at Jan.

"Anything for Trudy," Jan replied.

"So you're doing the parties together?" Mrs. Ferguson asked, turning her attention back to Trudy.

"Yes, but Kenny doesn't know it. He thinks he's just making a formal announcement about April and Matthew's engagement."

"That's really nice. How long has he been away?"

"He's been in Iraq for the past year. I was planning a surprise party for him, but it was April's idea to combine the celebrations since he's going to be arriving five days before her party."

"What a pleasant surprise it'll be for him," Mrs. Ferguson acknowledged.

"They're very close, so I think we'll have a blast."

"May I get you a beverage while we're waiting? A glass of wine, maybe bottled tea or water?" Mrs. Ferguson suggested.

"No, thank you," they both replied.

"By the way, Trudy," Mrs. Ferguson said, opening a folder. "Do you know the size for your husband's tux?"

"No, I would rather have him come by and get measured. With him being away for a year I'm not sure."

"That's fine. We have plenty of time with the wedding still four months away."

A sound behind them caught Trudy's attention. They turned toward the mirrored wall. Trudy watched as April stepped out into the room in a long, white, strapless gown, adorned with an elegant train. She stood where she could get a full view of herself in the mirrors. With her hands cupped together in front of her, she stared at her mother with a questioning look on her face, waiting for approval.

Trudy took a few steps forward and stopped. She lifted a hand to her lips and gazed at her daughter from head to toe. Her tall, thin body and her long, blonde hair cascading over her shoulders accentuated her graceful stance. April turned around slowly. When she came face to face with her mother again, her smile brought out the dimples in her cheeks.

"You're so beautiful," Trudy whispered. "So beautiful."

"Of course she's beautiful," Trudy's mother said, having come out of the dressing room with April. "She looks just like you did when you were her age."

An hour later, April, Jan, Trudy and her mother stood outside of the boutique discussing where to go for lunch. The Olive Garden was their choice.

"I'll ride with Trudy so she won't have to drive alone," Jan suggested.

"Then Grandmother and I will meet you there," April agreed.

"Ok. You two go and get a table," Trudy suggested, digging into her purse for her keys. "I need to run by the post office and pick up some mail from lost and found. It'll save me a trip back over this way after lunch."

"Then we're on our way." April waved, walking away.

"Drive carefully," Trudy reminded her.

As Trudy backed out of the parking space, Jan glanced back. "You're not taking work home, are you? That satchel looks awfully full."

"Actually, I'm trying to get caught up enough to call myself getting ahead. I don't want to work next week with Kenny coming home and April's engagement party. But I have so many girls looking for scholarships. I have more than fifty applications for colleges here in Lynchburg alone." She lifted one hand from the steering wheel. "I don't know what to do for them. Most businesses and clubs have reduced their contributions to the Foundation because of the economy." Looking to her left, she steered the car into traffic. "I've been writing requests for grants to try to get some state funding. But even if I come up with part of the money, these students might have to come up with ten to fifteen-thousand dollars each year they're in school." She sighed. "I just can't stand to see their faces when I tell them we can't help them as much as we would like to. I know some of them will never go to college unless I get assistance for them."

"You're always trying to do something for someone else," Jan remarked. "You'll figure out something."

"I remember when Mom and I moved back to Lynchburg. I was seventeen and we'd just been notified that Dad had been killed three weeks before he was to leave Vietnam and retire from the military. She was determined I was going to college. She worked full-time in the textile mill during the day and for an office cleaning service three nights a week. I helped her as much as I could."

"Your mother is a special person."

"Yes, she is," Trudy agreed. "It's been nice having her live with me this past year while Kenny's been away. I had almost forgotten just how close we were years ago after finding out Dad had been killed." She gave a shudder. "And then my life was shattered when I got a Dear John letter from the boy I thought I was going to spend the rest of my life with." She paused, thinking back. How had she ever made it through those terrible days and nights when everything in her life seemed so bleak? "It was just us taking care of each other until I met Kenny seven years later."

"It's obvious you and your mother are as close as two coats of paint."

"She's my best friend." Pulling to the curb and stopping, Trudy looked over at Jan and smiled. "Sorry, Jan. You're second in line."

"I could never compete with her," she giggled. "Second is fine with me."

"I'll pick up the mail and be right back."

Trudy found several people in line in front of her, but tried to be patient until it was her turn at the window. *Should've known if I came here in a hurry this was going to happen. Oh well, I'm here. Might as well wait my turn.*

Finally, several minutes later, she handed the postal clerk the notice she had received. "I'm here to pick up this."

"Sure," the young man replied. "It's right here." He reached behind the counter and grabbed a large, yellow envelope that read *Lost Mail Recovery.*

"I need you to sign for it right here." He pointed to the release form. "And would you mind signing a release for the US Postal Service to possibly use this incident in a news story if they so choose? Sometimes we like to release information to the press about mail delivery for public relations purposes."

"Sure, fine with me. It's most likely just a bill that didn't make its way to me. At least they didn't come and confiscate anything," she joked.

Back in the car, she read aloud the notice attached to the yellow envelope. "Listen to this, Jan. It says,

Please accept our apologies for the inconvenience this late mail arrival may have caused. Please know that your US Postal Service takes great pride in the prompt delivery of millions of pieces of mail daily. The Postmaster General."

She threw the envelope over her shoulder to the back seat. "I guess a few more hours won't matter. I'm sure April and Mom are wondering what's happened to us. Let's go have lunch."

CHAPTER 4

Twenty minutes later, the four women sat enjoying salads at the Olive Garden. Jan, being the bubbly person she was, added humor to the conversation.

Lifting her glass of water, she tapped it with her spoon. "I would like to propose a toast. April, may the man you're about to marry be more than you ever hoped for. May your life with Matthew become what dreams are made of. May all young maidens who see what your heart has sought and won be forever envious." She lifted her glass higher. "And forever remember to let the vows you're about to make conquer the trials you must endure."

They all clicked glasses and sipped water.

Their waitress, Sharon, overheard Jan and came to the table. "I guess congratulations are in order. When's the big day?"

"In four months…or exactly 114 days from now," April gleefully answered.

Sharon laughed. "It sounds like we have ourselves an anxious bride. I hope the next four months will be among the happiest and most memorable times of your life."

"Thank you. I'm sure they will be."

As Sharon walked away, Jan said, "April, share your love story with us. I know you dated Matthew some in high school, but what made you fall in love with him?"

April thought for a moment and tilted her head, blushing. "I'm not sure you really want to hear all that stuff."

"I'm not asking you to give us the juicy stuff," Jan giggled. "There's got to be that special event or moment that made you fall head over heels for Matthew."

"Hmm, maybe." April rolled her eyes. "I tell you what. I'll share my story with you if all of you will share your love story with me."

"My love story had a bad ending," Jan began, shaking her head, recalling she'd been divorced for three years. "I'm not sure if I want to remember anything about it." She hesitated, raised an eyebrow and then asked, "How about if we just talk about the first boy we loved or thought we loved."

Trudy hesitated. "I'm not sure I want to go that far back."

"Come on," Jan urged. "All of us had a first love. You don't have to tell us everything."

"I'll think about it," Trudy acquiesced.

"Okay, who's first?" Jan queried, glancing around the table. The waitress brought out their soup. Finally, April volunteered. "I'll go first. I think it was chicken noodle soup that made me fall in love with Matthew."

"Chicken noodle soup?" the three women repeated in unison and laughed.

"Matthew and I first met when we were in high school. I remember him as a quiet, skinny boy who sat beside me in ninth grade math and English classes. He was always so smart." She nodded and grinned. "It wasn't until my junior year that we actually started talking a lot. We had a friendship, nothing else. I used to go home and get on the computer and send him emails about little things that happened during the day. I remember telling him once about how hard it was to solve algebra problems Mr. Via, my teacher, had given us. He sent me a two-page summary, giving me step-by-step instructions on how to solve the problems." She took a sip of water and continued.

"We started dating when I was sixteen but only as friends." She smiled and went on. "Before we got serious, we dated other people a few times and talked about how awful the other dates were. Then we graduated and went off to different colleges." She smiled and shrugged her shoulders. "But we emailed each other every day.

"I remember studying for exams my freshman year and Matthew surprised me by sending a gift basket of fruit and snacks, with the sweetest note in it." She smiled and continued. "Once I came down with the flu. When he found out, did I get a surprise! The off-campus corner café sent a delivery boy knocking at my door with a quart of hot, homemade chicken noodle soup and cheese toast, from Matthew, of course. In one of our conversations, I had told him how much I loved their soup and cheese toast, and he remembered. I realized for the first time how special it was to have someone who actually wanted to take care of me, especially when I least expected it. From that time on, we spent every moment together when we came home on school breaks." She sat back and smiled. "That was three years ago, and it's only gotten better. Who's next?"

"That one's going to be hard to beat," Jan chimed in. "The first boy I *thought* I loved," she shrugged, putting emphasis on her comment, "sang in the church choir with me. We were both eighteen and I mean he was h-a-n-d...some." She leaned back in her chair. "He had this head of curly, black hair that you could only dream about. When I first met him, I told myself, he doesn't know it yet, but he's the guy I'm going to marry. I made breads and desserts for him, sent cards on every occasion, and invited him to everything I could possibly think of. But he moved on to bigger and better things," she sighed.

"What do you mean bigger and better things?" April asked.

"He fell for the girl who had larger boobs."

They all burst into laughter, causing the people seated near them to glance their way.

"Tell us about your first love, Mrs. Meyers," Jan said.

April's grandmother shifted her petite body as she sat up straight. "I'm not sure my love story will be as exciting as the ones you younger girls have. But I'll try." She took a sip of water and paused to think before beginning.

"My first love is the man I married. I was fourteen and we were living here in Lynchburg. Kurt lived on the same block as my family. When he was in high school, he worked part-time at J W Wood Wholesale, a food company down on the river. I used to sit at the window and watch him walk home from work, wishing I knew him. Finally, we were together in some classes in school.

"He started coming around the house. We sat together on the porch for hours. My dad often came out when it got late and said to Kurt, 'Son, don't you think it's time you went home?' He always made a beeline for the sidewalk." She snickered.

"He joined the army when he turned eighteen. We wanted to get married before he went to serve, but our parents insisted we wait. So we slipped off to Myrtle Beach one day while he was on leave and found an Indian preacher named Little John. He married us on a Saturday morning in the South Carolina State Park.

"A flock of ducks was sitting in the pond. When Little John started the ceremony they waddled up, surrounded us and didn't make any noise until we'd said our vows."

She paused and smiled. "When Little John said, 'You're now husband and wife,' they started quacking and strutting around. Little John told us God had sent them over to witness our union." She lowered her eyes and paused. "Your father was a good man," she said to Trudy in a quivering voice. Then she cleared her throat. "Driving back to Lynchburg, we were scared to death to tell our parents. But once they knew we were married, they accepted us with open arms."

"That was beautiful," April acknowledged, teary-eyed. "Thank you for sharing, Grandma."

Then their gaze turned to Trudy.

"There's not a whole lot to say about my first love," Trudy said, glancing down. "Only that I loved and lost."

"That's not fair," Jan insisted, leaning forward in her chair, sneering.

"Yes, Mom. You need to be a team player," April urged.

"Okay, if you insist. But please stop me if it gets boring." She gathered her thoughts and began talking.

"Each summer the last three years before Dad was to retire from military service, we visited Mom's sister, Aunt Margaret, and her husband, Uncle Harry. They had a farm in the Shenandoah Valley. Next to their farm was a large fruit and plant nursery owned by a wealthy Dutch family from the Netherlands. Uncle Harry helped me get a summer job working there part-time so I would have something to do and not be bored. They harvested seasonal fruits that were processed for canning and grew flowers and other plants they sold to florists and nurseries." Trudy paused briefly and shifted in her seat before continuing.

"That's when I met Richard. We were both fifteen. He and his younger brother, Raymond, came over from the Netherlands every summer to work and learn the family business their grandfather had started. When the harvesting was finished they returned to the Netherlands to continue their education." She paused and tapped her fingers on the water glass she held.

"It started out as me, the army brat, taking up for Richard, a tall, skinny boy who was being teased by the local boys because of his accent and the way he dressed. He and his brother always wore big-brimmed hats and baggy trousers held up by suspenders." She grinned. Glancing across the table, she found everyone raptly listening.

"The second summer we became close friends and spent every minute of our free time together. I think we started falling in love then. When he went back home we wrote letters to each other every week. I couldn't wait to see him again.

"When he came back that third summer he had become this most charming, handsome, young man I'd ever seen." She paused. "One thing led to another, and we kind of started talking about commitments to each other. I thought we really had something special since he often talked about our future together after he finished school and could return to the States. Call it intuition or whatever, but for some reason I had the impression his dad and grandfather didn't like me." She noticed her mother lower her gaze.

"In that third summer we became very close and talked about...our future together." She glanced at April who sat mesmerized. "He promised to stay in touch with me and said when he returned the next summer we would make our plans. I think his father and grandfather became aware of our relationship and, abruptly, he was sent home. Shortly afterward we got word Dad had been..." Trudy glanced at her mother who still had her eyes lowered. "We lost Dad in Vietnam," she finished.

"After that, we moved to Lynchburg to live. I continued to send letters to Richard, but they were all returned, marked UNABLE TO DELIVER." She paused and swallowed hard. "I didn't know what was going on, so I wrote a letter to his mother trying to find out. She sent me a letter saying Richard had quit school, and they didn't know where he was. She asked if I would please let them know if I found out." She grimaced. "She never told me why he quit school or left home."

Trudy shrugged and went on. "For several weeks I didn't hear from him. Then, finally one day in late September I got a letter forwarded to me from our previous home address in Fayetteville, saying he was sorry it was over between us. He wrote the letter as if it had been my choice." Trudy forced a smile trying to conceal the disappointment in her voice. "There was no return address on it, so I figured he left it off, not wanting me to know how to contact him. I never understood why and never knew what happened to change his mind about us."

They were listening intently when suddenly Trudy left her chair. "Okay, bathroom break for me."

"Did Mom get upset?" April asked, watching her walk away.

"April," her grandmother said. "Memories of a woman's loves are etched on her heart forever. Regretfully, for Trudy, that time and person in her life remains a scar."

Their waitress reappeared. "You ladies have been doing some serious talking over here. Have you gotten all of life's mysteries figured out?"

"No," Jan answered, laughing. "We've actually been talking about past boyfriends."

"Don't you know it's bad luck to talk about past lovers in the presence of a bride to be?" She glanced at April and winked. "They'll come back to haunt you. Maybe you'd like to try a dessert or coffee to add some flavor to the conversation."

"No, thank you," April answered. "I have to get back to work and review my material for tomorrow and Sunday's newspapers."

"Are you a writer for the paper here?" the waitress asked.

"I hope to be a real writer someday. Now all they let me do is write up wedding and obituary announcements." She laughed. "It's kind of challenging to jump from the bridal section to an obituary, though."

"Here's your tab. I'll watch for your engagement announcement in the paper. Good luck to all you ladies, and don't let any past boyfriends haunt you." She chuckled and walked away.

"What was that about?" Trudy asked, returning to the table.

"Nothing," Jan responded. "She's just teasing us a little."

"Okay, who's riding home with whom?" Trudy asked.

"I need to go home before going to work," April said. "I have to pick up a flash drive I left on my desk." She turned to her grandmother. "You may ride with me if you'd like."

"Then we girls split again. I'll see you this evening, April. Don't stay out too late with Matthew."

"I won't. Love you, Mom."

"Love you, too. Drive carefully." She watched April and her mother walk away, grateful that April was happy.

Riding home with Trudy, Jan looked at her friend. "Are you okay? You sounded a little unnerved while talking about the Dutch guy."

"I don't know what's gotten into me lately," Trudy admitted. "Every time I talk about something that's sensitive to me, I get all emotional."

"Most of us older girls are like that. I think it's one of those over-fifty things you and I deal with, called hormones."

"I don't know. I can't even sit down and watch a Hallmark movie anymore without crying." Lifting her hand from the steering wheel, she shrugged. "Even April picks up on my moodiness, and I know I worry her."

"She's mature for her age. She understands and knows what you're going through."

"Now I will possibly be forcing her to deal with a mother and father whose marriage self-destructed at her engagement party."

"Does she talk to you much about her dad?"

"More so now than she did a year ago. I know she wants us back together. She just doesn't come right out and say it."

"She's your daughter. Naturally she wants you two back together. Any child would. But you and Kenneth have to figure this out. No one else can do it for you."

"It doesn't make it any easier."

"I'm sorry I put you on the spot asking you to talk about your teenage love affair in front of her."

Trudy waved her off. "No, you didn't. But I should've talked about Kenny and me instead. April would have gotten more out of it. She didn't need to hear about her mother's teenage lost-love story. My mistake. I think I might have even upset Mother, too. That was a bad time in our lives."

"I think your mother handled it well," Jan's voice trailed off.

They sat silent for a moment.

"As a friend, may I ask you something and expect an honest answer?" Jan asked.

"Why do I feel like this is a loaded question?" Trudy frowned, knowing Jan always spoke her mind.

"Are you looking forward to Kenny coming home?"

"I suppose so…. Of course, I'm glad he's safe and coming home," she quickly added when she realized how nonchalant her answer sounded. "It's the *we* part I'm having trouble with."

"Since you and Kenneth have been separated for…?

"Fifteen months."

"Has it made a difference in what you're thinking about doing?"

"When we first separated, we both agreed it would be temporary until we could figure us out. I would like to think we still have a chance to make a go of it."

"Is that why you never took your wedding band off?"

Trudy glanced at her ring. "I'm not sure. Kenny wore his when he left for Iraq."

"Maybe you still love each other?"

Trudy hesitated before answering and noticed the condescending expression on Jan's face. "Why suddenly all of these questions?"

"Because I'm your friend and I care about you. You haven't been yourself lately and I know this has been bothering you. So I thought for a change I'd be the one to help you solve a problem. Just like you have been here for me for the last four years."

"It shows, huh?" Trudy said with a dry laugh. "Lately I can't eat, sleep or feel interested in doing anything. All I think about is Kenny coming home and what to do about us. And if we get back together will we be able to make it work?"

"What does your heart tell you?"

"I still care about him. Maybe we owe ourselves a second chance, if that's what he wants."

"What does Trudy want?"

"What I want doesn't matter anymore." She frowned. "I should go back to Kenny and be the good wife everyone expects me to be so everyone else can be happy."

"And you would never forgive yourself. It wouldn't work and you know it. Not unless you want to go back for you."

"I don't think I have a choice," she sighed.

"What would you do if he came home and wanted out of the marriage?"

"I...I haven't thought about that," Trudy stammered.

"Maybe this time away from each other will prove to be what you both needed and will give your marriage a second wind. The two of you going to counseling before he left showed how serious you were about saving your marriage."

"We talked about it the night he left. At that time I think he really wanted us to try. But after being away for a year...." She let the thought pass.

"You wouldn't be the first couple to separate and get back together. A lot of people have."

"I just wish I felt better about us." Trudy glanced at Jan. "I just need to figure out if staying married is what I really want. I can't imagine life without Kenny. But something's missing and I don't know what it is. I just want to be happy again and have things like they used to be."

"Trudy, you're going through a midlife crisis like the rest of us, for heaven's sake," she laughed.

"Whatever it is, I hope I hurry up and get over it."

"Well, let me give you some advice, girlfriend." Jan slapped a thigh. "You don't want to find yourself single and looking for love when you're over fifty, 'cause, honey, the good ones are already taken. All I seem to attract are sugar daddies wanting to drop in when convenient or old-timers with one foot already in the grave. I've decided that if I ever remarry it's going to be the real deal for me or I'll have to do laundry for only myself the rest of my life."

Late that evening Trudy sat alone on the back porch sipping a glass of wine. Listening to the crickets chirp, she thought of Kenny and wondered if he often thought of her. Back porch time together late in the evenings over a beer or glass of wine had been a routine they'd once cherished. Whether it was conversation about everything or nothing special or just bending an ear about coping with something at work, back porch time at night was a ritual that wove their lives together.

They had their share of disagreements over the last few years and had drifted apart, but their relationship had seemed to be improving while they were in counseling. In fact, the little surprises they sprang on each other and the token gifts that seemed to show up for no reason had become fun to do. They'd even competed to outdo each other.

Trudy remembered coming home from the airport after saying goodbye to Kenny when he left for Iraq. She had found a wrapped collection of seventies CDs—her favorite music—in the laundry basket. He knew she wouldn't find them until later and had left her a note.

I know things haven't been good for us lately and you will have a lot to consider while I'm gone. This music might help during those restless times. I'll think of you every day. Love, Kenny.

Now, Trudy wondered what their lives would be like once he returned home. Would they have the new beginning they had talked about before he left? Or would they slip back into the same old routine that drove them apart? She had been thinking about him, them, a lot lately. Feeling antsy, she went inside hoping for sleep tonight.

CHAPTER 5
The Lost Letter

Trudy finished her two-mile walk on the treadmill in the garage. April had gone to work early, and Trudy finished her chores so she could have most of the day to herself. Practically all of the preparations had already been made for April and Kenneth's party next weekend, so she thought she would enjoy a beautiful spring day on the back porch reading the last half of the novel she had started a week earlier.

On her way to the kitchen, she stopped by the utility room and grabbed an armload of towels from the dryer. She folded them and, as she walked through the kitchen to the linen closet, the telephone rang.

Seeing that it was Jan calling, she answered promptly. "Good morning, Jan. What're you doing up so early?"

"Have you seen the news this morning on Channel 13?" Jan blurted out.

"No, I haven't had the TV on."

"Quick, turn it on! They're going to talk about it again. I'll call later." The phone clicked, ending the conversation.

Puzzled, Trudy reached for the remote on the kitchen desk and turned on the television. Still holding the armload of towels, she listened attentively as the reporter began.

The US Postal Service always gets their mail delivered but perhaps not always in a timely manner. Last night they issued a press release about a letter that was delivered to someone here in

35

Lynchburg, Virginia. What's so unusual about this letter is that it's being delivered thirty-five years late. It seems it was originally sent in 1975 to a woman, perhaps then a young girl, named Trudy Meyers in Fayetteville, North Carolina. Ms. Meyers apparently had moved to Lynchburg and left a forwarding address that is still active. The letter evidently fell behind a wall cabinet when it arrived at the Lynchburg Post Office. During recent renovations the letter was found and forwarded to the woman's current address.

The envelope, postmarked August 15, 1975, was sent from the Netherlands, and simply had the name R. Vanderveer as the sender. The envelope was sealed with a heart, leading us to believe it may have been a love letter. If the woman who received this letter is willing to share, we at News 13 would love to hear the story behind it. Please contact us at News 13.

Trudy had forgotten about the envelope she'd picked up earlier. She dropped the towels on the table and ran to her car. Opening the door, she panicked when she didn't see the postal envelope on the car seat. Finally, she spotted it under the front seat. She tore open the postal envelope and found inside a faded, stained envelope, bordered with red and blue stripes and postmarked from Utrecht, Netherlands. The date caught her attention—August 15, 1975. After thinking about it a moment, she realized it must have been mailed prior to the last letter she received from Richard several weeks later in September. It was addressed to Trudy Meyers, her maiden name, and forwarded to her mother's address, the house her mother rented in 1975 when they moved to Lynchburg. Now, it was sent to Trudy's address, since her mother's mail was being forwarded there while she was living with her.

She walked back to the kitchen, turning the envelope over and over in her hands, curious and excited. She touched every part of the envelope, especially the glittering red heart that sealed the back flap. Slowly she slit the envelope with a letter opener.

She went out and sat on the back porch, staring at the faded envelope, almost afraid to pull the letter out. She still remembered how devastated she'd been after reading Richard's last letter thirty-five years ago.

She held her hand to her heart, thinking that maybe this would finally tell her why he'd suddenly called off their relationship as if it were her choice. She unfolded the brittle pages. Gingerly she spread them open.

Remembering Richard's handwriting, she began to read his words.

To my love, Trudy,

I write this letter to you with the utmost hurt and disappointment over what I've found out. Raymond came home from the States and told me what Father has done to separate you and me from ever seeing each other again.

First, he sent me home on the pretense that I needed to enroll in college early. I found that not to be true. Then Raymond overheard Father tell our grandfather he had given your mother a check for ten thousand dollars. He asked her to never bring you back to his farm. He told her there was no way he was ever going to allow us to have a future together and you would only be hurt more if you ever came back.

Trudy felt a knot building in her chest as she read the part about the money and her mother again. Was this possible? Her mother would never do such a terrible thing, would she? She swallowed hard, her throat went dry and she gripped the pages until her hands ached.

Trudy, I beg your forgiveness and understanding for the arrogance that my father has shown to you. I've made up my mind; I no longer wish to be a part of my family since they think they have the right to control me. I have quit school and left home to make my own destiny in life.

I have told no one where I am and left no forwarding address so they can't find me. I don't know what my new address will be since

I've yet to find a place to live. For the time being, I'm sleeping in a homeless shelter in Utrecht. I am working as a delivery boy for a florist and will get a room at the local boarding house as soon as I save enough money.

Trudy wiped at tears blurring her vision, trying to stay focused so she could read.

I've tried calling you, but all I get is a message saying your phone has been disconnected. I need you to call me and tell me what's going on. I so badly want to hear your voice and explain everything, but I don't know how to contact you. My number is 011-31-36-555-1212. If I'm not at the florist shop, leave a number where I can reach you and I will call you back as soon as I can. The florist's owner has agreed to take your call for me.

I will work day and night without rest until I save enough money to come back to the States to be with you.

My Trudy, I simply ask that you trust me. Call and give me a chance to explain how I'm going to make things work out for us. I can't sleep, work or do anything without thinking of you and spending the rest of my life with you. My love grows for you every day, and I can't imagine my life without you. I count the hours waiting to hear your voice.

Love always, Richard

Trudy pressed the letter to her bosom. This! This was why Richard had written the last letter telling her goodbye as if their parting had been her choice. Without hearing from her, he'd assumed she no longer wanted to continue their courtship. *It must have been awful for him thinking I had forsaken him.*

She sat staring, her vision blurring, remembering the boy she once loved so passionately and that day she first told Richard of her concern about his father.

—

Summer 1975

Trudy wiped sweat from her brow with the back of her hand as she walked on a carpet of wilted blooms she'd pinched from flowers in the afternoon heat. Glancing up, she noticed she had already picked through more than half of the plant beds stretching for several hundred feet. With her blue jeans cuffed so they wouldn't get wet or muddy from the frequent irrigation, she wore a light blue, sleeveless, cotton shirt with the tail hanging loosely over her hips. She'd clipped her long, blonde hair back to keep it out of her face in the sweltering summer heat.

Soon, since it was Friday, Mr. Vanderveer would ring the bell hanging from the packing shed post and all the hired help would ride in from the fields on wagons to get paid. She and Richard planned to go to Buena Vista later to get burgers and shakes and then go to see *Jaws*, the summer's biggest movie hit. She was looking forward to going to the drive-in that night. She had permission to use her mother's Chevy Impala, which was much nicer than the old Ford pickup Richard drove around the farm.

Never had Trudy imagined finding herself in love with this shy, timid boy from the Netherlands, whom she'd met three summers ago. Maybe it was his accent. Or was it his dark brown eyes, wavy, brown hair and his stout, tanned body that captivated her? She'd sympathized with him because he was an outsider, like she was. Her dad frequently moved them to different military bases all over the world. Whatever the reason for her fascination with him, ever since Richard had come back to the States for the summer to work at his grandfather's farm, Trudy had but one thing on her mind. And that was to spend every minute of every day she could with him.

Suddenly, water spewed everywhere. Startled, Trudy squealed and jumped around in a frenzy looking for the fastest way out of the plant beds. Seeing only one, she sprinted through the rows of flowers, sidestepping and jumping over plants as best she could. Since the irrigation system was controlled manually, she knew someone must have intentionally turned on the water.

Then it dawned on her. Earlier, she'd seen Richard ride over to the packing shed on his dirt bike. Always playing pranks on each other, he must have purposely turned the water on to get even with her after she'd grabbed his hat from the tractor seat and hurled it on top of the shed. Winking at the wagonload of workers waiting to be taken out to the fields, she'd hoped they wouldn't tell on her. She'd then gone down to the lower plant beds, working where she could easily watch his reaction.

Richard rushed out of the shed and climbed onto the tractor. He glanced around for his hat. Not seeing it anywhere, he climbed down and looked under the wagon. He searched diligently for several minutes before Raymond, his younger brother, finally told him where his hat was and pointed toward Trudy in the plant bed.

Watching him climb the ladder to fetch his hat, Trudy tried hard not to burst out laughing. She pretended not to notice as he looked her way, shaking his head and mumbling to himself.

Now, as she ran from the plant bed, soaked from head to toe, her clothes clinging to her curvy body, she imagined ways to get back at Richard for spraying her.

Knowing he expected her to run into the shed where he would laugh at her, she went around to the back instead. Now he'd have to come looking for her. She turned the outside spigot on full force but kept the nozzle lever turned off. She crouched down behind pallets of mulch with the hose ready in her hand.

When she heard footsteps, Trudy peeped through the stacked pallets and saw Richard looking around for her. She couldn't help noticing how handsome he looked in his baggy, gray trousers held up by suspenders. His white T-shirt fit his muscular chest snuggly. His wavy, brown hair stuck out under his wide-brimmed, gray hat.

He turned away as if to leave. Trudy threw a wood chip at some barrels in front of her. Turning back at the sound, he slowly walked toward the barrels. She waited with the nozzle ready, relishing her chance to wet him down. As soon as he came near enough, she sprang from her hidden spot and sprayed him with the full force of water from the hose.

"Ahh!" he hollered, stumbling back, waving his arms and knocking his hat off.

Every way he turned, Trudy stayed with him, spraying him from head to toe and laughing. "You thought watching me run from the plant bed was funny, did you?"

Unable to get away from the gushing water, Richard grabbed the nozzle and wrestled with Trudy. Both of them, soaking wet, tripped on the tangled hose and fell to the ground. Dropping the nozzle, Richard landed on his back with Trudy sprawled on top of him.

Propping himself up on his elbows and gazing at Trudy, he exclaimed. "Gosh! That felt great."

"Yeah! I'm sure you wanted me to wet you down."

Attempting to get the last word, he reminded her, "I say, Trudy, it looks like you've done gone skinny dipping again but forgot to take off your clothes."

Trudy glanced down at her wet, cotton pullover clinging to her breasts. "I still can't believe I did that with you last summer. You're never going to let me forget, are you?"

"I never want to forget anything about you," Richard conceded, lying back and propping his head with his right arm. "I don't know what I'm going to do with you half a world away while I'm at school." He grinned. "I won't have anyone to pick on."

"Does that mean you're going to miss me?" she asked, raising an eyebrow.

"Probably every hour of every day."

"I'm going to miss you, too." Trudy said, her eyes focusing on his. "Just make sure you don't look for someone else to pick on."

"Don't worry. If it were up to me, I would stay here and go to school. Father is just so set on me starting college in the homeland."

Trudy shifted off Richard and unclipped her hair, letting it fall around her shoulders, so that it would dry faster. She rested her chin on her hands, staring at the most handsome boy she'd ever met.

"Well, next year after I graduate from high school and we both turn eighteen, we'll have more say over what we want to do with our lives."

"That's almost a year away."

"Next summer will be here before you know it."

"It won't happen fast enough for me." His eyes narrowed. "Do you think your father and mother will approve of me taking you for my wife?"

"Sure they will," she responded enthusiastically. "Mom and Dad want me to go to college, but I can go to school and be married. I know other girls who're married and still in school."

With his free hand, Richard reached over and gathered strands of her hair cascading over her left shoulder and began rolling them into a bundle.

"What are you doing, Richard?" she asked, raising up and pulling her hair loose.

"I want to see what you'll look like with your hair rolled up under a bonnet. After all, you'll be a Dutch wife."

Trudy reached for one of his suspenders, pulled it out and let it snap back against his wet shirt.

"Ouch!" he hollered, sitting up and rubbing his chest. "What'd you do that for?"

"I see right now these suspenders have got to go. They're beginning to warp your mind." She giggled. "Yes, I think you'd look great in a pair of bell-bottoms and one of those fluffy-sleeved French shirts."

"Miss Trudy, you're a girl with a free spirit, I must say," he teased.

"What's wrong with that? After all, aren't you the one who's arguing with your father all the time?"

Richard rolled over onto his side. Trudy stretched out beside him. Staring into his brown eyes and his handsome face she couldn't resist leaning over and kissing him.

"Father and I just don't always see things the same way. He wants to get his way with everyone. All he thinks about is how to make more money," Richard said, petulantly.

"What's wrong with making money?" Trudy laughed. "You can't have too much of that, can you?"

"No, but Father uses it to control everyone."

Suddenly serious, Trudy narrowed her eyes. "Have I done something to upset your father or grandfather?"

"Why would you think that?"

"I don't know. They used to talk to me and pick on me all the time. They hardly speak to me anymore."

"Perhaps they have a lot on their minds since we're in the midst of harvesting."

"I'm not sure. Maybe it's intuition, but I feel like something's not right."

Richard reached over and brushed strands of hair from her face. "If something was wrong, I'd know about it."

"I know. But you and your father don't always get along. Maybe I'm the reason."

"Don't be silly."

"But it bothers me. Did you notice him and your grandfather staring at us while we were having lunch with the workers from the fields? I know they were talking about us."

"Grandfather talks about everyone here in the States," he snickered. "Trust me. If something's wrong, I'd know it."

"You know I trust you," she said, moving closer. Mesmerized by his intent gaze, she traced his broad, tanned face with a finger, beginning with his eyelids and then circling his eyes, nose and lips. She couldn't believe how much she loved this boy and thought about him every hour of the day. She imagined her life with him, forever.

Richard's arm cradled her. His hand moved up the small of her back, causing her to shiver, even in the July heat. He pulled her face toward his, ever so gently, and kissed her. Trudy melted in his arms and passionately returned his kiss. Knowing they should get back to work, she decided that a few minutes of making out with Richard wouldn't matter. After all, they were behind the shed. No one could see them.

Richard pulled her damp, curvy body closer against him. Yielding to the familiar passion, she responded to his advances. Richard's weight caused her to fall back as he leaned against her, his body pinning her down. Trudy savored the feeling he ignited inside her, her breathing becoming heavier.

Suddenly a noise, the sound of heavy footsteps got her attention. Trudy opened her eyes. Richard's father, Patrick Vanderveer, a husky man, was walking briskly toward them with a stern look on his face, intensified by his heavy, dark eyebrows. Richard's grandfather, a tall, lanky man with a gray beard, wearing a straw hat, followed close behind.

Trudy pushed Richard aside and sprang to her feet, her heart racing, almost falling in her haste. Richard jumped up in time to catch her. She noticed he was avoiding his father's eyes as he brushed loose grass from his trousers.

"Father," Richard said, "I'm getting ready to get the tractor to pull another load of berries in."

"I see what you're doing," Patrick shouted angrily. "Now get on out of here and back to work. I've got laborers waiting for you in the fields."

"Mr. Vanderveer, it's my fault," Trudy retorted. "I finished pinching the blooms from the flowers and saw Richard up here and sprayed him with the water hose."

"No, Trudy. You don't need to make excuses for me," Richard said. He picked up his hat.

"I see what you're doing, young lady," his father bellowed. "You need to go home, make yourself proper and put on some decent clothes. We don't run around on this farm looking like…" he gestured with his hand, at a loss for words.

The grandfather stood silently, shifting from one foot to the other, continuously pushing his heavy-framed glasses up on his nose. His jaw jerked every so often as if he wanted to say something but was holding back.

"Father, none of this is her fault," Richard exclaimed, raising his voice. "Don't take it out on Trudy. I turned the sprinklers on while she was in the flower bed." He turned to Trudy with a pleading look. "Leave. I'll take care of this."

"I'll go get the pruning tools to put back in the shed." She lowered her head and walked away, listening to Richard and his father arguing. She felt saddened that she had caused another confrontation between them.

Trudy felt she was to blame for at least some of their arguments since she and Richard were always conspiring some way to cross paths or spend time together while they worked. She tried not to let the intensity of her affection for Richard show when she was around his family, but apparently that hadn't worked. Lately, she couldn't help noticing the stares and mumbling that seemed to be directed toward her whenever they were together.

When the Vanderveers hired her three years earlier, Trudy noticed she was the only girl working at the farm and figured they'd given her the job as a favor to Uncle Harry. She worked hard to prove she could work as well as the boys her age, and Richard's grandfather had bragged about her work. Richard's father was pleased when he found out she was saving all the money she earned for college.

Everything seemed different now. Maybe it was because of the friction between Richard and his father or maybe it was because Richard had grown up and let his hair grow out and was more outspoken. Whatever the reason, Trudy was careful of what she said or did in front of his family. But it didn't stop her from spending every hour of every day she could with him. Soon it would be different for them.

Walking back toward the shed, Trudy saw Richard come around the building, his head hung low. Agitated, he threw something into the wagon, jumped onto the tractor and sped off without looking in her direction. She hung the pruning shears in their place on the back wall pegboard. Through the raised window she could hear Richard's father and grandfather talking, but she ignored them until she heard her name mentioned. She stood momentarily to listen.

"I don't think much of this. My grandson taking a fancy to some girl we know so little," the grandfather said. "Look at what's she's done to him. A hired field hand and she's got him talking back to you. It's downright disrespectful."

"I thought that by keeping the boys in school back home nothing like this would happen," Patrick admitted. "I guess I did wrong bringing them to the States to work summers. I had hoped it would be a good experience for them."

"Yesterday," the elder went on, "I heard Richard telling Raymond about a bunch of boys who make music calling themselves Three Dog Night and Creedence Creek Water Revival or something. It ain't right those young'uns over here making fun of animals and religion in their music."

"I know, Father," Patrick agreed. "It's not the same over here. I wish I could've kept the boys away from the local kids."

"Well, what are you going to do if he takes such a liking to that girl and wants to marry her? What are you going to do then?"

"Father, they're just kids. I'll talk to Richard about it, though."

Trudy heard them walking off. She rushed out of the shed and got into her mother's Chevy Impala and drove off before they could see her. Should she tell Richard about what she heard? No. It would only make things worse. She didn't want to cause another confrontation between Richard and his father.

—

Trudy sat stunned after learning what had happened. Tears welled up in her eyes. She reminded herself this was something that happened thirty-five years ago. *It was the distant past. It shouldn't matter anymore, should it?*

Tears flowed anyway.

CHAPTER 6

Trudy reread the letter over and over. During the last thirty-five years she had followed Richard's career closely by reading all the news articles about him that she could find. He had become a successful businessman, building an empire of food and floral companies all over the world. She never told anyone her secret that Richard Vanderveer was the boy who broke her heart.

Thinking about their lost opportunity of a life together, she felt cheated. Then she became angry. Her mother had taken money from Mr. Vanderveer and never told her. The more Trudy tried to ignore the letter, the more furious she became.

She got up and piddled at mindless chores around the house, trying to calm down, knowing that confronting her mother about something that happened years ago would change nothing. But it wasn't working. She couldn't control the hurt churning inside of her.

The telephone rang. She didn't want to talk to anyone but decided to answer it when she saw it was April calling.

"What do you want?" she blurted out.

There was a pause. "Mom, are you okay?"

"Yes, Sweetie, I'm sorry." She inhaled. "I just had something on my mind. Are you getting your work done?"

"Yes, but what I'm calling about is the mail you picked up at the post office yesterday. The story about the letter is on all the news media this morning. I wanted to see if you knew about it."

"Yes, I saw it on TV this morning."

"Since it's getting a lot of attention, our news office wants to do a follow-up story about it."

Trudy paused before speaking. "There's not a lot to talk about."

"When I told them that you were the one who received the letter they were ecstatic and wanted to know if you would do an exclusive interview with us."

Trudy thought for a second, not sure how to respond, but reluctantly agreed, "If it will help you."

"That's great. I'll tell them and be home in a few minutes. Are you sure everything is okay?"

"Yes, April. Everything's fine."

"I'm on my way. Love you."

Trudy hastily hung up the phone. She needed to get a grip on her emotions. Why was she letting something that happened so long ago rattle her? She decided to put it out of her mind and went back to doing chores.

Busy in the kitchen, Trudy recalled the time in her life when everything had gone wrong for her and her mother.

Trudy had been seventeen years old when she and her mother moved to Lynchburg after her father's death. She knew no one there except for a few distant relatives or cousins she had met at family reunions. With no friends to confide in, Trudy shared her mother's anguish and insecurity. She lay awake at night listening to her mother cry herself to sleep. Trudy clung to the hope that she'd have Richard to lean on. He would eventually rescue her from the sadness that gripped her. Weeks later, her world shattered when his letter arrived, marking the end of their relationship. Suddenly she had two losses to mourn.

Eventually, time eased the pain. She focused on her studies during a difficult senior year at Lynchburg High School. Her mother took a job at the local textile mill, since the money from her dad's pension wasn't sufficient for their needs.

Later, once they sat down and figured out what college was going to cost, her mother took a second part-time job to earn money for Trudy's education. Trudy tried to talk her mother out of it, but she reminded her, "It was your father's plan to send you to college. It meant a lot to him. I'm not going to let him down." That planted the seed in her life that eventually led her to volunteer with the FEW Foundation.

Trudy and her mother did everything together, supporting each other wholeheartedly. Eventually, mother and daughter became best friends.

Seven years later, Trudy met Kenneth and her heart reawakened. Because she and her mother were so close, she felt guilty telling her mother she was in love and wanted to marry Kenneth. When she finally broke the news to her, her mother surprised her by supporting her decision and shared with her the reason she'd never shown interest in any other men after her husband's death.

"When I married your father we were just two young, naïve kids and knew nothing about love, other than we couldn't live without each other anymore. I gave him my heart, and all of me. In return he loved me more and more every day. He made me feel special, and I never doubted he loved me just as much as I loved him. I knew no other man would ever be able to fill his shoes. I guess his love to me was enough for a lifetime and beyond.... Every time I look at you, Trudy, I know I still have a part of him with me. That has always been enough for me."

Trudy had always imagined her marriage would become like what her mother had.

But now, Trudy was horrified to even think her mother had known what Richard's father had done to separate them and had kept this awful secret from her. After all these years trusting her mother with everything, she felt betrayed.

"Morning, Trudy."

Startled, Trudy jumped and turned to face her mother at the kitchen counter. She poured a cup of coffee for herself and handed one to her mother.

"Morning, Mom...sleep well?" She struggled to get the words out.

"Yes, I did." Between sips of coffee her mother continued. "When April gets home, I'd like her to go with me over to my house. I want to give her some of my keepsakes since she and Matthew are going to have their own place shortly."

"Fine." Trudy's voice sounded distant to her own ears.

Mrs. Meyers studied her for a moment. "Your eyes are red. Have you been crying?"

Trudy waved off the question, fighting back emotions.

"Has someone done something to upset you?"

Trudy shook her head and turned away.

"Then what's wrong?" her mother persisted.

Overcome by a hot rush of anger, Trudy spun around, tempted to blurt out everything she now knew about the bribe her mother had taken and Richard's letter. Instead, she swallowed hard and spoke with restraint.

"Why didn't you tell me about Richard's father?"

"Richard's father?" Her mother shook her head as if she didn't understand.

"It's in the letter he sent, Mother! The one I picked up at the post office yesterday, thirty-five years late! Richard told me what his father did to separate us." Trudy saw confusion in her mother's eyes. She reached across to where she'd left the envelope on the kitchen table. "This is the letter." She held it up.

"Richard's father, Mr. Vanderveer." Her face paled. She set her coffee cup down on the island counter and spoke softly. "Trudy, I am so sorry. I had every intention of telling you back then. But I had just gotten word that your father had been killed. Then there was the move. I thought it was more than you could bear. It stayed on my mind but...." Her voice quivered as she paused. "When you got that letter from Richard ending your relationship, I just didn't want you hurt anymore than you already were. So I dropped it."

"Mother, I had a right to know!" Trudy insisted. "If I had known what happened I could have helped Richard. He left home and lived in a homeless shelter because of me."

"Trudy, I...I don't know what to say. I did what I thought was best for you at the time. I had no idea what Richard had done."

The front door opened. April called out. "Mom, Grandma."

She walked into the kitchen, chattering excitedly. "Okay, Mom, I have more details now about your story. A national news service is going to carry a follow-up article. Most likely it will be picked up by every major newspaper across the country and posted on every news web site." She hesitated, looking first at her mother, then her grandmother.

"What's wrong with you two? I was sure you would think this was cool."

Trudy glanced at her but had to look away. "Nothing's wrong, April. I'm glad for you."

"Mom, you've been crying. What's going on here? I wondered if you were upset when I called earlier."

"April, let's just drop it."

Mrs. Meyers turned and left the room, her head bowed.

"It's the letter, isn't it?" April stepped closer to her mother. "Something in the letter has you two upset."

"I can't talk about it right now. Okay?" Trudy muttered.

"Tell me what's in the letter that has you so upset," April insisted.

Hesitatingly, Trudy responded, "Please, I need time to sort this out. We'll talk about it later. Go check on your grandmother for me."

April left the room. Trudy stood staring out the window, wondering how to deal with what she'd learned today.

It was late evening and dusk had settled on what had been a perfect spring day. All day she tried to ignore the emotional trauma churning inside her, but nothing eased the anguish she felt. Finally, she called Jan, the one person in whom she could confide. April had left with her grandmother earlier. Trudy suspected April was purposely keeping her grandmother away until she knew what was going on between the two women.

She now sat on the back porch, pouring her heart out to Jan.

"You never told me that the boy you loved was *the* Richard Vanderveer," Jan said, after hearing the whole story from Trudy. "I'm sure you look at what he's become today and feel a little envious about not having your chance with him."

"I struggled with my emotions for a long time. Remember, I got the Dear John letter from him and didn't know why until this morning." She frowned. "Now I have Mom upset. I'm upset. And April wants me to do an in-depth interview for the media. All of a sudden it's gotten complicated."

"Well, let me put it in perspective for you, girlfriend. You lost your dad, you moved to a new city, started a new school, and Richard's father tells your mother that all you're going to get out of this relationship is disappointment. A couple months later, you got a Dear John letter from Richard, blaming you for walking away from the relationship." She held up her hands. "What would you have done differently?"

"I don't know." Trudy blinked several times. "Maybe she had her reasons, but Mom taking money from Richard's father floored me."

"Did you ask her about it?"

"No. I didn't mention it. I had already upset her enough over the letter and I was furious, so I figured the best thing was to not say anything about it. When things are calmer I'm going to ask her about it. It's just so out of character for her to have done something like that. It really hurt me knowing she did it and kept it a secret from me all these years."

"She didn't take it for herself. Can you imagine how insecure your mother must've felt with your dad gone and you getting ready for college within a year?"

"I suppose you're right." Trudy leaned back in her chair and relaxed. "I should have talked to you about this before going off on Mom."

"You would've figured it out. You didn't need me to do it for you."

"I don't know. Lately, I can't seem to make sense of anything. I'm already struggling with what to do when Kenny gets home…and now something that happened thirty-five years ago comes back to haunt me. It's more than I can deal with."

"You definitely have a lot on your mind now."

"At least you're listening to me."

"Whose ear did I bend for a year when I went through my divorce? I owe you big time, girl."

"I hope that's a debt I'll never have to collect on."

The phone rang.

"That might be Mom or April. At least I can let them know I've calmed down and make them feel better." Trudy stepped inside to the kitchen wall phone. She noticed Private Caller on the ID and hesitated but answered anyway.

"Hello?"

"I'm looking for Mrs. Trudy Quinn, please."

"This is she."

"Trudy, it's good to hear your voice. How are you?"

"I'm fine." She didn't recognize the caller's voice. He had an unfamiliar accent. She considered hanging up but asked, "May I help you?"

"I picked up the paper this morning, read about the lost letter, and have been thinking about you all day. I kept thinking about what the article said and finally went back and read it again. Then it hit me. According to the date on the envelope, the letter was the one I sent to you after I left school and went into hiding. The reason you never called me was because you didn't know how to get in touch with me. My letter never got to you!"

Trudy felt a lump in her throat and a shiver ran down her spine. She swallowed hard. "Rich...Richard? Is that you?"

"Yes, Trudy, it is." He laughed. "I didn't mean to surprise you. As soon as I read the paper this morning, I knew I had to call you. I hope you don't mind."

"No. No, not at all. I certainly wasn't expecting this."

"I've just got to see you."

"I'd love to see you, too. I mean it would be nice to get together sometime."

Feeling a little dizzy, Trudy leaned against the island counter for support. She didn't want to sound too excited and hoped that whatever she said wouldn't sound foolish.

"You know, if we'd had computers thirty-five years ago, with the click of a key none of this would have happened," Richard said.

"I guess you're right." She laughed.

"I felt awful this morning when I found out my letter never got to you, especially after writing the last letter to you ending our relationship as if it were your choice. I can only imagine how you felt."

"Yeah, that was a tough one. I couldn't figure out what I'd done. I really wanted to claw your eyes out," she jokingly said.

He chuckled.

"I've thought about you often over the years, wanted to call so many times, but had no idea how to contact you."

"I've thought about you, too," she murmured, smiling.

"When can I see you?"

"I...I don't know, Richard." She ran her fingers through her hair, unsure if agreeing to see him was the right thing to do. "My husband is coming home from Iraq next week; the following weekend I'm planning a surprise homecoming for him and an engagement party for our daughter."

"Then let's get together and have dinner tomorrow night. Maybe we can spend a day or so together and get caught up on what we've been doing with our lives."

"I wouldn't want to put you through any trouble or anything."

"Trouble?" he chuckled. "The timing couldn't be better. I'm actually in the States, staying at The Greenbrier in West Virginia for the next few days, trying to close a business deal. I'll send my driver down to pick you up. It's only a couple of hours from here to Lynchburg."

She nervously glanced around the room in disbelief. Was she really going to see him after all these years? "No, no need for that. I can drive myself up."

"Then, you can come up tomorrow?"

"Maybe," she said cautiously. "Let me talk to my daughter and mother first. Then I'll let you know."

"Sure. Here's my private number." He recited it. "If you're not comfortable coming up, then maybe I could come to Lynchburg and meet the whole Quinn family."

"No need for that," she said hastily, aware that she was suddenly very nervous and hyperventilating. "I'll try to work something out."

"Trudy," he lowered his voice. "We're meeting only as friends. Nothing more, okay?"

"I understand, Richard. Thank you." She relaxed.

"Then I'll hear from you in the morning?"

"Yes, you will."

"I look forward to seeing you, Trudy."

"Me too. Bye." She started to breathe more normally again and clicked the phone off, not sure what she had agreed to. Tearing the phone number from the notepad, she walked out to the porch where Jan sat, staring at her.

"Is everything okay?"

"I think so." Trudy sat down and rested her hands in her lap before speaking. "I just got off the phone with Richard."

"Not Richard Vanderveer!" Jan exclaimed, her eyes widening.

"He read about the letter in a newspaper this morning."

"What did he say?"

"Once he realized the letter that would have explained everything never made it to me, he wanted to talk to me."

"News really travels fast, doesn't it? I can only imagine how both of you must feel now that you know what happened. Where did he call from?"

"He's in West Virginia, staying at The Greenbrier, working on a business deal. He wants me to come up."

"Well, he certainly didn't waste any time. Are you going to meet him?"

"I'm not sure. I guess we owe it to each other after finding out what happened."

"What will April and your mother think? And what about his wife?"

"His wife was killed in a plane accident in Africa two years ago. I remember reading about it somewhere." She hesitated a moment. "I'm not sure how April and Mom will feel about me seeing him, though."

"Do you have to tell them?"

Trudy stared at her, appalled.

"You are legally separated, you know," Jan reminded her. "Why would they need to know?"

"Because I have a conscience and we're only meeting as friends. Besides, I'm not doing anything that needs to be hidden."

"Well, as your friend, I'm not sure whether to jump up and down for you or to caution you."

"I know. But maybe if we see each other, it will at least put closure on what was such a painful event in our lives."

"Or re-ignite the spark," Jan said skeptically, eyeing Trudy.

"No, I wouldn't let it come to that. Now, how to tell April and Mom will be the challenge."

"You're about to have your chance. I just heard them pull into the driveway. I'll leave so you girls can talk privately." She stood to leave. "Let me know how it goes. And remember, I'm just a phone call away if you need me."

"Thank you. I'm sure I'll be calling," Trudy replied with a playful smirk on her face.

Trudy met her mother and April as they came into the kitchen. Her mother carried several envelopes in her hand.

"Mom, April, may I talk to you for a moment?"

Both nodded and followed her out to the back porch.

Trudy sat across from them, her hands cupped in her lap. "I want to apologize to both of you for how I acted this morning. I overreacted to something that was in the letter I opened."

"Trudy, I want to…" her mother said, holding up her envelopes.

"No, Mother. Let me finish," Trudy interrupted. Directing her attention to April, she continued. "The letter was from a friend I knew when I was a teenager. I know you want me to give an interview to the paper about all of this, but first I need to sort out some things."

"The letter is thirty-five years old. What could you possibly have to sort out about it now?" April asked.

"The friend who wrote the letter to me read about it in a newspaper this morning and called."

"Oh," her mother said.

April blinked at her. "So?"

"He's in the country on business and is staying at The Greenbrier for the next couple of days. He's invited me to come up for dinner tomorrow. As friends only, of course," she quickly added.

"Why would you want to meet him?" April asked. "Isn't he the Dutch guy who jilted you?"

"I can't tell you a lot about it now. Only that at one time we were very close and thought we had a future together. This letter explains everything, and since it didn't get delivered, it changed our lives forever."

"Are you sure you want to see him?" her mother asked. "What good could possibly come out of meeting him and getting yourself upset again?"

"You should understand why we need to see each other," Trudy snapped, obviously agitated.

Feeling provoked but not wanting to sound defensive, she stood and took a couple of steps to the end of the porch, crossed her arms, and looked back at them. "Mother," she said calmly, "you know what happened between us. Maybe it'll be a chance for us to find closure for the relationship that ended so suddenly and painfully for both of us."

"You're freaking me out!" April stood, her voice quivering. "Dad's coming home after being gone for a year, and I'm having my engagement party next weekend and my...my mother is running off to meet an old boyfriend?"

"It's not like that, April." Trudy stood steadfast. "I'm not stepping out on your father."

She reached out to embrace April.

"No! Don't touch me," April shouted, stepping back. "How could you even think about doing this? I thought you and Dad were going to try to work things out when he got home!"

"We are, and this won't change a thing between us."

"Mother, I can't believe...." She angrily walked away without finishing.

Trudy turned to her mother, knowing she was also going to get an earful from her.

"Okay, Mom, your turn."

Her mother spoke softly. "I want you to understand something. When Richard's father came to Uncle Harry's farm and spoke to me, I wasn't prepared for what he told me. He said his family didn't approve of you and Richard getting close and figured it best you two didn't see each other again. It shocked me and I didn't know what to say or how to respond. After he left and I had time to think about what he told me he had done, I was furious. That night I made up my mind to go over the next day and give him a piece of my mind." She glanced down and paused. Her voice trembled when she spoke. "But before I could make it over the next morning I found out your father had been killed and my world fell apart. I forgot about everything else."

"Mother, I'm not blaming you for what his father did," Trudy responded. "I'm sorry for jumping to conclusions this morning. I've lived the past thirty-five years of my life wondering what I had done to change Richard's mind about me. Every time I heard his name mentioned in the news or read about him, I asked myself what happened. Don't you see? It'll be a chance for us to put an unfortunate event and time in our lives behind us. We at least owe it to each other to do that."

"Yes, I can understand. What happened between you two was unfair. Maybe it was destiny." She looked at Trudy with a grim expression. "I just don't want to see you hurt all over again and mess up your chance of working things out with Kenneth when he gets home. I would give anything now to have done something differently back then." She swallowed and cleared her throat. "But it was a difficult time for me with your father passing and watching you hurt so much. If I had it to do over again, I'm not sure I wouldn't do the exact same thing."

"Oh, Mother," Trudy sat down and reached for her mother's hand. "Forgive me for being selfish and thinking only of myself. I know that time in our lives was just as painful for you."

"It was hard on both of us." Her mother put her other hand over Trudy's and held it firmly. "I knew it broke your heart when you received that last letter from Richard. I just didn't want to see you hurt anymore than you were already." She paused before continuing. "You do what your heart leads you to do. I'll go up and speak to April and try to make her understand. But at some point you need to tell her everything so she'll know why you're thinking of doing this."

"Thank you for understanding," Trudy said, with heartfelt relief. She could always trust her mother to support her decisions. She always had.

She started to ask her about the money Richard mentioned in his letter. She had calmed down, and her mother was no longer upset, so now they could have a civil conversation about it. But maybe it would be best to wait. Maybe after she came back from seeing Richard would be better.

Watching her mother walk away, Trudy concluded that April needed her attention now. She had to convince April that her meeting Richard for dinner would be harmless. Yes. The money discussion could wait. She had to find a way to appease April.

CHAPTER 7

Trudy stood in her closet, eyeing clothes to pack. After pulling out several hangers, she finally decided to take soft, neutral colors, since they always complemented her light hair color, and a black silk dress in case formal wear was needed. With an armful of clothes, she pushed the closet door closed, assured that she was over-prepared.

She found herself primping more than usual in front of the bathroom mirror, trying to shadow her makeup just right and brushing her hair to get it to lay flat so the blonde highlights would be more visible. Wishing she still had the blonde hair of her youth, she gave it a last comb through with her fingers and proceeded to pack her cosmetic bag.

On her way down the hall, she remembered she had one more thing to take care of before leaving. She saw April in her room at her desk. Tapping on the door, she stepped inside as April looked up.

"Got a few minutes for me?"

"Sure, come in."

Trudy sat on the bed, cupped her hands together, and spoke gently. "I didn't mean to upset you last night."

"I just didn't understand why you need to go and see this guy." She glanced down. "I'm still not sure I do."

"Did Grandmother tell you about him and what we meant to each other thirty-five years ago?"

"Yes." She looked up. "But you and Richard were seventeen years old. How could you have even known what love was then?"

Trudy smiled. "Why do I feel like I'm talking to my grown-up daughter?"

"I'm sorry, Mom. I just don't want anything to happen that might come between you and Dad getting back together when he gets home. That's if you want to," she timidly added.

April waited for Trudy to respond.

"Look, if it were anything more than meeting for dinner, then I would run from him. Besides, Richard even mentioned we would be meeting only as friends."

"But you and Dad went through marriage counseling before he left. What if…" She trailed off without completing her thought.

Trudy stepped over to the window to look out. "I'm sorry your father and I put you through that. Yes, we've had our share of problems, but I would never let another man come between us."

She paused and turned from the window, knowing she needed to convince her daughter to trust her. "Richard was the first boy I loved. And, yes, I loved him very much even if we were only seventeen years old. Our time together happened a long time before your dad and I ever met. Then when our relationship ended, even to this day, I've always asked myself why." She moved closer to April. "Because of me, Richard quit school and left home, and his family didn't even know where he was. It changed his life, our lives, forever because that letter didn't get to me."

"I understand that, but…" April stood up, hands on hips, and spoke more firmly. "I'm still concerned about my mother running off to see a former boyfriend."

"April, you've got to trust your mother on this one."

"What if Dad finds out?"

"Why do you think I told you and Mom? I'm not hiding anything. When your dad gets home I intend to show him the letter and tell him about Richard, meeting him and all. If we're going to have a chance at mending our marriage, there has to be some trust between us."

"It's not that I don't trust you." April frowned. "Look at all that's happening next week. Dad's coming home and my engagement party is next weekend." Flustered, she rolled her eyes.

Trudy reached for April's hand and held it in hers. "I know the timing isn't good, but I'll be gone for only one night. When I get home, I'll give an interview to the paper and we'll put all of this behind us."

April did her best to smile.

"So promise me you won't worry," Trudy said, squeezing her hand and letting go.

"You're my mother, and I have a right to worry."

Trudy chuckled to herself. On her way out the door, she smiled, thinking, *What can I say? She's all grown up now.*

—

Walking into the kitchen with packed bags, Trudy found her mother seated at the table reading Sunday's morning paper and sipping freshly brewed coffee. She poured a cup and sat at the table as her mother pushed the front section over for her to read.

"You might want to see this."

Trudy glanced at the headline. Winchester Apple Fruit Company Rejects Vanderveer Enterprise Buyout Offer. Now she knew which business Richard had referred to. She ignored it.

"I spoke with April. I think she's a little more tolerant of me now." She sipped her coffee.

"I'm glad. I tried to calm her down last night. She was very upset."

"I know," Trudy sighed. "I wish I could've put this off for a few weeks."

"Why don't you?"

"Because Richard's going to be in the country for just a few days. If we don't see each other now, we might never have another chance."

"Does that bother you?" her mother asked, watching closely.

Trudy sat back, flustered. "I don't know." She could always count on her mother to ask tough questions. "We're just meeting for dinner. That shouldn't cause any harm."

"When are you coming home?"

"I'll be home sometime tomorrow."

"You know Richard's a wealthy, powerful man now," she reminded her. "He's not the same tall, lanky boy you knew thirty-five years ago."

"I know." She met her mother's unwavering gaze. "I'm sure he's got a harem waiting for him all over the world. Besides, we're meeting as friends. That's all."

Her mother reached over and patted her hand. "Trudy, I hope this works out for you."

"I'm sure it will. I'm going to get started now so I can be up there by midday."

"Drive safely. Call me if you need me."

She kissed her mother on the cheek. "Love you, Mom."

She picked up her bags and left.

~

Restless during her two-hour drive to The Greenbrier, Trudy fidgeted with the radio to find the right music to soothe her anxious and weary mood. Nothing seemed to work as her thoughts jumped from the excitement of seeing Richard again, to Kenny coming home from Iraq, and April's engagement. Finally, at the point of wanting to scream, she opened her sunroof to let fresh air blow in. Remembering the seventies CDs Kenneth had given her that she kept in her CD player, she hit the play button. Once the music started, she relaxed and thought about her childhood and events that led to her meeting Richard.

She had lived near or on army bases most of her childhood because her dad was a career soldier. Since he was in Special Forces, he often went on tour to many parts of the world, leaving his wife and daughter alone for months at a time.

When he did come home, he would change out of uniform and into civilian clothes as soon as possible. A lot of the young boys who had parents in the army often talked about the fighting and killing their dads were doing. Trudy finally figured out that for her dad, changing to civilian clothes was his way of separating his private life from military life and sheltering them from the reality of what he was doing. He never spoke about his tours or missions.

Except for one time.

— ⌣ —

She was six years old. Some of the boys at school told her that her dad killed enemy soldiers. It bothered her so much she sat on the porch that day, waiting for him to come home so she could ask him. He drove up in his Jeep and hesitated before walking onto the porch when he saw the solemn face she wore.

"What's wrong, Trudy?" he asked.

Trudy dropped her hands in her lap and looked down, not sure what to say.

He squatted down beside her and touched her cheek. "What's got my princess unhappy today?"

Trudy raised her eyes and asked, "Daddy, what kind of job do you have?"

He thought for a second, reached for her small hands, and guardedly chose his words. "I protect the borders of America, so all little boys and girls can wake up every morning in a free country. Does that bother you?"

She shook her head no.

"Has someone told you differently?"

"Some of the boys at school say their dads do bad things to other people. I told them you didn't do those things," she said, shaking her head.

"Trudy, sometimes I have to do things I don't like doing." He moistened his lips. "But I do them so I can help other boys and girls somewhere else in the world wake up to a free country and go to school like you do every day. Do you think that is a bad thing?"

"No."

"Well, let's the two of us make each other a promise."

"Okay."

"I promise I will do only what I have to do to protect the people in the world who love freedom, and you promise me that you won't worry about this anymore."

"Don't we have to cross our heart and hope to die to make the promise real?" Trudy murmured.

Her father laughed. "I think you and I can trust each other enough to seal this promise with a big hug. What do you say?"

"Okay." She scrambled to her feet and hugged him.

She turned toward the door and found her mother standing and smiling as she listened to them.

—

Her mother often worked at food commissaries at the army bases to keep busy and earn money for the extras they enjoyed. When her dad came home on leave, she often surprised him with vacations she had planned and paid for to get him away from army life for a while.

Trudy made a lot of friends on the bases. Some of them she knew for years and some for only several weeks as new recruits often rotated on and off the base. Trudy remembered all too well when news came in about someone's dad or husband being killed while on active duty. There was always a lot of grief and sadness around them, and her mother did all she could to comfort a family that lost a loved one. The families often moved away quickly, and Trudy never saw them again.

During the last three years of the Vietnam War, her mother tried hard to keep her away from army life as much as possible. That was the reason she visited Aunt Margaret and Uncle Harry's farm every summer where she met the Vanderveer family.

She reminisced about the first time she met Richard and their three summers together. Their last day together etched in her heart forever, she remembered well.

—

Trudy and Richard sat on a blanket on the grassy Maury River bank, listening to Casey Kasem's *American Top Forty Countdown* on a transistor radio. Richard lay back, his hands cupped behind his head. Trudy sat with her legs crossed, feeding him grapes and sharp cheddar cheese she had brought as part of their picnic.

"I can't believe summer is almost over. I dread going back home to start school." Richard chomped down on the last bit of cheese Trudy placed in his mouth and leaned over on his left side, propped up on an elbow. "I'm going to miss our weekend afternoons here on the river."

"I'm going to miss you, too, Richard." Trudy cleared the food out of the way and lay face down on the blanket beside him. She spread the grass apart with her fingers, looking for four-leaf clovers at the edge of the blanket, believing if she found one it would bring her good luck. She knew Richard would be leaving and going back to Europe the next day to start college. She felt uneasy knowing he would be meeting a lot of girls from all over Europe.

"Richard…" she tried not to sound concerned, "what if you like going to college in Europe and decide to stay and finish school there?"

"That's not going to happen. I'm coming back so I can be with you." He reached over and toyed with the hair falling over her left shoulder. "Next spring when I turn eighteen, I'll apply for college somewhere here in the States and transfer."

"But a year is a long time, and we'll be far away from each other. A lot can happen between now and then," she reminded him, as she pulled a cloverleaf from the grass. Seeing it had only three petals, she tossed it away.

Richard dropped his hand from her hair and spoke seriously. "Promise me you won't let anything come between us while I'm away."

Trudy glanced over at his intense gaze, glad that he, too, was concerned about being away from her.

"I'll promise if you'll promise not to fall in love with any of those fancy European girls who I'm sure will have their sights set on you."

He chuckled. "No, I'm all about you. When I come back, we'll start making plans to get married as soon as we can."

"Once we do, we'll have to find jobs, and it'll be difficult for us to stay in school," Trudy replied, trying not to sound pessimistic.

"I'll do what I have to do. You know that. If I have to work day and night so we can be together, then I'll do it."

"I know you will," Trudy agreed, turning to her side. "That's the reason I love you so much. You're always so confident."

"Someday, we're going to have us a big, white house on a farm." He lifted his hand, painting a picture in the air. "And a front porch with rocking chairs and lots of handsome little boys wearing hats and suspenders to hold their britches up." He grinned.

"No, Richard." Trudy shook her head and raised an eyebrow. "We're going to have little girls wearing bright colored bows in their hair, and they'll take ballet and music lessons and be sought after by charming princes from far away places once they're all grown up."

"I say, Trudy," he snickered. "We may need to have a lot of babies so we both can get what we want."

"That's easy for you to say," she giggled. "You're not the one who has to have them." She paused at the thought. "What will you do if your father won't let you transfer to a school here?"

"As long as I stay in school somewhere he shouldn't care. Besides, I can help grandfather with the farm if I'm over here. That should make him happy, I reckon."

"What if he doesn't approve of me?"

"It doesn't matter, Trudy," he emphasized strongly. "I won't need his permission. Once I'm eighteen, I can do what I want. Besides, I'm not letting him pick the girl I marry."

"I know, but it worries me knowing that he might not approve of us marrying." Trudy glanced away, suddenly feeling sad.

"We've talked about this," Richard reminded her, reaching over and brushing strands of hair from her face. "You have to quit letting this bother you. Let me worry about Father. If he doesn't agree to us getting married then I'll just leave home."

Trudy held his hand against her face. "I love you, Richard. But I would never want to come between you and your family."

"Then trust me. I'll make it work out. I promise."

"I know you will," she smiled, sliding up close to his body and putting her arm around him. "Will you always love me?"

"Always."

She fell back on the blanket when his body shifted against her. They passionately kissed. Richard tenderly caressed her body and Trudy knew that she should stop him, yet she yearned for his touch and the way it made her feel inside. Their breathing became heavier. He slid his hand under her shirt and up to her breast.

"No. No, Richard. Not like this. We can't." She pulled his hand away from her and pushed herself up.

He leaned on his side and frowned.

"Oh, Richard, I'm sorry," she apologized. "Some day we'll be together always and it won't have to be like this."

Richard left for the Netherlands the next day. That summer, all she thought about was Richard and what life would be like as his wife. She relished the thought of planning her life with him, and knew her life was becoming what dreams were made of.

What happened a week later, on a hot August day in 1975, had lived in her mind ever since. She sat on the back porch with Aunt Margaret and her mother, snapping half-runner beans for canning. Uncle Harry came out of the house with a grim look on his face.

That's when she noticed the black car with *United States Army, Official Government Business* on the door that had pulled up to the farm house. Two men in uniform came to the door and asked to see her mother. Trudy watched as her mother sat there, expressionless, her hands clasped together, tears rolling down her cheeks as they told her that her husband was a hero. She knew her mother was being strong for her sake.

Two weeks later, having moved to Lynchburg, Trudy had no friends to confide in as she endured the anguish and grief she shared with her mother. Earlier, she had mailed a five-page letter to Richard pouring out her sorrow and insecure feelings, only to discover two weeks later it was the first of several letters to be returned and stamped *UNABLE TO DELIVER.*

~

Startled, Trudy jerked the car back into the right lane at the blast from an eighteen-wheeler. She had let the car drift into

71

the neighboring lane. Noticing that she was driving faster than the speed limit, she took a deep breath and slowed down. Her heart raced from the scare, as she looked for a sign to see where she was. The mileage marker told her she was only a few miles from The Greenbrier.

Her thoughts filled with anticipation, Trudy turned at the next exit listening to "Yesterday Once More" by The Carpenters on the radio.

CHAPTER 8

Trudy pulled her Acura up to the loading zone in front of the stately white hotel nestled at the foot of a towering mountain range. An array of uniformed men and women were busy loading and unloading luggage from cars and SUVs. Someone opened her door, and a young man dressed in a black uniform and white shirt greeted her.

"Good morning, or midday, ma'am. Will you be checking in with us and would you like valet parking?"

"Yes, I'm checking in. And valet parking would be appreciated."

Another uniformed bellhop stepped up with a cart. "I will get your luggage, ma'am."

He pulled a pad from his pocket. "Your name please?"

"Trudy Quinn."

"One moment, please." He left and walked over to the service stand and spoke to a short young man dressed in a dark gray uniform. He followed the bellhop back to Trudy.

"Ms. Quinn, I've been expecting you. My name is Kwan," he introduced himself.

He spoke with an accent, and she figured him to be Korean.

"I am Mr. Vanderveer's assistant. He's expecting you. Your travel here today was good, I hope?"

"It was, thank you."

"If you're ready to go to your room, I will take you up."

"Yes, but first let me give them a tip for parking my car." She dug in her purse.

"I have taken care of that, Ms. Quinn."

He held up a room key. "If you're ready, I'll lead you up to your room."

"Okay," Trudy responded, following him into the hotel lobby that opened into a luxurious foyer with high ceilings, colorful walls and bright carpeted paths that stretched in every direction. Wingback chairs and sofas were placed throughout the rooms where a number of people were milling around. Wide paned windows trimmed with floral draperies towered to the ceiling. Some people sat and gazed at the mountains surrounding them or watched people skating on the outside skating rink. Trudy marveled at the colorful interior as she followed Kwan down the hallway to the elevator. She hadn't expected her room to be ready or to be ushered in by Richard's personal assistant.

In the elevator, Kwan asked, "Ms. Quinn, may I bring you a cocktail, a beverage, or maybe some hors d'oeuvres?"

"Yes, something light would be great." She had been so focused on her trip today that she hadn't taken time to eat. "But I can order room service so you won't have to bother. And please, call me Trudy."

"Yes, Ms. Trudy. I'll take care of the order for you once you're in your room."

Trudy smiled, realizing she wasn't going to get him to drop the Ms. in front of her name no matter how hard she tried. She followed him down the hall past several doors, and finally he slid the key into her room door. She stepped inside and was overwhelmed when she saw the size and appearance of the room. It had green striped carpet and flowered wallpaper, pink wingback chairs, and cherry wood furniture was placed throughout the room. On a table was a large vase of fresh cut flowers. To her right was a separate room with green carpet, light-green wallpaper, white furniture, and a king-size bed. The bathroom had marble countertops, a shower, and a bathtub that was as large as her bathroom at home.

"Ms. Trudy, are you pleased?" Kwan asked.

"Very much so," she said, turning around in a circle.

"Your luggage arrived and I've placed your bags in the closet. Your personals in your travel bag, I can put them away for you also."

"No need for that. Here, let me get you something." She opened her purse.

"No, no, Ms. Trudy. Mr. Vanderveer takes care of me." He waved her offer away. "I'll order room service for you. What would you like?"

"Hmm...Maybe some veggies, fruit with yogurt and water will do. Just charge it to my room. I will cover it when I check out."

"No need for that, Ms. Trudy. I'll go and order for you."

"Thank you, Kwan. And I need to let Richard know I'm here."

"I'll let him know. Have a pleasant evening, Ms. Trudy." He let himself out the door.

Trudy walked to the window and gazed out at the flowers in mulched beds. The gardens were surrounded by a lawn bordered with greenery and towering trees that looked picture perfect. She remembered the one time, her only time, she and Kenny had come here for their fifteenth wedding anniversary in late October, nine years earlier. They had recently moved into a newly purchased house. April had just gotten braces, and they had spent all of their savings on furnishings for their new house. Money was tight, but Kenny insisted they splurge and spend a night away to celebrate their anniversary. They drove up from Lynchburg and stayed in a deluxe room at The Greenbrier for one night.

Smiling, she remembered Kenny picking her up and carrying her into the room when they arrived. Then he went down to the bar and bought glasses of wine. When he returned, he also brought a single pink rose to her. Trudy reflected on how hard he tried to make their romantic night special. She had always remembered that weekend. Their life was full of play, and just being together was all they needed to have fun.

Her thought of now meeting Richard here clouded her mind. Suddenly she felt apprehensive. She turned away from the window, and the vase of fresh cut flowers caught her attention. She walked over to the cherry wood table where they set. Beside them was a silver tray with assorted chocolates and a folded card. She picked up a chocolate and bit into it. Savoring the rich strawberry cream filling, she reached for the card and read:

My dearest Trudy,

I can't begin to tell you how much it means to me for you to have come today. I hope to make our time together just as special for you also. Meet me at the North Terrace Patio at two o'clock. Perhaps we can walk around this beautiful place and catch up on what we've been doing with our lives. After all, we have thirty-five years to cover.

Always, Richard

Trudy checked the time and saw it was only noon. That gave her two hours to relax and calm down, she hoped. Before relaxing she laid out her clothes for the afternoon: tan pants and a light-blue pullover blouse accentuated with a white beaded necklace and a cream-colored, knitted sweater that hugged her hips.

CHAPTER 9

A robin flew from a tree and perched itself on the rail that Trudy leaned against. She had come out to the North Terrace a few minutes early to wait for Richard. The robin flew down to the ground, picked up something and flew back to the tree limb. Trudy leaned forward, straining to see the nest to which she was sure the robin had flown to feed its young.

"And the forest looked back at the lady and said, 'ah... what a beauty she is.' "

Trudy spun around and there, standing in front of her, was Richard. He wore a light tan cashmere jacket, a collared white shirt, and black trousers. He looked even more handsome than the pictures she had seen of him in magazines or clips she often caught on television. She had prepared what she would say, but all of a sudden she was speechless.

"I was watching a robin," she finally stammered, struck by his presence.

He smiled and stepped closer.

She noted that he was about eight inches taller than she was. He still had his full head of brown hair, cut short, now peppered with gray. His face was smooth, with just a few age lines showing, and his body was heavier with wider shoulders than she remembered. However, he was just as handsome as he had been when a young man.

"Trudy, you're absolutely stunning," he exclaimed as he gazed at her from head to toe. He reached out for her hands and clasped them as their eyes locked. "I couldn't have begun to imagine how beautiful you are."

"Thank you. But I am half a century old, you know," she managed to say with a smile.

"Then life has really been good to you." He continued to hold her hands, his stare fixing her in a trance.

"I had prepared what I was going to say to you, but now I'm speechless and maybe just a bit nervous," she honestly replied.

"Nervous?" he chuckled. "I was afraid to come out, thinking you might still want to claw my eyes out. Why do you think I'm standing here holding your hands?"

She laughed heartily, and he let loose of her hands.

"Also," he said, as he opened his coat, "I remember what a free spirited young lady you used to be so I was very careful with what I chose to wear."

She laughed harder, remembering how she used to pull his suspenders out and let them snap back against him. He had always made her laugh, one of the many reasons she had fallen in love with him.

He gestured toward the terrace rail and they walked over.

"It never dawned on me that you might not have gotten that letter. I was overwhelmed when I read the newspaper article yesterday. I cannot comprehend that we lost each other over a lost letter."

"I actually cried. I think it was one of the worst moments in my life," Trudy acknowledged, feeling relaxed to have been so honest.

He leaned forward, resting both arms on the railing, looking out and away with a solemn expression on his face. "I remember writing that last letter to you in late September, after I didn't hear from you for several weeks. My heart was broken. I thought the reason you didn't call me was because you wanted out of our relationship." He turned back toward her. "My intentions were for you not to feel guilty for making that choice. I wondered whether it was the money Father had given your mother or the fact that I was homeless and had quit school and was barely able to feed myself. I surely didn't want you to think it was your fault for my decision to leave home after what I'd brought on myself."

"I didn't know about the money until I read it in your letter. Mom never told me. A week after you left, we got word Dad had been killed in Vietnam. We moved to Lynchburg almost immediately since that was Mom and Dad's hometown. I had sent you a letter to the address you gave me to let you know what had happened. It came back to me, along with all the other letters I sent, stamped *UNABLE TO DELIVER*. I had no idea what was going on and my life was in turmoil."

He looked visibly upset. "I never knew about your father. I'm sorry."

"If I'd known what happened and how to reach you, I would have," Trudy said. "I could have sent money or anything you needed. Once you turned eighteen, you could've come back to the States and applied for citizenship without your father's permission."

"I know you would've helped. I know that now."

"I sent a letter to your mother trying to learn your whereabouts. She simply wrote back that you had quit school and asked me to let them know where you were if I found out." Trudy shrugged her shoulders. "I didn't have a clue about what happened."

"I tried calling you several times but always got a message saying your phone had been disconnected." Richard spread his hands out in a gesture of defeat. "I never suspected that you weren't getting my mail."

"I guess we were half a world away with no way to get in touch with each other." Trudy paused and reminisced. "Richard, I was utterly shocked when I opened your letter yesterday."

Richard stood silent for a moment and then asked, "Do you feel up to a walk? If I stay out here and we keep talking about this, you're going to see a grown man cry."

"Then let's walk," she readily agreed.

They crossed the terrace into the hallway and down to the lobby. Kwan was standing in the corner at the bellhop's desk. He came over.

"Trudy, would you care for a bottle of water or maybe a beverage of some kind?" Richard asked.

"Water will be fine."

"Sparkling or regular?"

"Regular for me."

"Kwan, two waters, please." Richard held up two fingers. "One regular and one sparkling."

"Yes, Mr. Vanderveer." He walked away.

"Kwan is very likeable," Trudy commented.

"I have to agree. His father worked for me as a foreman in one of the food processing plants I own in Korea. One day, for no apparent reason, there was a riot by a group of workers. His father was killed when someone threw a wrench and hit him in the head. I continued to pay his family the wages his father earned and helped send Kwan to college since there weren't many social programs over there to help them."

"That was generous."

"Kwan and his mother, being proud, refused my help unless Kwan could work for the money. So I let him follow me around the world, taking care of my meetings and a lot of the juggling I have to do. It worked out so well that I hired him as one of my permanent assistants."

"Then I'm sure he must be a busy person."

"Yes. He's actually quite capable of doing all I need him to do. And it doesn't hurt that he's a master tae kwon do. He's gotten me out of some tough spots."

"I can see he enjoys working for you."

"I let him work and travel with me for six months and send him home for six so he can help take care of his mother and spend time with his brothers and sisters. However, I pay him for the entire year."

"He's got to be happy about that, I'm sure."

"It's good for him to see parts of the world he never could have on his own, and I've gotten so accustomed to him taking care of my needs that it's hard for me to send him home."

Kwan returned with the water.

"After you, Trudy," Richard gestured toward the door.

They walked away from the resort, down a path lined with flowering gardens.

"How did you find me so fast?" Trudy asked.

"The article noted that you lived in Lynchburg. So I did a Google search. I never knew any other girl named Trudy so I thought your name, being unique, would pop up and you'd be easy to find. But I didn't have any luck." He shrugged. "Then I searched the local newspaper web archives, and your name popped up several times with your picture. You're a busy person with the work you do for the FEW Foundation and all the local charities with which you've worked."

"It keeps me busy," she agreed with a nod.

Richard stopped walking and turned toward her. "Trudy, it doesn't surprise me that your career is about helping others. I saw that in you when we first met."

"I was a teacher before retiring and now I have a full-time position with the Foundation. However, I've been involved with them ten years or more, trying to find scholarship money for girls to go to college." She kicked at a pinecone that lay at her feet. "It's just so hard to find help in this economy. A lot of students won't be able to continue their education unless I find the funds to help them."

"I'm sure you're going to make it work."

"What happened after you left school?" Trudy asked. "It had to be a struggle for you."

"Yes." He took a sip of water as they began strolling again. "I got a job at a floral shop in Utrecht. It was a hundred miles or so from home and no one knew me. I was determined not to let Father find me. I slept in a homeless shelter until I got a room at the local boardinghouse. I worked during the day with the florist and I helped with the cleaning and cooking at the boardinghouse in the evenings in exchange for board. I worked seven days a week, saved every guilder I made, determined to make it on my own."

He stopped and looked at Trudy. "My heart was broken when I didn't hear from you. I knew I could never go home and live a normal life again after what Father did. I sent that last letter to let you know I wasn't mad or holding it against you." He stared at Trudy and groped for more words. "I kept hoping that you might change your mind about me and call." He paused and glanced away. "After you didn't, all I had to look forward to was work."

Trudy's eyes teared up. She felt saddened. She longed to reach out and hug him. Instead, she tried to control her emotions.

"Hey, I didn't invite you up to make you cry." He brushed a tear from her cheek. He took her hand and put on a smile for her. "I thought we could get together and share a bottle of wine with dinner and reminisce about the fun we did have together."

"I'm sorry," Trudy murmured, blinking her eyes dry. "I had no idea I was going to react this way."

"No apology necessary." He glanced around, then pointed. "Look at the springhouse. Let's go over for a closer look."

They walked over and down the steps.

Trudy began touching the flowers around the springhouse wall, hoping the distraction would keep her from getting emotional again. Richard leaned against one of the columns, sipping water as he watched her.

"Tell me about your life after moving to Lynchburg."

"Oh, there's not a lot to tell." She continued walking alone around the springhouse, inspecting the flowers, her back to him. "We were devastated when we got word that my father had been killed just weeks before he was to retire. I know Mom moved to Lynchburg because a lot of family members whom she knew we could count on for help if we needed it were still living there." She turned to face him. "For me, it was just another school and new friends. I was used to that because of moving around so much during Dad's army career. Mom got a job at the local textile mill and eventually got a job cleaning office buildings in the evenings. I helped her with that as much as I could. She was determined to make sure I had enough money to go to college."

"What about the money my father gave you. Did it help?"

Feeling uncomfortable, Trudy glanced away, not knowing how to respond.

"I'm sorry." Richard put a hand on her arm. "I didn't mean to say that or make it sound the way I did."

Trudy shrugged. "It's not your fault, Richard. I didn't know about the money until now or why my letters were returned or why..." she searched for words and spoke openly, "you and I ended."

Richard placed his hands on her shoulders and spoke soothingly. "If I could change all that and make it right, I would. I know that as long as we look back, we're going to find a lot of disappointment. We can't change what fate did to us. Why don't we start putting our past where it belongs? Behind us. Let's talk about our lives and what's happened to us between then and now. I want to learn everything I can about the free-spirited, beautiful, young girl I loved."

She wiped at tears streaming down her face. "I promised myself I wasn't going to cry."

He pulled her close. "That's all right, Trudy. I understand." He held her head to his chest as her hands unconsciously clasped his shoulders. A moment of contentment rose between them as they embraced, neither saying a word, the quiet broken only by birds chirping nearby. Trudy felt his chest expanding as he breathed with her body against his. She tried to remember how it used to feel when he held her just like this years ago. Even though his arms comforted her, it felt strange.

Finally, she stepped back. Their eyes met as Richard grasped at her fingers sliding through his palms.

"Are you okay?"

"I'll be okay," she affirmed with a nod.

"I knew this wasn't going to be easy, but thank you for coming."

She forced a smile. "I know, Richard. I know."

"Well, let's go make dinner reservations. This place is crowded."

They walked toward the hotel, close enough to be holding hands.

"What time will dinner work for you?" he asked.

"Anytime's good for me."

"How about I make early reservations?" He checked his wristwatch. "Say at six and we meet for cocktails at five-thirty?"

"Sure, that's fine."

"Good. Then we can have the whole evening to ourselves. We've got a lot to talk about."

When they entered the lobby, Kwan met them. "Mr. Vanderveer, there's an urgent call you need to take."

"Sure, I'll get right to it." He turned to Trudy. "Thank you for being here. I know we're going to have a wonderful evening."

"Thank you for putting up with my crying and all. I'd planned for it to be different."

"No," he responded. "You were honest and sincere. But remember, tonight is a new beginning. No more looking back. Only forward."

"I'll try," she smiled.

He walked her to the elevator. Their eyes locked, and they gazed at each other until the doors closed.

On the ride up, Trudy tried to put their meeting today in perspective. Feeling a little disappointed about how emotional she had gotten, yet fascinated at Richard's understanding and sensitivity, she exited the elevator and went to her room.

On a table inside she found a bottle of chilled water and champagne on ice, along with a platter of appetizers. A note lay beside it. She ate a fruit-filled tart as she read.

Mrs. Trudy Quinn,

Please know that all spa services, including a massage of your choice, await you any time of day or night. There is no need for scheduling and you may call to make arrangements at our spa or we can arrange in-room service for your convenience. Our staff is on continuous call. Let us know what we can do to make your stay more pleasant.

The Greenbrier

Trudy knew Richard had set this up. She was pleased that he was so generous in thinking about her. She looked forward to dinner with him.

CHAPTER 10

The Queen Anne cheval mirror reflected her curvy figure as she slid her hands from her waist and over her hips. Turning sideways, Trudy could see the results of her exercise routine that kept her weight down and her figure firm. Dressed in the black silk dress that hugged her curves, accentuated with gold, hoop earrings and a matching single-braided gold necklace, she stepped into a pair of black stiletto heels and glanced in the mirror one last time. Then she locked her handbag in the room safe and picked up a small black purse on the way out the door.

Promising herself she wouldn't get emotional again, she stepped off the elevator into a lobby full of people sipping wine, laughing and seemingly competing to see who could speak the loudest. She had taken only a few steps when Kwan approached her.

"Good evening, Ms. Trudy," he greeted her.

"Good evening, Kwan. I'm a few minutes early. Have you seen Richard?"

"Mr. Vanderveer is on the back patio waiting for you. Follow me and I'll show you the way."

Trudy followed him down a long hallway. They made a left turn, and the chattering voices were left behind. When they came to two large doors, Kwan held one open and Trudy walked out onto the tiled patio. Richard stood alone with his back to the door, speaking to someone on his cell phone. He wore a black jacket, white shirt with a brown suede tie and tan trousers.

"If they won't come to the table and talk, then I'll just change the rules on them," he sounded aggravated. "When I get through with them they'll be glad to give me what I want on my terms at any price. Who do they think they're dealing with?" He glanced around when he heard Trudy approaching. "I'll call you back later." He put his phone away.

A smile crept across his face as he turned to her. "I didn't know you could get even more beautiful." He took her hand and held it.

"You're going to spoil me if you don't quit saying that," she said, blushing behind the smile creeping across her face.

"There's nothing wrong with telling the truth. What's your wine preference?"

"Merlot is good."

"Merlot for the lady and Pinot Noir for me," he told Kwan, then addressed Trudy. "I hope you didn't mind coming out here where it's quiet."

"No. It's nice to be able to hear when you speak."

He dropped her hand. "Is your room okay? I wasn't sure of your preference."

"It's lovely."

He stuck his hands in his pockets. "You just don't know how many times I've thought about you over the years."

"I've often thought about you, too, Richard," Trudy chimed in, shifting on her feet. "Every time I heard your name mentioned in the news or I picked up a magazine and saw your picture or some article written about you, it always made me stop and think about." she paused.

"Us?" Richard finished the sentence.

She nodded in agreement.

"I guess neither of us could stop questioning what happened," Richard added.

"I think you're right."

A young girl dressed in a barmaid's uniform walked through the door and handed them crystal stems of wine.

"I propose a toast," Richard said, holding up his glass. "To a most beautiful woman with whom I get to spend this evening. Let us not fret over the years we've been apart, but let our presence with each other tonight bear memories that warm our hearts."

They clicked glasses and sipped.

Richard filled the short silence. "Trudy, I want to know everything about you. Where do we begin?"

"My life has been kind of quiet compared to yours...you're the one who's been making headlines all over the world."

"The media can be a blessing or a curse." His eyes narrowed. "You've been keeping tabs on me?"

"No." She shook her head and smiled. "It just seems every so often I pick up a paper or hear a journalist talking about your endeavors to buy or take over some company somewhere in the world."

He laughed. "They love a story, don't they? Especially when they can twist the truth and make it sound like it's the powerful against the weak."

"I've never thought that about you." She paused. "Richard, how did you do it?"

"Do what?" He raised an eyebrow.

"What made you start your own business and turn it into what it has become?"

"Because of you, Trudy," his eyes narrowed again. "You inspired me to do so."

"Me!" She laughed.

"Yes. I'm serious. When I left home and went to work for the florist in Utrecht, I was determined to make something of myself. I was convinced you never called because I was homeless, penniless and appeared to have no future."

"Richard, you didn't!" Her eyes widened.

"I was just as devastated as you and didn't know what to think." He grimaced. "After losing you, I threw myself into work seven days a week. When I wasn't delivering flowers, I researched all I could about the business end of the floral industry."

"You started your own floral shop?"

"It wasn't quite like that." He sipped his wine.

"I worked for a florist in Utrecht for two years. He always paid me fair wages and gave me extra when he could. He didn't have a clue that I was a son of the wealthy Vanderveer family. He thought I was just a naïve kid trying to make it on my own." He swished his wine around in the glass. "Eventually, when his business slowed down, he came to me and said he could no longer employ me and thought about closing his shop. A large floral franchise had come in and set up several shops all over Utrecht, putting a squeeze on the smaller independent florists there. Since he'd taught me so much about the business, I didn't want to see him lose what he had worked for all of his life. So I told him I would work for free, if he'd give me a chance to turn it around for him. He agreed."

"You always loved a challenge. I saw that in you at an early age."

He laughed. "Yes, that's what kept me in trouble with my father. You remember?"

"Oh, yes. I remember all too well," she laughed.

"I went to all of the growers and nurseries that sold plants and flowers to us and asked them if they would sell their entire crop to me at a discount. It guaranteed them a sale of all their stock. They laughed at me but agreed to the deal, thinking I couldn't do it." He sipped his wine and looked down, smiling as he remembered.

"Then I went to all the independent florist shops within fifty miles of Utrecht and formed a co-op and convinced them to lend me the money to buy out the entire crops of the plant nurseries."

"What did you have to gain by doing that?" Trudy asked.

Richard grinned. "In order to get fresh cut flowers and plants daily, our competitors also had to buy locally, but the local nurseries had sold their entire crops to our co-op. We let them resell the flowers to our competitors for us but at a higher price that we set. The growers were making money for us while they got paid an extra commission."

"I always knew you were smart but not that savvy." Trudy smiled.

"Every time our competitor purchased a flower or plant, we made money on it. It took us less than one year to put them out of business."

"That's wonderful," Trudy exclaimed excitedly.

"We started branching out into other cities doing the same thing with other independent florists. In five years we had more than two hundred florists in our co-op."

"You must've been proud of that accomplishment."

"Eventually, someone from London found out about our co-op and convinced us to go public with a stock offering so we could grow more rapidly." He smiled. "Guess who they wanted to be president?"

"Richard, I'm so proud of you."

"Vanderveer Enterprise was born. We now own floral and food companies on five continents."

The door opened and Kwan appeared. "Mr. Vanderveer, your dinner reservation is ready."

"Thanks, Kwan. We're on our way." Richard reached for Trudy's wineglass and handed both glasses to Kwan. "How did we get to talking about me? I wanted to talk about you."

Smiling, as they entered the hallway, she told him, "I was a teacher for thirty years. I know how to get what I want out of a conversation."

He smiled.

CHAPTER 11

After walking through the long floral designed carpeted hallways, encased with lovely-papered walls, illuminated with chandeliers hanging from high ceilings, Richard ushered Trudy into the dining room. White tablecloths, china, crystal glassware, and lit candles complemented the table settings in the dimmed lighting. A violinist played near the table where Richard and Trudy were seated.

A petite young lady with blonde hair came over to greet them. "Good evening. My name is Chiantia. I'm your server tonight," she spoke with an accent.

"You're French, aren't you?" Richard asked.

"Yes, I am." She perked up. "How did you know?"

"I spend a little time over there now and then."

"Where do you like to go when you're in France?"

"I stay mostly around Voiron. I own a chocolate company there."

"Not Vanderveer Chocolatier Enterprises?"

"Yours truly," Richard replied, smiling.

"I grew up in that city and I love your chocolates." She grinned. "And here I am, meeting the most famous entrepreneur half way around the world."

"It's a small world, isn't it?" Richard chuckled. "How long have you been in the States?"

"For two years now. I got a scholarship from a foreign student exchange program to go to the university here. I've got two more years to go."

"Good for you."

Trudy sat listening, wishing she could find money for the girls she was trying to help send to college.

"May I start you off with a glass of wine, maybe a cocktail?"

Richard lifted his eyes toward Trudy. "Do you have a preference?"

"No. Anything is fine. Just one glass for me anyway."

"Red, Chardonnay, a blush?"

Trudy's knowledge of wine was usually the supermarket sale of the week.

"Surprise me," she smiled.

"Brave woman. Give us a bottle of Solaia Antinori 2001."

"Excellent choice. I'll get your wine. When I return, I'll give you our chef's choices for the evening." Chiantia walked away.

"What's on your mind?" Richard asked. "You seem to be in deep thought."

"I was just thinking how wonderful it would be to have the money to fund the scholarship requests I get. I have a lot of students who want to continue their education but won't be able to if they don't get help."

"That means a lot to you, doesn't it?"

"I know what Mom and I had to do to get me through school." She paused. "And now I know your father helped."

"No." He held up his hands. "Let's not go there. Maybe he made a contribution, but for the wrong reasons." He reached over and placed his hands over hers. "How about we never bring this money thing up again? Didn't we agree to look forward, not back?"

"You're right," she nodded. "I'm sorry."

Chiantia brought their wine. She named off several menu favorites for dinner. They chose beef Wellington, baked halibut, veggies, sauces, soups, and salads.

"Okay, Trudy; it's your turn."

"My turn for what?"

"I want to hear about your life."

"I can sum up my life in a couple of sentences."

"No. I'm not going to let you off that easily," he chided, before sipping his wine. "But I'll help. Tell me about your children."

Trudy perked up. "I have one daughter, twenty-two years old."

"You mentioned something about an engagement party next weekend, if I remember correctly."

"Yes, that's right." Trudy couldn't remember what she'd told him when he called.

"What's her name and does she look like her mother?"

"Her name is April." She grinned and spoke proudly. "Mom says she's the spitting image of me when I was her age."

"Then she has to be one beautiful girl. Is she going to be a career girl like her mother?"

"She works for the local newspaper now. She majored in journalism and wants to be a serious news writer someday. But she's getting married in four months, so who knows what direction her life will take."

"Good for her. I mean the journalism thing, of course. She's got plenty of time to figure out what she wants. Let her enjoy the honeymoon for the next couple of years."

"I've thought of telling her the same thing," Trudy added.

"What kind of news stories does she write?"

"They have her writing about weddings and obituaries." Trudy picked up her wineglass. "I know that sounds weird, but she realized she had to start somewhere. She's waiting for her chance to move up and write seriously. She's really excited that her office has been asked to do a follow-up story on the lost letter for the news wire services. They all have requested it."

"Then we need to make sure we give them something to write about." His eyes gleamed.

"Richard! I'm married. Remember?" She glanced at him sharply with a sassy smile.

"Yes, to my regrets," he chuckled.

Chiantia brought out their food.

"Would you do something for me?" Richard asked Chiantia.

"Sure."

He motioned her close and whispered in her ear. Pulling his wallet out of his jacket, he slipped her a folded bill.

"What are you up to?" Trudy asked, curiously.

"You'll find out shortly." He grinned.

She could only imagine since she knew how he used to love playing pranks on her.

"Do you have children?" Trudy asked.

"Yes." Richard laid his fork down and sat up straight in his chair. "Trudy, you jinxed me. I swear you did."

"What do you mean I jinxed you?" Trudy asked, leaning forward.

"Thirty-five years ago you told me I was going to have girls with bows in their hair and all that crazy stuff." He waved his hands in the air. "I swear you jinxed me, and you were right."

Trudy sipped her wine and smiled. "Then you must have a daughter."

"I have two wonderful, spirited daughters."

"Tell me about them."

"Elin's twenty-three years old. She's the creative one. She's in London doing theater, writing screenplays and wants to have her own production company someday."

"Sounds pretty ambitious to me," Trudy remarked, cutting into her asparagus.

"Amanda's twenty and a bit more conservative. She looks like her mother." Richard paused and grinned. "She wants to save the world. Always emailing me a bunch of news articles on green technology and wants to know if I've upgraded all my food production plants to green. I think if I turned her loose, she would bankrupt me by converting everything I own."

He laughed. "I think she's going places, though. She's very outspoken."

"I'm sure she'll take after her father and do quite well."

"I can only hope so." He forked a cut of beef into his mouth.

A familiar sound caught Trudy's ear. She thought briefly and then it dawned on her. The violinist had started playing songs by The Carpenters. This song, one of her favorites, was "Close To You." Her eyes widened and she perked up. Richard must have remembered they were one of her favorite music groups in the seventies when they were together. She noticed he was watching her closely.

"So that's what you had Chiantia do. You told her to get the violinist to play The Carpenters' songs for us."

"You catch on fast."

"I can't believe you remembered!"

"I remember it all, Trudy. I remember it all." He spoke persuasively, gazing into her eyes.

She smiled, blinking several times, fascinated by this man she'd not seen for so long.

After an hour of conversation, laughter and reminiscing about their teenage lives, Trudy began to tire from sitting so long. She was relieved when Chiantia walked up.

"How are we doing? Ready for a coffee, brandy, and one of our signature desserts?"

Richard waited for Trudy to answer.

"No more for me."

Chiantia turned to Richard.

"I'm fine, too."

"Are you sure about dessert? We make everything fresh."

"We'll pass for now but maybe come back later," Richard suggested.

"Very well. I'll get your check."

Trudy saw Kwan walk into the dining room, looking around anxiously. Once he spotted their table, he came over and bent to whisper in Richard's ear.

Richard's face tensed, and he tossed his napkin on the table. "Trudy, I have to get on a conference call for a few minutes. Would you mind meeting me at the lobby bar in about fifteen minutes?"

"No, I don't mind. Is something wrong?"

"It's just business as usual. Regretfully, though, it can't wait." He sounded annoyed. "Kwan, stay here and sign the check for me. Trudy, I'll make this fast."

He pushed his chair back and stood up as Trudy offered, "I'll browse the gift shops and meet you at the bar."

"Okay." He walked away briskly, obviously irritated.

Trudy strolled through the shops while waiting for Richard. A necklace, with pink and blue stones caught her eye in the jewelry boutique. As she admired it, the sales lady approached her.

"Would you like to try it on?" she offered.

"I'm just browsing while waiting for someone." She noticed it wasn't priced and that usually meant it was out of her range anyway.

"Well, there's no harm in trying it on." The woman unlocked the case and had it in her hand before Trudy could say no. "Here, let me put it on you." Stepping behind her and clasping the necklace, she reached for a mirror and handed it to Trudy.

Reflected in the mirror, she saw Richard leaning against the door column watching and smiling. She turned to face him.

"How long have you been there?"

"I actually just walked by and saw this most gorgeous woman. I stopped for a closer look, hoping I wouldn't get caught by my date."

Trudy smiled at the stunned expression on the woman's face.

"Maybe with a little urging I'll drop her and stay with you instead," Richard went on. "That's if you're in agreement."

"I'm not sure that would be a good idea. I might not be as much fun as your date." She tilted her head and gave him a quick smile.

"Umm, I'm willing to take my chances. By the way, that necklace looks great on you."

Trudy took the necklace off and handed it back to the clerk.

"Would you like to know the price?" she asked, shifting her eyes to Richard.

"No, thank you," Trudy interjected. "I was just window shopping. It's beautiful, though."

"You're welcome to take it and wear it tonight. If you're not pleased with it then you can return it for a full refund," she persisted.

"No, I don't think so," she responded. She turned around and hooked her arm into Richard's. "Come on. You've got to quit saying those things in front of people. Someone who knows me might see us and then I will really be in trouble."

"Years ago, if someone had said there was trouble to be found, you would have run to find it."

"Let's just say that I've gotten a little older and a lot wiser."

"I can relate to that. Now, we can go to the lobby bar or go for a walk."

"I can't walk in these heels, and I don't need anymore wine."

"Then why don't we go find us a nice spot to park ourselves."

"Sounds good to me."

CHAPTER 12

Finding a quiet room with murals painted on the wall, Richard and Trudy sat on a burgundy-colored sofa in front of a stone fireplace.

"Are you in a hurry to leave tomorrow?" Richard asked. "I have something planned I'd like for us to do together."

"No. As long as I get home tomorrow evening is fine. I've got a few things to work on before Kenny gets home."

"He's a lucky guy. I think I'm a little envious of him."

"Well, you probably wouldn't say that if you'd been married to me for as long as he has."

"I could only hope to have that chance." He eased back into the sofa, broke into a smile, and started chuckling, then finally laughing.

"What are you laughing at?"

He shook his head and laughed harder.

Trudy slapped him on his arm. "Richard Vanderveer, are you laughing at me?" she demanded.

"No, no, never." He waved his hand while trying to control his laughter. "I'm just trying to remember what you called those boys who were making fun of Raymond and me when we met for the first time."

She smiled as she remembered. "I called them rednecks."

"That's it! I just knew Raymond and I were going to have to fight our way out of that one."

"You didn't have anything to worry about." She turned to directly face him. "You could've handled them if it had come to that."

"It wasn't them I was worried about. It was what Father would've done to us if he found out we'd been fighting."

"He was kind of strict." She shifted her position and leaned toward Richard. "What's Raymond doing now?"

"He stayed with Father and Grandfather in their business ventures and has done quite well for himself."

"I remember how he used to tag along with us every time we got together."

"And we tried everything to get away from him."

"You remember the first summer when we were picking blackberries, and he followed us around so he could hear everything we talked about?"

"Oh, yeah," Richard nodded.

"He got a thorn in his finger. I pulled it out and his finger started bleeding."

Richard laughed again. "You told him he was going to get an infection and would have to get his finger cut off. You had him scared to death."

"Then I told him to run home, put some milk on it, and let the cat lick it so it wouldn't get infected."

"I got a nice lecture out of that one from my mother. At least we had some time to ourselves."

"And I wondered why your father never liked me," she giggled.

He laid his arm across the couch and turned sideways to get closer to Trudy. "You were one free-spirited young lady back then."

"Living on an army post with kids from all over the world, there was no room for the meek. How are your father and mother?"

Richard eased back into the sofa. "I lost Mother fifteen years ago. Father is mostly into charity work now and lets Raymond pretty much run the businesses. They're coming by Tuesday morning to see me while I'm here in the States."

"How did your father react when you left school and he couldn't find you?" she asked, curiously.

"Mom said he was devastated. It was two years before they found out where I was living. It was five years before I spoke to him again. Whenever I called home, if he answered the phone, I hung up." Richard grimaced. "When I finally spoke to him, I did it only for Mom's sake. It was fifteen years later before we actually tried to restore our relationship."

He paused before continuing. "We were both at Mom's bedside and she'd gotten so weak she couldn't speak. Before she passed away, she took my hand and placed it in his. It was her way of telling us to take care of each other. We were both at a loss for words and stood there looking at each other, knowing we had to do something to mend our relationship."

Trudy reached for Richard's hand and wrapped her fingers around it but said nothing as he continued to speak.

"We talk to each other often and have remained cordial. That's as far as our relationship goes. I kind of let him and Raymond do the father-son thing. I've always stayed my distance, but we all manage to meet for the usual birthdays, holidays, and special happenings."

"Do you have any regrets?"

"I don't know what I could have done differently." He turned his gaze to meet hers. "I just never felt close to him after what he did to us…me."

"I'm sorry that happened between you two." Trudy spoke softly, dropping her gaze, knowing that she had caused the rift between them.

"I think we all paid a price for what happened."

They sat quietly for a moment.

"Come on." Richard stood up. "I've got to move around. Let's walk."

"I won't be able to go far in these heels," Trudy reminded him.

"No problem." He leaned over and pulled them off her feet. "I'll carry them for you."

Together they began walking, Richard carrying her heels.

"Where is home for you now?" Trudy asked.

"I have homes in Zurich, Interlaken, and London. I stay in London most of the time. That's where Iona, my wife, was from."

"What did your father do when you married outside the Dutch community?"

"He seemed happy for me and never said much about it." Richard stopped walking and turned to Trudy. "That was nine years after I left home. I think he was glad just to have been invited to the wedding."

"Did he ever mention giving the check to my mother?"

They began strolling again.

"He never mentioned it, and I never questioned him about it. I figured enough damage had been done and bringing it up would resolve nothing." He shrugged. "Remember, I pretty much kept my distance."

"Did Raymond marry a girl from the Netherlands?" Trudy glanced at him.

"Three years after Raymond graduated from college, he married the love of his life. She was from Ireland, a longtime college friend with whom he'd stayed in touch."

"Did anything turn out the way your father wanted it to?"

Richard stopped walking again. "I think my leaving home devastated him so much he realized that controlling our lives wasn't going to work."

"It usually doesn't."

"Father and Raymond inherited all of my grandfather's businesses and have built them into quite an enterprise. Grandfather cut me out of the inheritance when he found out I left home."

"Did that bother you?"

"Not at all. Besides I was busy chasing my own destiny. Lately, they've asked me about merging the family companies into my corporation."

"Would that be a good move?"

"There would be a lot of good synergies between them, I suppose." He shrugged. "But I don't need them. Raymond would gain more from it than I would. Hey, there we go, talking about me again. I want to hear about your life."

"I'm sorry. Your life is so much more interesting than mine."

"Let me be the judge of that." He grinned. "Tell me about this lucky guy you married. How did you meet?"

"I worked at a 4-H Camp at Smith Mountain Lake during summers when I wasn't teaching school. The lake is about an hour's drive from Lynchburg. I was driving out of the park one night when a herd of deer ran in front of me, and I stopped suddenly. The driver behind me rear-ended my car." They walked to an island in the hallway, and Trudy leaned against the counter. "The state trooper who investigated the accident said there was no way I could drive my car. He waited with me for an hour until a wrecker came to tow my vehicle. As he was ending his shift, he offered me a ride home because he knew it would take another hour for someone to drive from Lynchburg to get me. I rode home with this good looking trooper and talked about everything with him for an hour." She smiled.

"He called twice to check on me to make sure I was okay. The third time he called, I laughed and told him, 'I can assure you I'm all right.' He laughed and said he wasn't calling to check on me but wanted to know his chances of taking me out to dinner." Trudy's eyes twinkled. "We dated for two years and then I became Mrs. Quinn."

"Sounds like a sly move to me," Richard suggested. "I don't think I could have done better."

"We've had a lot of good years together. I have no regrets," she said, with a hint of pessimism in her voice, and began walking again.

"Are you still happy?" Richard asked, eyeing her closely.

The question caught her by surprise. He had asked the one question that had plagued her thoughts for the past year. Unsure of how to respond, but wanting to give him some kind of answer, she chose, "Just as happy as anyone who's been married for a quarter of a century, I guess."

"So things could be better?"

Trudy thought to herself. *Why did I let myself get led into this? Maybe I ought to tell him the truth and be done with it.*

She sighed and plunged in. "We've had problems over the last couple of years, but we're working on it. We actually separated three months before he went to Iraq. But we've gone through the counseling routine and seem to be getting it worked out. We both thought that time away from each other would be good for us and make us realize what we have is important."

"You've been separated for over a year?"

Trudy nodded. "Fifteen months or so."

"And you're still wearing your wedding band?" He glanced down at her hand.

Trudy glanced at it. "I guess I haven't given up on us yet."

"So you're separated but married?"

"Something like that I guess," she responded, feeling uncomfortable.

"Has it made a difference for you?"

Unsure of how to answer, Trudy remained silent.

"I'm sorry, Trudy." He reached out, knowing he had hit a tender spot with her. "It's none of my business. I didn't mean to pry. I just asked out of concern. Please forgive me."

Trudy forced a smile. "It is what it is, Richard. I understand." She stifled a yawn. Their conversation had taken on a more serious tone than she wanted it to. "I'm sorry, Richard; I need to call it a night. I didn't rest well last night. I think I was too excited about meeting you."

"No coffee or dessert?"

"Thanks, but I don't need the sugar or caffeine. I want to sleep."

"Come on. I'll walk you to your room."

They walked toward the elevator.

"What time do you want to start in the morning?" Richard asked.

"I'm an early person. Any time works for me."

"How about eight-thirty?"

"Sure."

"Did you bring jeans or casual wear?"

"I think so." She looked at him curiously. "What do you have planned?"

They stepped on the elevator, and Richard pushed the third floor button.

"Something I've been meaning to do for a long time." He leaned back against the wall and smiled. "I think you'll like it."

The door opened and they walked down the hall to her room. Trudy put her key in the door and turned back to Richard.

He held up her shoes. "If the slipper fits, don't I win the heart of the princess?"

Blushing, she tried to figure if he was inviting himself in.

"I know. I know." He grinned. "You're a married-separated, or something, woman."

"Good night, Richard." She reached for her shoes.

"Good night, my Trudy," he replied, imitating his boyish Dutch accent.

She watched him walk down the hall. Before he turned the corner, he glanced back and hesitated when he saw her still standing at her door. Trudy tossed him a little wave and went into the room.

She leaned back against the door in a daze. Their evening together had gone nothing like she'd imagined. It was as if the thirty-five years apart were melting away. She felt warmed by his gentleness and was captivated by his candor. She wondered what he had planned for tomorrow.

CHAPTER 13

Trudy finished putting on her makeup as she listened to the morning news. Then she looked into the mirror to make sure her hair was in place. Dressed in a white cotton top and blue jeans, she reached for her cream-colored tennis shoes. Sitting down to put them on she realized she needed to check if there were any messages from home. She slipped on her shoes and turned on her phone.

A local news brief caught her attention.

On Friday we brought you the news that the Winchester Apple Fruit Company rejected the buyout offer from Vanderveer Enterprise, stating that the offer was far below current market value.

However, over the weekend, Vanderveer Enterprise launched a hostile offer for the Winchester Fruit Packing Company. Calls to the Vanderveer corporate office haven't been returned. Vanderveer Enterprise owns floral and food companies on five continents.

Trudy wondered why Richard would do something like that. After all, his enterprise was already worth millions. Why would he want more by taking over some small Virginia company? It didn't make sense to her.

Her cell phone rang. She noticed it was Jan.

"Hello."

"Well, how did it go?" Jan blurted out.

Trudy smiled, not surprised that Jan got straight to the point. "It was okay. I felt a little awkward at first, but he put me at ease."

"Was he what you expected him to be?"

"I don't know what I expected." She rolled her eyes and laughed. "He seems to be easygoing, sincere, and still has a sense of humor."

"Sounds like the perfect man to me. And he's rich." Jan giggled.

"Indeed, but you'd never know it." Trudy stood to look out the window to see what kind of day it was. "He seems to be the same man I knew years ago. Just all grown up and mature and a bit more serious."

"Have you heard the news this morning?"

"Yes. I just heard them talking about the buyout offer he made."

"I mean on the national news. They're talking about the lost letter. It seems some Internet news bloggers are trying to solve the mystery as to whom the letter is from and who is this Trudy Meyers to whom the letter was sent."

Trudy perked up. "No. I haven't heard that."

"They're speculating that the letter was from either Richard or Raymond Vanderveer. They've already learned that the boys worked on their grandfather's farm in the Shenandoah Valley back in the seventies."

"I never thought it would draw that much attention." She turned away from the window.

"You know America," Jan remarked. "They love a mystery, and everyone's speculating the letter was a love letter because of the heart on it."

"I guess I need to hurry up and give the paper an interview so I can put this to rest."

"When are you coming home?"

"Not until later. Richard wants me to go somewhere with him today. I should be heading home by mid-afternoon I would think."

"Then I'll see you tonight and you can tell me everything."

"Would you mind letting Mom and April know what my plans are so they won't worry?"

"Sure. I'll call them. And don't give the bloggers anything to write about," she jokingly said.

"Quit picking on me." Trudy laughed.

"Be careful driving home."

"Bye, Jan."

One last glance in the mirror, and Trudy grabbed her lightweight, white-cotton jacket and left to meet Richard. On the way down she promised herself she wouldn't get emotional again. After all, they had broken the ice and knew each other's feelings about their misfortune. It was time to move on, she thought, stepping off the elevator.

Walking across the floor into the café, she glanced around to see if Richard was already there. Kwan sat at a table by the window. After noticing her, he stood and waved to get her attention.

"Good morning," she called.

He pulled out a chair. "Good morning, Ms. Trudy. Your night's rest was pleasant, I hope?"

"I don't remember a thing once I went to bed," she responded, seating herself.

"Oh," he responded, wearing a confused expression.

"It's just a figure of speech. I slept great."

"Good for you, Ms. Trudy."

A waiter walked up. "May I bring you coffee or juice?"

"I'm actually waiting for someone. Kwan, have you seen Richard this morning?"

"He left to take a conference call about ten minutes ago. He should be back soon."

"Then I will start with a coffee," she told the waiter. "I'll wait for the rest of our party before ordering breakfast."

Trudy noticed several folders of papers in front of Kwan. "Can't get away from work, can you?"

"I'm just taking care of some things for Mr. Vanderveer that arrived last night and reviewing our schedules for the next two weeks."

"Will you be going home or traveling more?"

"We're going to Guadalajara, Mexico, and from there back to Korea," he said, shuffling papers.

"Do you like working for Richard and traveling with him?"

"Yes, Ms. Trudy." He nodded. "Mr. Vanderveer has been good to my family, and I want to help any way I can."

Trudy reached over and touched his arm. "Richard is really fond of you, too, Kwan. He told me so."

Kwan returned an even bigger smile.

When Trudy's coffee arrived, she sipped it and glanced around to make sure Richard wasn't in sight, then asked, "Does Richard have a significant other in his life?"

Kwan looked puzzled.

"I mean," she said, gathering her thoughts, "does he have a steady girl or lady friend that he spends a lot of time with?"

"No, Ms. Trudy. Since his wife...." he hesitated.

"I'm sorry. That's probably too personal," Trudy interjected, noticing that the turn in conversation was making him nervous.

"When he lost Iona," Kwan continued, "he mostly just worked, worked, worked. When he's not working, he visits his daughters."

"Does he visit Raymond often?"

"They talk on the telephone, and when there's a family gathering they spend time together. I don't know what he does when I'm not traveling with him, though."

"Looks like you might be waiting on me to start breakfast," Richard said, walking up to the table. "I'm sorry," he added, sliding into a seat beside Trudy.

"I've enjoyed sitting here and talking to Kwan," she responded.

Kwan stood and gathered his folders.

"Don't let me interfere with something you two may need to take care of," Trudy offered.

"We've just finished some scheduling and dealing with things that came up last night," Richard assured her.

"I was ready to leave anyway," Kwan added, smiling at her. He turned to Richard. "I'll go and make sure your ride has arrived and take care of these other matters."

Richard focused his gaze on Trudy. "You look rested this morning."

"I slept wonderfully."

"Good for you."

The waitress returned and asked, "Will you be having breakfast from the buffet or menu?"

Richard nodded toward Trudy.

"I'll have fruit, yogurt and wheat toast with one scrambled egg."

"I'll have the southwest omelet, fruit, and wheat toast," Richard added.

She poured more coffee for Trudy and a cup for Richard and then walked away.

Richard gazed at Trudy with a slight smile.

Trudy felt his stare, ignored it for a few seconds, and then lifted her eyes to meet his. "Okay, something's on your mind. What is it?"

"I was thinking that every time I see you, you always look stunning. It doesn't matter what you're wearing or what you're doing. It just comes out naturally for you."

"Oh, Richard." She waved him off with her hand. "You're just fascinated with meeting a long lost girlfriend."

"No, I'm serious."

"You know what they say, don't you? Love is blind."

"Is that what this is about?" Richard asked, grinning. "Love?"

"No, I mean…." she tried to backtrack her words. "Maybe we're both just a little fascinated meeting each other after…" she paused, realizing she was entrenching herself even more.

He held up his hand to stop her. "I know what you meant, Trudy."

After the waitress brought their breakfast, Trudy decided to question Richard about the news story she'd heard earlier. "You made the news this morning," she commented, gauging his reaction.

"The media loves a story, especially when I'm involved. They like to try to make me sound like a corporate raider."

"I didn't think it sounded like that."

"I knew this company would try to use the media to persuade the co-op to vote against me. I have another plan if they wish to try to stop me," he added.

"They're such a small company." Her curiosity aroused, she asked, "Why do you need them?"

"I don't. They've got great brand recognition here on the East Coast, but I could give them worldwide distribution through my food channels and grow their market tenfold." He leaned back in his chair.

"Why can't they recognize their potential with you as a partner?"

"I have no idea," he answered, dismissively. "I used to love doing acquisitions and putting deals together, but lately it just wears me down. All I get out of it is more negative publicity. I'm beginning to wonder why I put myself through it." He looked up from cutting his omelet. "I guess for me it's the challenge of making a deal work."

"I can certainly understand that."

"I'm glad you're on my side." He chuckled. "Hey, let's get off this subject. I'm ready to spend a day away from work with a lovely lady."

"Fine with me!" She gleamed in agreement.

Walking outside with Richard, Trudy looked around for the car that would take them on their day's adventure. Kwan met them with two leather jackets in hand.

"The Harley you requested is over there," he pointed. "I have it packed and ready to go."

Trudy stared at the large, black, chrome trimmed Harley motorcycle in the parking area.

Richard turned to her. "You don't mind riding a Harley, do you?"

"I don't know. It's been decades since I've ridden on a motorcycle."

"Are you willing to take a chance with me?"

Reluctantly, she said, "I suppose."

"If you don't like it, then I'll turn around, come back, and we'll get a car." He gave her a pleading look. "Fair enough?"

"I suppose it'll be okay."

"Kwan will take your jacket back in for you. It'll be a little too cool for you to wear it. These leather jackets will keep us warm."

They put on their jackets and helmets and mounted the bike. Without another word, Richard cranked the motor and drove off.

"How are you doing back there?" Richard asked, after turning into the street.

Surprised that she had speakers and a microphone in her helmet, she responded, "I'm hanging on for dear life. Can't you tell?" She clutched him tighter.

"If you need me to stop, let me know."

"Rest assured, I will."

Music started playing through the helmet speakers. It was The Carpenters. Obviously, Richard was making every effort to please her with things he remembered she liked. Trudy tightened her grip on him as he sped up.

Leaning her body against his back so she would be shielded from most of the wind, she reminisced about a time long ago.

She could still see Richard and the other boys on the farm racing dirt bikes. He always competed hard at everything he did, even to the point of taking risks. Once he tried to pass some boys by running his bike up a bank to get around them but flipped it and took a bad spill. She ran to him as fast as she could, only to find his body lying motionless. She gathered his head into her arms and begged him to speak to her.

Finally, becoming conscious, he looked up. "Now I know what I have to do to get your attention."

Startled, she had jumped up and shouted, "Richard Vanderveer! Don't you ever scare me like this again!"

It was long, long ago, when the only thing that had mattered in her life was being close to him. With her arms now wrapped around his waist, she held tightly, listening to The Carpenters music and riding down Interstate 81 on a perfect spring day.

CHAPTER 14

After riding for more than an hour, Richard took an exit leading to Buena Vista, a small city nestled between the Shenandoah Valley and Blue Ridge Mountains. Trudy guessed Richard was taking her back to what used to be his grandfather's farm, where they'd met and spent three summers. The farm was located just outside the city on the banks of the Maury River.

"Ready to stretch your legs?" Richard asked.

"Yes," Trudy replied, "and to give my arms a rest. I think they've gone to sleep, I've been holding onto you so tightly."

Richard pulled the Harley over to the curb of the small downtown and stopped. Trudy stepped off the bike and would have stumbled backward, had not Richard reached out to hold her arm and steady her. Then they both stretched for several moments in the full sun that had warmed the day.

Looking up the street at the same stone and brick buildings he used to see, Richard squinted from the bright sun. "Kind of brings back memories, doesn't it?"

"It surely does," Trudy agreed.

"I've always wanted to come back and visit but never had a reason until now." He turned toward her. "I couldn't imagine coming back here and not seeing you."

"It looks like you got your wish." She smiled.

"Let's get these jackets off and walk a couple of blocks."

Pulling their leather coats off, Richard put them in the bike compartment and locked the helmets to the Harley. They began strolling up the sidewalk past what used to be a busy downtown grocery market, hardware mercantile, and a drug store, but now they'd become an art gallery, law offices, and an AT&T cellular store.

"I can still see Raymond following us every step to keep up when we came here on Saturday evenings. I didn't realize it back then, but he absolutely idolized you, Richard. Are you two still close?"

"No. I guess there have been too many miles and too much time between us." He winced. "We talked a lot on the phone for the first few years. He even worked for me on break from college. But eventually he grew up and found his own calling."

"If you two merged your companies and he could work with you, wouldn't that give you a reason to be close again?"

Richard stopped walking and stared at her without speaking. Thinking that she might have intruded on a personal matter, she elbowed his side. "Come on. We're just having conversation. Nothing wrong with that, is it?"

She noticed a coffee shop up ahead. "Let's get a latté. I'm chilled from the bike ride."

For the next couple of hours, they walked to familiar places and talked about events and moments they had shared that had woven their lives together during those three summers. They walked by Aunt Millie's Kitchen where everyone who lived within twenty miles came to dine. It was known for its pones of cornbread, pan-fried chicken and half-runner snap beans that were canned every summer so they could serve them year round.

There was the old theater that was now an antique store. They walked inside and even though it was stripped of its worn leather seats and burgundy draped walls, Trudy walked over to the section near the back of the building to where she and Richard used to sit. She remembered when she was sixteen years old and they were sitting on the back row holding hands and watching a John Wayne movie. Richard had leaned over and kissed her tenderly on her lips for the first time. It excited her and when he put his arm around her, she snuggled closer.

"Brings back memories, doesn't it?" Richard said, interrupting her thoughts.

"Yes it does," she said, turning toward him, blushing, wondering if he had the same thoughts.

"Are you ready to go? There's one more place I want us to visit before we leave."

"Yes."

Back at the Harley, they geared up and rode out of the city through what Trudy remembered was once open farmland. Now developments of condos, shopping malls, fast food restaurants and buildings of all shapes and sizes lined the highway. She knew they were headed toward what used to be Richard's grandfather's farm.

Richard drove down a side road that led to the river. He stopped and they got off the bike. He grabbed a packed bag that was strapped to the Harley and they strolled down a trail to the grassy riverbank.

"Does this spot bring back memories?" Richard asked, setting the bag down.

Trudy took a couple of steps forward and looked out over the river, remembering it well. "Yes," she turned around, smiling. "This was our favorite spot when we wanted time to ourselves."

Richard pulled a blanket from his tote bag and spread it on the grass, then placed a small tote on it.

"Here. Come sit." He extended his hand. "It's time for lunch."

"Well, aren't you full of surprises!"

They removed their jackets.

"The last time we came here, you packed lunch. I figured I owed you one."

"I just can't get over how you remember everything."

She sat beside Richard as he unpacked bottled water, cheese cubes, chicken salad, crackers, and a fruit medley of strawberries, grapes and blueberries.

"Well, I did have the best-looking girl in the States with me back then." He took a toothpick, pinned a strawberry, and handed it to Trudy. "And that's something one doesn't easily forget, my dear."

Trudy took a toothpick, plucked a cheese cube and stuck it in Richard's mouth, remembering how she used to feed him just that way when they were young. "I have a confession to make. I remember that day, too. Everything about it." She plucked a cheese cube for herself.

They sat and ate while facing each other.

"There's something I've always wanted to ask you."

Trudy lifted her gaze and nodded while chewing.

"When we were sixteen and came here to the river," a slight smile crept across his face and his eyes narrowed, "had you already decided to go skinny-dipping or was that an impulse that hit you?"

She burst into laughter, placing her hand over her full mouth. "I should've known you would remember that." After almost choking, she swallowed her food and went on. "I'd heard some of the older girls and boys talk about skinny-dipping here. So you know me," she shrugged. "I wasn't going to be outdone. I decided to try it, but only with you, of course."

"When you dropped your clothes and waded into the river, it blew my mind." He sat back and grinned as he lingered on the thought. "I never expected you to do that."

"And it blew my mind when you followed me in, naked." She smiled. "I was actually nervous but felt safe with you."

"That was the first time I'd seen a real girl naked." He smiled, obviously savoring the thought. "So, you thought I was harmless, did you?"

"Not at all. I just knew I could trust you." She poked him with a finger. "Don't you remember I nicknamed you Octopus

Man? At times you had more hands than I could possibly fend off."

"Yes, I remember." He grinned. "I guess when you're young that's part of falling in love. In fact, I think it works at any age," he chuckled.

"I suppose it does." She lifted her eyes from putting chicken salad on a cracker and saw Richard staring at her with a slight grin on his face.

Their eyes met and lingered as though they were reading each other's thoughts.

"Does your family still own the farm?" Trudy asked, wanting to change the subject.

"No. When my grandfather died, Father leased it out for a while. When the real estate boom hit in the nineties, he sold it to developers who turned it into an asphalt and concrete jungle."

"That's a strange way to put it."

"And they call it progress. Look at all the empty buildings here now." Richard stuck a toothpick in his mouth. "Let's get this food out of our way so we can have more room."

After putting the food away, Richard folded his jacket and placed it behind his head as he lay back and stared up at clouds rolling by. Trudy sat beside him, her arms resting on her crossed legs, watching him and remembering seeing him lie back this same way when they were young.

"Thanks for coming here with me. It's meant a lot," Richard said.

"It means a lot to me, too."

"Thirty-five years doesn't seem to have changed much about us."

"It seems like only yesterday when you and I were making plans to...." Trudy hesitated once she caught what she was about to say.

Richard reached and squeezed her hand. "I remember, Trudy."

"What was she like?"

"What was who like?"

"Iona. How did you meet?"

Richard let go of her hand. "A couple of years after Vanderveer Enterprise became a public company, the investment bank that took us public asked me to do an in-depth interview with the business community to acquire more recognition for our company." He chuckled. "All they really wanted was for me to get our stock price up. I hadn't given anyone an interview since going public." He hesitated for a second. "I think it was because I had disciplined myself so well from doing anything that would draw attention to me that would have let Father know where I was or what I was doing."

"You really were serious about cutting him out of your life."

"Iona was a writer for *The Business Journal International*. She was chosen to do the interview. When I spoke with her, I told her that the only way I would oblige her was if she'd come to Interlaken for a weekend."

"And you said Kenny was sly," Trudy laughed.

"We had several meals together, drank a little wine and went skinny-dipping." Richard tried but failed to suppress a smile.

"You didn't!" She slapped his arm with a backhand.

"I'm just kidding. You were my first and only." He turned serious again. "We stayed in touch and started checking our schedules to see where and when we'd be close enough to rendezvous so we could spend time together. A year and a half later we got married."

"Sounds like a fairy tale to me."

"After that, I pretty much quit giving any interviews about the business. I told corporate the last one got me in trouble. It got me married."

"I'm surprised they let you get by with that."

"They had plenty of people who could fluff the media better than I. They needed me more to do strategic planning and to negotiate acquisitions." He paused for a few seconds. "In fact, Iona always told me it wasn't about the money for me, but simply making a deal work."

"I remember how determined you were, Richard. I can see why she saw that, too."

Richard sat up, looking past her. "We had a lot of good years together. I found myself always flying her to some far corner of the world to meet me so we could squeeze in a couple of days together. When the girls came along, it became harder for Iona to travel." Richard swallowed hard and continued. "I was waiting at the airport in Cape Town to pick her up. She was flying in on a small corporate jet we owned that tried to land during a thunderstorm." Pain registered in his expression. "I saw it all, Trudy. I saw it crash."

Momentarily stunned, Trudy leaned toward him and placed her hand on his. "I'm so sorry, Richard."

He paused for a moment. "I'm sorry for bringing that up." He turned his gaze back toward her. "She reminded me of you. Always mischievous, making me laugh and challenging me the way you used to do."

"I'm glad you found someone good for you and that she made you happy." Feeling compassion for him, she squeezed his hand. Their faces were only inches apart. Trudy opened her mouth to speak, but words escaped her. His stare unnerved her.

Suddenly, a loud boom of thunder rumbled, distracting them. Looking south, Trudy saw dark clouds building on the horizon.

"We'd better find shelter. I forgot to check the weather before borrowing this bike." Richard jumped up, looking concerned. "The storm is south of us, but I think we can beat it since we're going north. Do you want to try to make it back to The Greenbrier or should I call Kwan to come get us?"

Trudy knew that waiting on Kwan would most likely delay her at least another three hours before starting home. She figured it was best to try to leave then. "If you want to try to make it back, it's okay with me."

They gathered everything together and rolled the blanket. Hastily, they made it back to the Harley. After they'd put on their coats and helmets, Richard sped away with Trudy clinging to him.

Captivated by this man she'd spent the last twenty-four hours with, she was convinced that the last thirty-five years apart had dissipated. She almost dreaded to see her visit end. It felt as if a part of her that she'd long buried had been awakened. She wondered if she would still feel cheated and betrayed or would their time together be enough to put her past behind her where it belonged?

CHAPTER 15

On the way back to The Greenbrier, the dark clouds approaching from the south crept around the mountain to the west and lay directly in their path. With no towns between them and The Greenbrier, Trudy doubted they could make it much further without running into heavy rain. Knowing from the sound of thunder that rain would surely follow, Richard slowed down, searching for shelter.

Suddenly, a headwind gusted, forcing Richard to drive even slower. Whiting out all visibility ahead, a wall of rain moved rapidly toward them.

Trudy saw an old shed on a hillside. She patted Richard's side and pointed to it.

Richard slowed and turned off the road into a grassy meadow, trying to make it to the shed in what was now a sheet of rain sheered sideways by the force of wind. Struggling to keep the bike upright, he drove slower until he finally guided the Harley into the open shed.

Kicking down the stand, he turned the engine off and glanced around to assess where they were. They were surrounded by large cylindrical bales of hay.

Pulling off his helmet and wiping more water from his face, Richard reached for Trudy's hand to hold her steady as she slid off the bike. "I'm sorry about that. Are you okay?" he shouted above the rain pounding the metal roof.

With her hair and face soaked, she shouted back. "Yes, I think so! But I'm soaked!"

They removed their leather jackets that had done little to stop the rain from running down their necks. Richard laid their coats on a bale of hay to dry out. Then he suggested, "If you want to get those wet clothes off, I'll get out the blanket for you. It should still be dry since the tote bag is waterproof."

"No, that's okay. They won't dry and I would only have to put them back on once we started traveling. This will probably blow over in a few minutes."

Richard unzipped the tote bag strapped to the Harley and pulled out the blanket. He wrapped it around her. "Maybe this will at least keep you from getting chilled."

She pulled the blanket tighter around her.

"I'll call Kwan and get him to drive out to get us."

"There's no need for that. This should let up soon enough. We're only a few miles away and you won't have to leave the Harley here."

Suddenly, a flash of lightning lit up the shed and sky. Trudy screamed and jumped into Richard's arms, knocking him off balance. They fell onto a collapsed hay bale. A clap of thunder roared, shaking the shed as Richard held Trudy sprawled out on top of him.

They lay motionless for a moment, letting the scare of the thunder subside. Trudy's heart was still pounding when she finally rose up enough to look at Richard, the blanket laying partly over them. She started to speak but let the pounding rain fill the silence. Their gazes fixed and bodies nestled together, neither moved away.

Gazing into her eyes, Richard moved his hand up the small of her back, over her wet top exposing her full-figured body. Trudy held her breath, knowing she should stop him. His fingers ever so gently caressed the back of her neck and then moved around to caress her face. Trudy wanted to say something but she didn't know what. With the slightest tug he pulled her face toward his. Briefly, Trudy resisted but when their lips met she closed her eyes and yielded to his advance.

Cradled in Richard's arms, she no longer felt chilled from the cool air and her wet clothing. The heat from Richard's body warmed her as she lay against him, her heart racing, oblivious to the storm raging just a few feet from them. His kiss excited her and seemed to linger on and on.

Richard's gentle caresses to her tense body released her pent-up passion even more. Breathing hard, she clung to him, pressing her body to meet his advance, realizing how much she missed responding to a man's touch. She hadn't felt this aroused for longer than she could recall.

Kenneth! She thought and panicked.

Her hands moved from grasping Richard to pressing against him. He held tightly, not responding as she tried pushing herself from him.

"No. No, stop!" she uttered, rolling to her side, trying to break his hold. But Richard rolled with her, pinning her body between him and the hay.

Panicking, she turned her face away from his kisses.

Her cell phone rang. She reached up blindly for her coat laying on the hay bale behind her, grasping it and pulling it down.

Startled by the noise and her thrashing movements, Richard let go and sat up with a confused expression on his face. Catching her breath, Trudy sat up, too, reached for the phone and answered when she saw it was April calling.

"Hello, April," she answered, trying to sound calm while catching her breath.

"Hello, Mom. Are you okay?"

"Yeah...yes, I am," she said, brushing her wet hair back and glancing at Richard. "I was just looking at something, and the phone ringing startled me, I guess."

Richard stood up and walked toward the shed opening. The rain shower had almost stopped.

"When are you going to start home?"

"Probably within the next couple of hours." She picked loose strands of hay from her wet clothing.

"Have you heard the latest weather report?"

"No, I haven't. What are they saying?"

"They're calling for bad storms and there's a tornado watch for all of southwest Virginia until nine o'clock tonight."

Trudy looked outside to see what Richard was doing. "I wasn't aware of that."

"Do you think it's safe for you to drive?" April sounded concerned.

"I'll see what it looks like when I get ready to leave. If it's bad, I'll call and let you know."

"Has your visit with Mr. Vanderveer been what you expected it to be?"

"Yes, pretty much so," she said, realizing it had been anything but what she expected. "Is Mom doing okay?" Trudy changed the subject.

"Yes. I've been helping her put pictures of her and Grandpa into an album." She paused. "I think she's thinking a lot about him now for some reason."

"Your grandfather was a wonderful man. She loved him very much." Trudy smiled as she remembered him.

"Call me before you start home, and I'll let you know what the weather looks like here."

"I will, Sweetie."

"Love you, Mom."

"Love you, too. Bye."

Trudy walked outside and found Richard talking on his cell phone and realized he was talking to Kwan.

"We'll try to drive on in. It's not raining here now." He glanced back at Trudy and continued. "I'll drive to the back of The Greenbrier and come in through the service area. They won't see us coming in that way. Maybe you can get some house robes for us to slip into. We are soaking wet."

Richard flipped his phone shut. "Is everything okay?" he asked.

"Yes. That was April. She said we're under a tornado watch until nine tonight."

"I picked a good day to go bike riding, didn't I?"

"I wouldn't have missed it. It brought back a lot of memories," Trudy said, glancing away, feeling awkward about their intimate moments earlier.

"Kwan said reporters with cameras have shown up at the resort, asking questions. I guess now that they've found me, they will press me about the buyout."

"What do we need to do?"

"Kwan's going to meet us at the service area with robes to change into. Anybody seeing us will think we've been at the spa. They won't expect me to be riding in on a Harley." He reached over and brushed strands of hair from her face. "Are you okay?"

"I'm fine," she nodded, not meeting his eyes, glad he hadn't brought up what had just happened, knowing she'd disappointed him.

"Then let's get on the road before we get caught in another downpour."

He mounted the bike and gave Trudy his hand.

Riding behind him on the bike, Trudy leaned into him closer since the wind from the bike ride chilled her wet body. She thought about their passionate encounter and wondered why she'd allowed herself to let things go so far. But being with Richard had brought back tender memories of their youth. She had felt like a teenage girl again, and making out with him seemed the most natural thing to do. It had been years since she'd felt excited by a man's touch. *I'm fifty-three years old now and married to another man,* she reminded herself, as they turned into The Greenbrier and drove to the back service entrance just as another burst of rain poured down.

Making a dash through the service docks, they found Kwan waiting with a couple of house robes and slippers.

"Ms. Trudy, Mr. Vanderveer, here are your robes. Put your wet clothes in these bags. I'll have them cleaned and returned to you."

"Thank you, Kwan."

"Would you like a beverage or maybe hot tea to help warm you?"

Trudy, shivering from the bike ride, let Richard answer.

"That would be great, Kwan. We'll get out of these wet clothes and go to the spa and wait for you there." He looked at Trudy. "Let's go in these bathrooms here and change. That way we won't draw attention to ourselves. I don't want to face those vultures upstairs until I have to."

She knew he meant the news reporters who were lurking around to interview him.

Trudy went into the women's bathroom and changed. Trying to brush her hair so it wouldn't look so windblown, she became frustrated and gave up. She folded all of her wet clothes, placed them in the bag and went back out to the hallway to wait for Richard.

A young man walked by, talking on his cell phone. He glanced toward her and smiled as he passed.

Richard appeared and remarked, "You look better than you did a few minutes ago."

"Thanks for the kind effort." She frowned, knowing how awful she looked.

"I'm sorry we got stuck out in the storm. I should have checked the weather before leaving."

"It's not your fault. You know how thunder showers pop up here in the mountains. Besides, I enjoyed our day together. It brought back a lot of memories and..." she hesitated, searching for the right words to say.

"About how things used to be or could have turned out for us," Richard finished for her with a solemn expression.

"Yes, something like that," she agreed, refusing to meet his eyes.

Richard took her hand and pulled her around in front of him. "Also, I need to apologize for what happened out there today. I know I got carried away."

"It was just as much my fault," she acknowledged, feeling relieved that he had broached the subject.

"I guess we took our reminiscing a little too serious." He grinned.

"Right."

"I'm beginning to realize what I've missed by not being around you for the last thirty-five years."

Trudy snickered and raised an eyebrow. "Like I said before, you probably wouldn't say that if you had lived with me all those years. But thanks for the compliment."

He squeezed her hand. "Why don't we go find that hot tea and get ourselves cleaned up so maybe we can find something else to reminisce about? Who knows, we may even find ourselves in trouble again."

Trudy stood on her toes, reached up, and took the collar of Richard's robe, then pulled his head down to her forehead. "Richard, I swear I don't think you've changed at all." She laughed.

They heard a commotion nearby and looked around to see the young man who had passed her earlier. Trudy stepped back from Richard as he walked by them, seeming to purposely avoid looking in their direction.

"Let's go get that tea Kwan has waiting for us," Richard suggested.

They walked down the hall, talking and laughing as Trudy playfully elbowed Richard for adding bits of humor to their conversation just as he had always done so many years ago.

CHAPTER 16

Wave after wave of rain pounded the window. Trudy glanced outside, listening to the weather channel's report. A tropical depression had changed directions and was causing havoc with flooding and tornadoes in the mountain area. Unable to start driving home, she and Richard were meeting for dinner. They had decided to dine at the resort café since she'd brought only one formal dress and refused to wear it twice. Richard understood.

She glanced at the room clock and saw it was almost five o'clock. Sitting in her room for the last hour, Trudy thought about the intimate encounter she'd fallen into with Richard. She felt uneasy about having lost control the way she did. Her thoughts bounced back and forth between Richard and Kenneth. It seemed as though the storm raging outside was also creating havoc in her heart. One minute she was calm and the next she couldn't sit still.

Trudy decided to go to the lobby and wait for Richard. Anything was better than pacing the floor and listening to weather reports that she now could repeat word for word. She wore a light blue dress and glanced in the mirror to make sure she looked okay after her disastrous run-in with the weather earlier. Checking her cell phone, she noticed the battery was beeping low after two days of use. Not wanting to open the safe to get the charger out of her handbag, she turned it off, deciding to charge it later.

Sitting on a corner sofa in the lobby listening to guests talk over tea and cocktails, Trudy noticed several men walking around the room with cameras and figured they were reporters waiting to corner Richard.

A few minutes later, Richard walked into the room dressed in a brown and blue plaid sport coat, white collared shirt, and blue trousers. Immediately, the crew with cameras descended and started questioning him while snapping pictures and filming with video cameras.

He held up a hand to stop them. "I'm late for a dinner meeting, gentlemen. But if you'll ask only a few questions and make this quick, I'll try to oblige you."

Trudy was within hearing range and knew that Richard hadn't noticed her yet. She watched as he answered the reporters' questions with ease and confidence and seemed to steer the conversation where he wanted it to go.

"Mr. Vanderveer," one of the reporters asked, "since the Winchester Apple Company has rejected your offer to sell to Vanderveer Enterprise, why are you still pursuing them?"

"We can give them international recognition and sell their brands through our existing food supply chains. That will generate business for them that they could never do on their own as an independent company. The growth potential for them would be enormous."

Another reporter asked, "Mr. Vanderveer, we understand your people have been calling all of the apple growers in this region, offering to buy out their crops at a premium price for the next three years. Is this how you plan to force the co-op to sell to you? Without the local orchards supplying them, you know it would put them out of business."

Richard hesitated before speaking. He frowned and then replied aggressively, "Look! There's nothing wrong with offering these growers a fair market price. That's just another way everyone wins if we become partners through this acquisition. Now, please excuse me. I'm late for dinner."

Suddenly a young reporter stepped in front of him, preventing him from walking away. "One more question, please."

Richard ignored him and tried to pass around him.

Trudy noticed it was the same young man they'd seen down at the service entrance earlier.

"It's not about the buyout," he quickly interjected.

Richard stopped to listen.

"A few days ago there was an article released by the US Postal Service about a lost letter mailed in 1975 to a woman named Trudy Meyers. Since the letter had R Vanderveer as the sender and was mailed from the Netherlands, your place of birth, was the letter sent by you? If so, who was this woman, Trudy Meyers, the letter was mailed to?"

Richard caught sight of Trudy. He stepped back, paused, and put his hands in his pockets. "I remember reading about that somewhere." He chose his words cautiously. "I can't remember who I was with last week, much less thirty-five years ago. Maybe my brother Raymond and I need to get together and see if we remember that name. We had a lot of friends back then, as you can imagine." He pulled his hands from his pockets as Kwan walked up.

"Excuse me. I have a dinner reservation I need to keep."

The reporter started to follow, but Kwan stepped in his path. He pulled a camera from his pocket, held it up, and called out to Richard. "Mr. Vanderveer, one more question, please!"

Richard ignored him. Walking past Trudy, his eyes made contact with her and he gestured with his chin for her to follow.

When she stepped into the hallway to follow, the reporter hollered, "Mrs....Mrs.!"

Not wanting to draw attention to herself, she didn't look back. She caught up with Richard as they turned the corner at the end of the hall.

"Sorry about that. I knew they were going to catch up with me sooner or later."

"You handled it well. Wasn't he the same man who passed us in the hallway at the service entrance when we came in?"

"I thought he looked familiar. It's probably some kid wanting his few minutes of glory by posting a blog on the Internet about me." Shrugging, he reached over and caressed her arm. "Come on. Let's get something to eat. I'm famished, and I bet you are, too."

Seated by a window in the café, they gazed at the torrential rain pounding the window.

"I doubt if I'll be able to drive home tonight."

"Then stay over another night. We'll find some music and relax," Richard suggested.

"That would be nice, but I must get home." She made a tent of her fingers on the tabletop. "I have to get things ready for Kenny and April's party next weekend."

"Maybe someday I can meet this man who's won your heart." He scrutinized her closely as he waited for her reaction.

"That would be nice," Trudy said, imagining what Kenny's reaction would be at meeting Richard.

"Okay, back to you and me." Richard decided not to press her. "Where did we leave off?"

"Somewhere between 1975 and now." Trudy reminded him and relaxed at the flow of conversation.

For the next two hours they reminisced about anything and everything. Dreams they'd sought and lost, challenges that reshaped their lives. Sometimes they laughed and other times they sat quietly, gazing at each other as if reading each other's thoughts.

Listening to Richard talk about his life in-depth, Trudy wondered how different her life might have been with him. *Would I still have had the chance to pursue my own career, or would I have been at his beck and call, flying all over the world to spend time with him? After all, he seemed to want to control everyone and everything, needing to prove to himself and everyone in the world that he was the best at what he did.*

If I'd married him, would he still have become this self-driven man, whose focus in life was to get everything he wanted at any cost? Could I have loved someone whose passion in life was driven by wealth and a daunting desire for success, always lurking for the next opportunity that was never enough? What would have been his expectations of me? Would my expectations of him have made life impossible for us?

She doubted they'd ever have been compatible. She knew she couldn't have given up her independence or career choices to be a kept woman for him, anymore than he could have given up his desire to become successful and wealthy that had become his priority in life. She needed someone who understood the importance of her having her own career goals, who would support her making her own decisions, and experiencing with her the things she was passionate about. *Someone, who would let me be me, like Kenny.*

Someone like Kenny?

Richard seemed to notice the distant expression on Trudy's face and suggested, "Let's go for a walk. I'm getting stiff. I think the Harley took a toll on me."

Trudy glanced at her watch, then out the window at what was now just a steady rain. "I really need to decide if I'm going to drive home tonight, then call Mom and April to let them know."

"Let's go for a walk first. It's only seven o'clock. The night's young. If you need to get home tonight, I'll have a driver take you. I don't want you driving alone in this weather and I can get your car to you tomorrow."

"No need for that. I'll make up my mind shortly."

Strolling through the hallways of The Greenbrier on the lobby level, almost deserted because of the storm, and the weekend crowd having left, Trudy found herself unconsciously brushing against Richard. She felt comfortable with him.

Down a green carpeted hallway leading to the west wing, they came upon red carpeted steps that led up to a half-moon foyer of white and black checkered marble flooring adjacent to an outside patio. Live piano music played over the intercom system. But no one other than the two of them was there to hear it.

Richard glanced around. "Let's dance," he suggested, holding out his hand.

Trudy stared at him, hesitantly.

"Come on. Let's not lose the moment," he insisted, flashing a smile.

"Okay," Trudy conceded, lifting her hand to his.

Richard led her onto the marble floor, pulled her close, and they danced. Trudy kicked off her heels so she could move more freely. They swayed to music playing for them alone in the deserted foyer.

After several songs, Trudy found herself leaning into Richard's embrace, her head against his shoulder. They were silent as their bodies nestled together in the harmony of the moment, encompassed by the piano medley. Richard held her with his face pressed against her hair. Trudy closed her eyes, savoring the moment, as she tried to remember the last time Kenny had held her in a dance. In fact, she couldn't remember the last time they had even danced. Moving to Richard's lead, she wondered if she and Kenny could ever again find the intimacy that once wove their lives together.

Finally, the music stopped. Trudy lifted her gaze to meet Richard's. Without speaking, he held her close.

Suddenly, a noise in the hallway distracted them. They separated and stepped back from each other as a young couple walked by.

Without speaking, Trudy strolled over to a tall glass door and stared out at the night that had now become calm. Feeling a little apprehensive, Trudy worried that once again, she had allowed herself to get too comfortable with Richard. But she reassured herself that she'd soon be leaving. She let the thought pass.

Richard followed and stood close behind her, placing his hands on her shoulders. "I need you to close your eyes," he instructed her.

Trudy met his eyes in the reflection of the glass and hesitated, but finally closed her eyes. She felt something cool and solid being placed around her neck. When she opened her eyes she reached up and touched sparkling stones, then met his gaze again in the glass. "It's beautiful."

"You make it beautiful."

"Richard, you are very thoughtful, but I can't accept this."

"Why not?"

"Because we're just two…" she searched for words, "acquaintances from the past that have been fortunate enough to spend a couple of days together."

"I think we're more than just two acquaintances," Richard said softly. "I think it's been a lot more and we both know it."

"What do you mean?"

"Have you ever wondered what life would have been like for us if given the chance?"

"Yes, of course I have," she said, blinking several times, confused at what Richard was insinuating. "But that's our past and we can't do anything about it now."

"Why not? What's stopping us from trying to pick up where we are with what we once had and make it a reality?"

"I'm married, Richard." She spun around. "I have a family to consider."

"But are you happy?"

"Happiness is what one chooses to be."

"Trudy." The tone of Richard's voice changed. Placing his hands on her arms and gazing into her eyes, he continued, "The last couple of days have made me happier than I've been in a long time. Now that fate has brought us back together, I don't want to let go. Let's give us a chance."

"We've been together for only a couple of days." She shook her head. "Even if I weren't married, we wouldn't know each other well enough to consider a commitment like that."

"I understand what you're saying, Trudy. But if given the chance, we could rekindle the feelings we once had for each other. We just need to give us time." He dropped his hands and spoke more urgently. "We're not strangers who just met. You're the girl I loved thirty-five years ago. I never stopped loving you. Even when I thought...."

"No," she interrupted him. "You never quit loving the girl you knew thirty-five years ago." She hesitated and lowered her voice. "Just like I never stopped loving the boy I once knew. But we have both changed. We're two different people from two different worlds now."

"No, we're not. I know we both moved on and eventually loved other people. But it was because we thought our chance at a life together was lost. How many times have you reflected on us and wondered what life would have been for us, if we'd had the chance?" He spoke persuasively.

"Look at what you're asking me to sacrifice." Trudy's entire body tensed. "You're asking me to walk away from my marriage. You know that's not possible."

Richard dropped his gaze and threw his hands up and spoke more intensely. "Trudy, you never answered my question. Are you happy? You said yourself that you two have been separated for over a year and were looking for a second chance. Look at what you could have with me. I could give you things dreams are made of."

"No, Richard," she responded firmly. "I said we were looking for a new beginning with each other. Not going our separate ways. And you know me well enough to know I could never be a kept woman."

"But what if your marriage doesn't work out? Then what? If Kenneth is looking for a settlement of some kind, I can help with that. I'm sure he would be more than content with what I can offer him."

Trudy couldn't believe what Richard was suggesting. He thought he could buy her love, just as his father had paid off her mother thirty-five years ago to remove Trudy from his son's life. It infuriated her. She clenched her teeth to keep from shouting. "Richard, don't you see what you're doing and what you've become? In your quest to become independent of your father, you've become just like him. Wanting to control everyone, everything and..." She paused, searching for the right words. "And taking what you want regardless of the consequences or harm it does to other people."

Richard's eyes hardened. "Is that what this has been about and why you came to see me? Did you come up just to fabricate some reason for not liking me? Is this your way of getting even with me for what happened thirty-five years ago?" His face flushed red. "And what do you mean I've become like my father?"

"Look at the things you're doing," she shouted back, determined not to be intimidated. "Trying to force some little corporation to cave in to your wish, to own them because you think you have to prove something. And you won't even consider a merger with your own brother because you're afraid he's going to gain more out of it than you." Her voice quivered. "Now you're asking me to turn away from people I love so you can have me." She shook her head in disbelief as tears welled in her eyes. "Richard, I'm not a piece of property you can buy or manipulate! I'm a human being with feelings."

His face winced with anger. "Forget it, Trudy," he scoffed, throwing his hand out. "Forget this ever happened." He raised his voice. "Forget about me, us, this weekend and everything that happened thirty-five years ago. It meant nothing then..." he spoke softer as if asking himself a question, "apparently it means nothing now."

Trudy felt a rush of bitterness, then hurt, sweep through her. "You're not the boy I once knew, Richard." She glared at him, tears blurring her vision. "You wouldn't have asked someone you cared for to do what you just asked of me. Richard, I'm sorry for you. I really am."

He scowled at her briefly, then turned away and stared into the distance.

Overwhelmed with emotions, Trudy reached down, picked up her heels and gave him one last look before briskly walking away.

With each step, she considered her angry words, and regretted losing control of her temper. Her anger subsided. *He didn't deserve that. I have no right to tear him down about the way he lives his life. Maybe he's just lonely and that's why he said what he did.* She couldn't walk out on him like this after what they'd been through. She'd never forgive herself.

Abruptly, she stopped. Trying to regain her composure, she wiped her eyes while considering what to say to him. She turned to go back and saw him walking briskly toward her. Dropping her heels, she ran down the hallway to meet him. They rushed into each other's arms. Neither spoke. Only her sniffling and their breathing broke the silence.

Finally, Trudy looked up through teary eyes. "I am so sorry. I didn't mean for it to come out that way. I have no right to criticize your life. Please forgive me."

"No. It was me," he replied, his voice cracking. "It was selfish of me to think we could go back to what we had so long ago. I should never have mentioned it."

Trudy reached up and held his face with her hands. She swallowed hard to clear her voice. "I wish it could be yesterday once more for us and we could go back to what used to be. But we can't. Don't you see what would happen?" She winced. "We would be tearing each other apart. Neither of us would ever want that."

He bowed his head. "You're right. You were always right, Trudy. Please forgive me."

"Oh, Richard, don't blame yourself; I understand. We just never had a chance to grow up together, to play, or even have disagreements like people who love each other. It's those things that bond two people together."

Richard composed himself. "I understand. Please don't hold what I said against me."

"I would never do that."

Richard tilted her chin up with two fingers. "I wish nothing but the best for you…and Kenneth. I know you two will get back together and make your marriage work and have a wonderful life together. Just don't blame me for trying. Okay?" He forced a smile. "I'm just so damn envious of him. I hope he knows what he's got."

"I think he does," she declared with a trace of sadness and a smile through the tears streaking down her cheeks.

"Now, this is the Trudy I once knew. Not so serious and always smiling." He reached up and wiped tears from her cheek with his fingers.

"Has my mascara run?" She touched her face and looked at her fingers.

"Hmm, a little."

"I'll go clean up. I need to call home anyway. I'm sure Mom and April are worried about me."

"Call and tell them you're staying tonight. You don't need to travel out this late by yourself. The weather could get bad again." He lifted her hands, squeezing them. "I promise. There will be no more episodes like this. When you come back down, we'll get coffee and dessert."

She looked at him tenderly. "Thank you for not staying mad over what I said. I don't think I could've lived with myself if you had."

"I could never hold a grudge against you, my Trudy," he said in his boyish, Dutch accent.

She couldn't help but smile as she stepped back, her fingers slipping from his grasp.

"I'll meet you in the café."

She nodded and walked away. Picking up her heels from the floor, she glanced back and saw Richard deep in thought. She felt calmer, but couldn't believe they'd just had such a terrible spat. Why had she allowed herself to get into a confrontation with him? And more importantly, why had he suggested using his wealth to lure her from Kenneth?

She reasoned that most likely his money was the only tool he thought he had. Manipulation and wealth were the weapons he'd learned to use to build the life he now had. Added to that, he was a lonely person. With all the traveling and distractions involved in his work, he probably didn't have time for romance anyway, she thought. Maybe she'd temporarily filled an emotional void in his life. Was that it? Was she just an entertaining weekend to him or was he being honest with her about his desire to be with her and build on the relationship they once had? If he truly loved her, how could she hold that against him?

Would she still long to see him once Kenny returned and would she still yearn to know what life could've been like with Richard? How would she bring their reunion to closure so she'd have no lingering regrets? Did she do the right thing by coming to meet him and how was she now going to say goodbye forever? Those thoughts burdened her mind as she entered her room.

CHAPTER 17

Ten minutes later, Trudy looked out the window of her room to find the rain had completely stopped. She picked up her cell phone to call home to inquire what the weather was like in Lynchburg. Immediately, the phone started beeping from a low battery. She went to the room safe to get the charger from her handbag. Pulling the bag from the safe, it snagged the door lock and fell to the floor, dumping out most of the contents. Stooping over, she hurriedly began stuffing everything back into the bag. A long, white envelope sticking partially out of the bag caught her attention.

Curious, she opened it and pulled a letter from it. She recognized her mother's handwriting. Within the folded letter was an old discolored check for $10,000 made out to Mrs. Janet Meyers. The date was August 4, 1975, just one day before they received word that her father had been killed. The signature on the check was that of Patrick Vanderveer, Richard's father. Noted on the bottom were the words, *For Trudy Meyers.*

Trudy felt a knot building in her chest, as she had when she first opened the lost letter she'd received from Richard. It was now obvious. Her mother had never used the check Patrick Vanderveer gave her. She remembered her mother holding an envelope when they were on the back porch talking about her going to meet Richard.

She began to read her mother's words.

Trudy,

I wasn't sure if this check was mentioned in Richard's letter but I intended to show it to you and tell you about it, until I found out you were planning to meet Richard. I didn't want you hurt even more over what you found out and knew this check had nothing to do with your desire to meet him anyway. It was simply a scar left on your heart that drove you to want to see him again.

Richard's father spoke to me about you and Richard and how you were going to get hurt if the relationship didn't end. He rambled on something about you two being from different cultures and more that I didn't understand. I was shocked and dumbfounded at what he told me.

He asked me to never bring you back to the farm and simply said he wished you the best, handed me an envelope and walked away. When I found this check, I assumed it was given as a token to keep you away from Richard. I was furious and planned to take it back to him the next day and give him a piece of my mind. But on that day I found out your father had been killed and my world fell apart.

When I thought about it again, we were already living in Lynchburg. I have waited my whole life hoping for the opportunity to meet Patrick again so I could give this check back to him and tell him that no amount of money could ever buy my daughter's love for or from any man. Regretfully, I never got that chance.

I was determined that if, someday, Richard asked for your hand in marriage, then I would do everything in my power for you two to have a life together, regardless of what his father threatened. I never got the chance because of the letter you received from Richard, ending your relationship. It hurt me watching my little girl hurt. I know you've lived with that scar on your heart for a long time.

I pray that your meeting Richard will erase the hurt and disappointment you both had to endure, then both of you can forever put the past where it belongs. Behind you.

Love, Mother

Trudy leaned against the wall, fighting back tears. Another reminder that she and Richard had lost their chance for a life together. After spending time with him, it was obvious he still had feelings for her. Whether intentional or not, her feelings for him, too, had blossomed during their reunion. She'd thought that she could simply walk away and put her past behind her. It wasn't working. Richard had been honest about his longing for her and had simply tried to win her over in the only way he knew how. Yet she had fought him all the way.

Her knees weak, she slid down the wall to the floor. She longed to run down to Richard and throw herself into his arms, knowing that he would comfort her. But she also knew a relationship with him could never be. With three other people in her life who meant so much to her, she again realized that the check her mother received did nothing to seal their fate. It was simply a letter that never made it to her. Tears blurred her vision as she fell to the floor sobbing, her face buried in her hands.

〜

The room telephone rang several times before jolting Trudy back to reality. She reached for it and cleared her throat in case it was Richard calling to check on her. She didn't want him to know that she'd just had a complete meltdown.

"Hello," she answered.

"Hello. Is this Ms. Trudy... uh," the caller paused. "I'm sorry; I forgot your last name."

"It's Quinn," Trudy replied quickly, not recognizing the caller.

"I'm sorry. I have the wrong person." The phone clicked dead.

Trudy sat down to pull herself together. She felt a sudden urge to leave as if she needed to run from someone or something. No longer sure if she could trust herself with Richard, she grabbed her bags and was packed within minutes. She thought it best not to see him again because she could not trust what she might do. She went to the desk in her room and, choking back tears, wrote him a note. She would leave it at the front desk, to be delivered after she was gone. Hoping he would understand, she hastily stuffed the note and the check into hotel envelopes, since the one her mother had the check in was drenched from her tears. She glanced in the mirror one last time and noticed the necklace he had placed on her neck. Hastily taking it off, she put it in an envelope, grabbed her bags and left the room.

Exiting the elevator, she hurriedly made her way to the bellhop's desk and instructed him to get her car.

"Do you have your car voucher?" the bellhop asked.

She fumbled for the voucher, then remembered that Kwan had her car parked and held the ticket. "Mr. Vanderveer's assistant took care of that for me when I arrived. I can show you my ID, though."

"No need for that. He's outside helping Mr. Vanderveer unload. We'll get it from him and bring your car around."

Trudy thought it strange that Richard was unloading something at this time of night. Not wanting him to see her leave, she figured she'd just have to deal with it as best she could.

She went to the registration desk. "I'm leaving and need to check out. What do I owe?"

The desk clerk checked the computer. "Mrs. Quinn, your charges are forwarded to Mr. Vanderveer. All your expenses are covered."

"Also, I have something that I need to return and have credited back to Richard Vanderveer's account." She placed the envelope with the stone necklace on the counter. "The lady at the jewelry boutique said I could return this if I wished. I'm in a hurry and it will save me a trip downstairs if you can do it for me."

"I'll be glad to handle it for you, Mrs. Quinn. If you have your receipt, I will call the jewelry shop to verify the purchase and issue a credit for you."

"I don't have the receipt." She became frustrated and then asked. "Can you see if Mr. Vanderveer charged it to his room and take that as a receipt?"

"Sure, I can do that." He began searching the computer.

"Ms. Trudy, is something wrong?" It was Kwan, standing behind her.

She turned to face him. "No, Kwan. I just need to leave. Is Richard outside?"

"No, Ms. Trudy. He's at the café waiting for you. I'll go get him."

"No, no!" Trudy stepped away from the registration desk, holding up her hand. "I don't want him to know I'm leaving. Not yet anyway."

Kwan looked puzzled.

"It's hard to explain." She tried to find words to make him understand. "It's time for me to leave. If I stay any longer, it's just going to hurt Richard, or both of us, more. I don't want him to have to go through that." She saw that he didn't understand what she was trying to tell him. She reached into her handbag and pulled out the envelope with the letter that she had written to Richard. "Give this to him, please. It explains everything. He'll understand."

"Yes, Ms. Trudy, I will. At least let me take your bags out and put them in the car for you." He picked up her bags and left.

Trudy turned back to the desk receptionist.

"Mrs. Quinn, I called the jewelry boutique and they verified the purchase so I have issued a credit to Mr. Vanderveer's account in the amount of $9,247.00. Would you like a receipt showing the refund?"

"Give it to Mr. Vanderveer when he checks out, please."

"Very well, I shall," he replied.

Trudy started to leave but heard a familiar voice from the center of the room. Looking around, she didn't see anyone she knew. An elderly man with gray hair spoke out again. Shivers ran down her spine when she recognized the heavy eyebrows, now gray, the accent, now cracked, and the old and wrinkled face of Patrick Vanderveer. She froze for a second, wondering if he would recognize her. Then she remembered what her mother had written in the note.

Walking toward him, she pulled the envelope from her handbag that held the check, determined to confront him.

He glanced up when she stepped in front of him.

"Mr. Vanderveer, my name is Trudy Quinn. But you may remember me as Trudy Meyers. I have something to return to you." She handed him the envelope. "We never wanted your money. My mother and I both want you to know that no amount of money could have bought my love from Richard. What you did to us was wrong. I hope you've lived well with your guilt." She turned and walked away.

He didn't have time to respond and she wasn't sure he knew what she was talking about. But she felt good for her mother's sake.

Outside she found Kwan standing by her car.

"Kwan, take care of Richard. He's...." She paused, not sure what to tell him, then simply said, "Take care of him for me."

"I will, Ms. Trudy."

Trudy glanced inside to see Patrick Vanderveer still standing in the foyer, looking dazed. He was staring at her through the glass wall.

"Goodbye, Kwan." She got in her car and drove off.

Plugging her cell phone into the car jack, she called home.

"Hello, Mom," April answered.

"Hello, Sweetie. Has it stopped raining in Lynchburg?"

"Yes, about an hour ago. When are you coming home?"

"I'm on my way. I should be there in a couple of hours."

"You sound funny." She didn't wait long enough for a response before asking, "You've been crying, haven't you?"

Trudy sighed, realizing her daughter could detect her every mood. "I'll tell you about everything later. I'll be there by eleven o'clock or so."

"Mom, please be careful."

"I will. Don't worry about staying up. Everything's fine. Love you."

"Love you, too, Mom."

Trying to avoid crying again, Trudy searched the radio channels, looking for a distraction to clear her mind so she would be able to continue driving. She had thought the trip to The Greenbrier was stressful, but she felt even antsier now that she was leaving. She couldn't get the fight with Richard out of her mind.

And what about her mother? Guilt overtook her, thinking that she actually thought her mother would have ever taken money from Richard's father to keep her away from Richard. How could she have doubted her mother's integrity after what they had been through together? She was relieved she hadn't confronted her mother about it.

Her mind continued to churn with questions. Had she done the right thing by going up to meet Richard? Would he think badly of her for leaving without saying goodbye? Would she ever hear from him again? And how much should she tell Kenny? After all, the news media would likely continue to follow the lost letter story until she gave the paper an interview. Did the world need to know about her and Richard's teenage love affair?

As she set the cruise control, all she could hope was that she'd have everything resolved before Kenny arrived home.

⁓

Richard looked up to see Kwan walking into the café.

"Have you seen Trudy? She went to her room almost an hour ago and was supposed to meet me here."

"She just checked out and left."

"She did what?" Richard lurched from his seat. "Is something wrong?"

"She said no," Kwan paused and then added, "but she did seem a little upset. I told her I would come and get you, but she insisted I didn't." Kwan handed him the envelope. "She wanted me to give this to you and said something about this would explain everything and you would understand."

"I don't understand," Richard murmured, as he pulled from the envelope what looked to him to be an old scrap of paper. As he read it, he saw it was a check made out to Mrs. Janet Meyers for $10,000 and signed by his father. On the bottom was scrawled the words For Trudy Meyers and he noticed the date, August 4, 1975.

Richard gasped when he realized what he held in his hands.

Kwan, noticing his reaction, asked, "Is everything okay?"

"No! I mean, I'm not sure." Richard fumbled with a reply, trying to sort out what Trudy's intentions were by giving him this check that was never cashed.

"What do I need to do, Mr. Vanderveer?" Kwan asked. "You're upset."

"Nothing!" Richard turned away. "I just need some time to myself."

"I'll be in the lobby if you need me. By the way, your father and Raymond just checked in. They said they were tired and would get with you in the morning."

Richard replied, "Sure, Kwan. I'll see them later."

He sat down and stared at the check, remembering all that happened between Trudy and him over the last two days. *Why didn't she tell me she had the check and never used it? Why did she let me think she knew nothing about it and then give it to me and leave without any explanation? Maybe she's still angry over what had happened thirty-five years ago, and it was all a scheme to get even with me. I have to admit I never saw it coming. She'd had me convinced there was something special between us. I guess I misread her and her intentions.*

The café waitress walked over. "Are you still waiting for your friend?"

"Not anymore," he answered sharply.

"Would you like more coffee?"

"No." He stood and tossed a few dollars on the table. "I'm going to the bar. It'll fit my mood better."

CHAPTER 18

She was floating through a dream. Voices in the distance sounded familiar. Everything was peaceful and all the thoughts that plagued her mind earlier were thoughts that would simply go away since they were part of her dream. The aroma of freshly-brewed coffee filled the air. Trudy shifted positions and held her pillow tighter. Then it dawned on her. *You can't smell in a dream.*

Trudy opened her eyes to daylight. The clock read eight-thirty. Always an early riser and up by six every morning, she'd slept late. Then she remembered as she sat up in bed that it had been eleven-thirty when she arrived home and midnight before she went to bed. The last thing she remembered was checking the time at two o'clock, trying to calm all that was on her mind so she could sleep. After a couple of stretches while yawning, she headed for the kitchen to join her mother and April.

They turned from the television news as soon as she entered the kitchen.

"Morning, Mom, April," she said, reaching for an empty cup from the cabinet.

"Good morning," they replied, watching her closely.

April walked over and gave her a hug. "I was worried about you. You sounded upset last night."

"I know you were." Trudy returned the hug. "Everything's fine now."

"Was meeting Richard what you expected?"

Trudy rolled her eyes up before speaking. "Hmm...yes and no."

April stared.

"Someday you and I will have a mother-daughter talk and I'll tell you all about it." She wanted to change the subject. "Is your father still scheduled to be home tomorrow?" She poured a cup of coffee, determined to keep the conversation off her and Richard.

"Yes," April replied, excitedly. "The city and veteran groups are encouraging everyone to come out to welcome the troops home."

"Then while we still have time, and we're all together, let's make sure our plans for the party this weekend are ready so we won't have to discuss them while your father's around." They made themselves comfortable in their usual chairs at the table.

"How do we keep it a surprise?" April asked.

"Your father thinks there's going to be an engagement party for you and that it won't start until three o'clock. I've told him that we'll have light refreshments and hors d'oeuvres, and it's just a get together for our families and close friends for him to formally announce the engagement of his daughter."

"Won't he know something's up once all of his friends and the neighbors start showing up?"

"No problem," Trudy added. "I'm thinking about renting a house for us at Smith Mountain Lake for a week. We will leave Thursday evening and won't come back home until Saturday morning. We'll do the decorating for your party and then slip out for a light lunch and do a few errands that will keep us away until three o'clock. You and Jan can take care of setting out beverages and hors d'oeuvres for everyone and putting his welcome home banner out. The caterers will have the barbeque here and set up by four."

"Does this mean you and Dad are getting back together permanently?" April asked, her eyes brightening.

"Don't you trust your mother to make the right decision?" She rolled her eyes at April. "Remember, this has to be your father's decision also. But I plan to influence him a little," she teased with a smile.

April beamed at her. "I'm sorry I went off on you about going to meet Richard. Will you forgive me?"

"You only did what any responsible, twenty-two year old daughter would have done. And you are forgiven." She sipped her coffee.

"What else can Matthew and I do to help at the party?"

"Nothing, Sweetie. Just enjoy your evening. Are you two still thinking about driving down to Orlando on Sunday to visit his grandparents?"

"Yes. They won't be able to make the trip up so we thought we would go visit and share the news of our engagement with them. Maybe we can also do some fun stuff while we're there."

"I remember when your father and I used to take off on trips spontaneously."

"Why did you stop?"

"You came along and," Trudy reached and touched April's cheek, "our priorities changed."

"I'm no longer an excuse now."

"You're right."

"Are you and Dad going back to the lake after the party?"

"We are, but not until Monday morning. That'll give him a chance to visit with some of his work buddies and friends over the weekend. I'm sure he has war stories to tell." Trudy looked at her mother. "Are you okay with all of us being gone for a few days?"

"I'll be fine. Besides, I'm going to move back home over the weekend."

"Why?"

"Because you and Kenneth need your time alone and I need my own space," she said, holding her head high. "Remember, I agreed to stay here only while he was away."

"You don't have to leave. There's plenty of room in this house for you to have your own space."

"In another twenty years I may need to take you up on the offer. But as long as I can get around as well as I do, I intend to live in my own house," she declared.

"Okay, Mom." Trudy, knowing her mother was strong-willed like herself, decided to drop the subject. "But why don't you wait until we get home next week and we'll help you move?"

Her mother thought for a second. "I suppose I could wait till then. Maybe I can help you with the party since I'll be here."

"Okay, that takes care of that." Trudy turned to April. "What are your plans for the next couple of days?"

"Susan, one of my bridesmaids, wants me to come over and spend the night with her."

"Why does she want you to do that?"

"Well, she's kind of throwing a bachelorette party for one of her friends who's getting married this weekend." April grinned. "I promised to help with it since she's in my wedding."

"Now we know the real reason." Trudy laughed.

"And I thought you and Dad might want some time to yourselves."

"Oh, don't be silly." Trudy waved her off.

"Maybe I'll go over and spend a night at my house," her mother added. "It'll give me time to tidy up before I move back."

"What's gotten into you two thinking Kenny and I need to be left alone?"

Her mother reached and patted her hand. "Trudy, I may be old, but I'm not naïve."

"Mom, you're blushing," April giggled.

"Okay. Okay, girls. Whatever you say," Trudy agreed and got up to pour another cup of coffee. "When do you want to sit down with me and do the interview about the letter?" she asked April.

"One of our staff writers will have to do the interview and write the story," April advised, as she took her cup to the sink. "I would like to, but it would be an ethics violation if I did."

"That's not fair. You won't get credit for it."

"My time will come. I have to pay my dues like any other news journalist." She checked her watch. "How about doing the interview over lunch? The newsroom is on me to get it to them. They're scared someone else will beat them to the story. It's still being covered by the national media."

"Don't worry. My lips are zipped." Trudy reflected back to her time with Richard. "Besides, I would really like to get this behind us before your father gets home."

"I'll bring Courtney Emerson with me for the interview. She's the staff writer who's writing the story. You remember her. She's the petite, bubbly girl I interned with at the paper during my finals in school."

"Yes, I remember. I can only imagine what she'll write. I guess I'll have to be careful with my words."

April sharply cut her eyes at her mother. "Mom, you know it'll be done professionally and we aren't allowed to spin anything."

"I'm just teasing, Princess. I know she'll do fine. Now, you and Matthew go take care of your errands and I'll plan to give you girls a good story over lunch."

April left, and Trudy sat with her mother again. Two television news commentators were talking about Vanderveer Enterprise. She listened attentively.

"Apparently, Richard Vanderveer plans to get what he wants at any cost. Rumor has it that Vanderveer Enterprise is offering a premium price to buy out all of the orchard crops in the valley for the next three years as a way to force Winchester Fruit Company to sell to them. Richard Vanderveer has not returned our calls to confirm or deny these allegations."

The other commentator continued, *"Vanderveer has always been a private man who likes to keep a low profile when it comes to media attention. It's been impossible to get an interview out of him for years.*

And I remember someone once jokingly said that Richard wouldn't do interviews anymore because doing it had gotten him in trouble. He did an interview with Iona Landon and eventually they married." He chuckled as he faced the other commentator.

"Wouldn't you like to know the story that's driven this man to be one of the most successful businessmen of the century? His story would certainly be compelling. Especially what drove him to leave home and drop out of school as a seventeen-year-old kid? And what made him so determined to make it on his own? It's been said that he actually lived at a homeless shelter until he could make enough money to live in a boarding house."

"His family was very wealthy, but he never relied on them for help," the other commentator added. *"What a fascinating story his life would tell."*

Indeed, it would, Trudy thought. She turned to her mother and found her staring intensely at her.

"You still love him, don't you?" her mother asked, her eyes narrowing.

"I guess I'll always love the boy I once knew." She confessed. "After all, he was my first love. Doesn't it work that way for everybody?" She tried to sound convincing, looking away from her mother.

"April said you'd been crying last night when she spoke to you."

Trudy sat tight-lipped for a second and knew she wasn't going to fool her mother. "It kind of got emotional for us toward the end of the evening. We both said some things that were upsetting." She quickly added, "But we both apologized for it."

"Will you two be able to put this behind you now?"

"I hope so. I left *The Greenbrier* after I found the note you left me. Oh!" Her voice rose with excitement. "I saw his father coming into the hotel while I was checking out. I gave him the check and told him what we thought about it."

"I wish I could've seen his face," Mrs. Meyers chimed in.

Trudy recalled the scene. "He never said anything. He just stood there with his mouth wide open, looking dumbfounded. I don't know if he understood or even remembered me."

"I'm sure it'll sink in sooner or later."

"Forgive me for jumping to conclusions about you, Mother. I can only imagine what you had to deal with back then. I know I would've done the same thing."

"It's behind us, Trudy. I'm just glad to see that you've gotten through this unscathed." Her voice was solemn. "I was afraid something might happen that would've come between your and Kenneth's chances of mending your marriage."

"It could have gotten out of hand." She paused in reflection. "But I remembered what you always told me to do."

"What was that?"

"You told me that whenever I was in doubt about something to always follow my heart."

"Yes, that usually works." She pushed herself up from the table. "I'm going up to my room and start packing some of my keepsakes."

"Need some help?" Trudy stood and carried her cup over to the sink.

"No. You take care of what you need to do." She walked across the room. Placing her hand on the doorframe, she turned back. "I don't have anything to do tonight, and the only parties I go to anymore are the church circle parties. Maybe something different would be good. What's a bachelorette party?"

"Nothing, Mom. It's just a bunch of girls getting together, making a lot of noise and staying up all night."

"Well, I reckon that would be too much for me. Maybe I ought to just stay at home."

Trudy sighed and shook her head at the thought as her mother left the room. She heard the news commentators bring up Richard's name again.

"Richard Vanderveer has no trouble making the news lately. A blogger, who claims to have solved the mystery as to who sent the lost letter that has been in the news for the last several days, has posted his findings on the Internet. He said that Richard Vanderveer sent the letter and has met the mystery woman at The Greenbrier Resort over the weekend. We have no way to confirm or deny if that information is correct."

Trudy contemplated the interview to be done so she could put all of the gossip and assumptions about the lost letter behind her. Once the truth came out, she hoped everyone would let the story drop. She would tell Kenny everything so he wouldn't be surprised when he read the story.

She paused and thought of Kenny. For the first time in a year she actually looked forward to seeing him. It was as if a burden had been lifted and she no longer doubted whether they should try to mend their marriage. Would Kenny remember the new beginning they talked about before he left? And could they again find the companionship and intimacy that once wove their lives together? Could they make it happen? She would try. Yes, she would try, hard.

CHAPTER 19

Trudy sat on her back porch admiring the foliage and flower decor she had added to the patio for summer. Since they ate most of their evening meals outside when it wasn't too hot, she thought a garden would look great. She had placed a fern on a stand in the corner against the wall, a palm tree in a basket caught the full sun on the left wall corner, and a couple of large colorful leafy plants in clay pots sat on the front corners. In the mulched areas beside the porch, she had put assorted flowers that bloomed all summer, with a rose tree in a large clay pot in the center.

Trudy heard a car in the driveway. It was only a little after eleven o'clock, so she walked around the side of the house, thinking April must have come home early. She saw Jan getting out of her car.

"I couldn't stay away any longer. It was killing me. How was the rendezvous?" Jan blurted out.

"Well, let me see," Trudy teased, rolling her eyes and putting her hands on her hips. "I got wined and dined and danced all night until I fell out. How else would you expect the rich and famous to live?" She laughed.

"Now tell me, really, what happened?" Jan asked.

"Follow me. I think we're going to have some serious porch time. Care for a beverage? I made lemonade tea for lunch. I'm having April and her friend Courtney Emerson over for lunch to give them the story about the letter."

"No, thank you," Jan said, taking a seat. "I told April to call me last night if she heard from you. I was worried about you driving home because of the storms. She called and said you sounded upset when she spoke to you."

Trudy leaned forward. "I never was any good at hiding my emotions, especially from April. I'm beginning to think she can read my mind. Even better than I imagined."

"So, what happened?"

"It was wonderful. It was doubtless two of the most memorable days of my life." She turned her wandering gaze to Jan. "Until he asked me to leave Kenny for him."

"He what?" Jan asked, startled.

Trudy stood, walked to the edge of the porch and stared out into the back yard. "It wasn't entirely his fault." She turned back to Jan. "I think the spark kind of got re-ignited between us."

Jan stared, but remained silent.

"We reminisced, we cried, and talked about each other's lives, so it just seemed the most natural thing to pick up where we left off. He's the same boy I first loved, only an adult version now."

"What are you going to do?"

"It kind of fell apart and we had a big fight. We were dancing by ourselves one minute and the next we were verbally tearing each other apart." Trudy walked over and sat down. "I said some really bad things to him. Now that I've thought about it, I'm totally ashamed of what I did."

"How did he react?"

"He got mad. I got mad. Then we both realized what we were doing and all of a sudden we were in each other's arms making up and apologizing."

"That had to be an emotional roller coaster for you," Jan said, shaking her head.

"That's not the worst part," Trudy replied in a halting voice. "I left without saying goodbye."

"Why?"

"I went to my room to call home and found the check in my handbag that Richard's father had given Mother thirty-five years ago. She never used it and had put it in there for me to find, with a note that tore my heart apart."

"Did you tell Richard?"

"No. I completely fell apart once I found it. I guess the reality that the check was not the reason Richard and I didn't have a life together got to me." She swallowed hard. "It was simply a lost letter that kept us apart, nothing more."

"You okay, girlfriend?" Jan asked.

"Yes, I'm sorry," Trudy answered, composing herself. "Anyway, I had a good cry, wrote a note to Richard, and gave it to his assistant to give him and I left. At the time I wasn't sure what I might do or what my emotions would've led me to do, or say. I felt vulnerable and emotional and thought it was best to leave right away."

"Do you have any regrets about meeting him?"

"No." She blinked a few times. "Richard's a wonderful man. I'm grateful that we learned the truth about what happened because both of us still lived with that missing piece in our lives."

"Will you be able to move on now?"

"Mom asked me the same question." She sat up straight. "Now that I know exactly what happened, I won't be questioning myself every time I hear his name mentioned anymore."

"So you have no regrets about how your life has turned out?"

"My last twenty-five years have revolved around Kenny. I know we've had our share of problems lately but when I think about how much he has always supported my careers and all, I know he's my soul mate. I know I'm lucky to have someone who lets me be me. I just hope we can get back to how things used to be." Grinning, her eyes brightened. "Maybe re-ignite the spark."

"This would make a wonderful love story. You ought to get someone to write a book about it someday."

"Yeah, and what would we call it? The Past Adventures of Trudy?"

They both laughed.

"Mom, I'm home!" April shouted from inside the house. "We're here to do the interview."

"We're on the back porch, girls!"

"I'll leave so you can talk," Jan suggested.

"No. I've got homemade chicken salad and a fresh fruit medley for lunch. Stay with me while I go through this. I may need some moral support." She touched Jan's forearm.

"Okay. You've talked me into it. I'll do anything for homemade chicken salad."

Walking onto the back porch, April introduced Courtney to her mother and Jan. She was a petite girl just a few years older than April. Her shag-cut, auburn hair hung down to her shoulders and she wore a pair of light-framed designer glasses that gave her a professional appearance. She wore a light tan blouse and a long, brown skirt with a flowered border and brown slippers. She brought a recorder, along with her laptop, for the interview.

"Hello, Courtney," Trudy greeted her, smiling. "I'm glad you're the one who's writing this story."

"I'm glad they chose me," she said, enthusiastically. "Very seldom does one get a chance to write a story that's gotten as much national exposure. I can hardly wait to hear it."

"Well, you may think it's rather boring once we finish." Trudy laughed.

"No way, after what April has already shared with me."

Courtney turned on the recorder and April began. "Okay, Mom. State your full name and give us your consent to record this interview."

"I'm your mother, for heaven's sake. You don't need all that stuff to interview me."

"Mom," April firmly stated, "the paper won't touch it unless it's done professionally and by the book." She gave her mother a hard glare. "Now! Let's try this again. State your full name and consent please."

"My name is Trudy Quinn, and I give my consent for this interview to Courtney Emerson and my wonderful daughter, April, whom I love very much." She winked at April. "Good enough?"

April rolled her eyes as Jan and Courtney sat, smiling.

"Tell us the story behind this lost letter, Mrs. Quinn," Courtney opened the interview.

"It was the summer of 1973. I was fifteen years old and had just gotten my first job working at the Vanderveer Farm in the Shenandoah Valley," Trudy began.

For the next hour Trudy shared with April and Courtney bits and pieces of her teenage life. Sometimes laughing, sometimes pausing to reminisce, she told the story of how she and a Dutch boy became friends only to find it blossoming into a passionate love in the summer of 1975.

"If that letter had been delivered on time, it could've changed my life. And that's the story behind the letter," Trudy concluded.

April and Courtney sat speechless. Finally, April spoke. "Now I know why you went to see him."

"This is a beautiful story," said Courtney, staring at her notes. "I just hope I can do it justice."

"I'm sure you'll do fine," Trudy assured her.

"I need to try to sum this up into an abbreviated version for the paper," Courtney said, closing her laptop. "I'm going to work on it for the rest of the day but it will probably be the following day before I can have it ready to print."

"Don't hurry for my sake," Trudy replied. "I'm just glad to get it behind me."

"I'll let you know our reader's response to the article. I'm sure they will be captivated."

Jan stood to leave. "I hate to leave the party but I have a manicure appointment. Thanks for lunch and letting me sit in on the interview. I loved it."

"Let me walk you to your car," Trudy suggested. She followed Jan around the house.

"As I sat and listened to you, I couldn't help notice the tone in your voice whenever you mentioned Richard," Jan remarked, stopping at her car and eyeing Trudy closely. "There's still something there for him, isn't it?"

"I guess I still have us on my mind." Shrugging her shoulders, she continued. "Once a part of your life, always a part of your life, I suppose."

"If Kenneth wasn't in the picture, would you try to make it work with Richard?"

"No, what we had happened a long time ago. It's long gone and we could never make it work. Besides, I'm really looking forward to working things out with Kenny. I've really been thinking about him lately."

"All of a sudden, you've become committed to your marriage again. What happened?"

Trudy hesitated. "A year ago maybe something different might have happened between us," she mused. "Maybe it's the year I've had to think about us or maybe it's seeing Richard and knowing I had a choice that helped me make up my mind. Whatever the reason, the whole time I was visiting Richard, I couldn't get Kenny out of my mind." She looked at Jan wryly. "I know it sounds weird, but it was as though I was comparing him to Richard."

"They were the only two men you ever loved," Jan reminded her.

"Maybe so. Kenny and I just have so much in common. I really want us to have a chance to make our marriage work when he gets home."

"Kenneth is a lucky man; I hope he knows what he's got."

"I think he does." Trudy replied as Jan slid into her car seat.

Jan looked back at Trudy with a wry grin.

"What are you getting ready to say?" Trudy asked, hesitantly.

"I'm trying to figure out what it is that's held you and Kenneth together. Anyone else would have given up long ago and moved on."

"If you find out, I would really like to know."

"You'll be the first to know," she laughed. "See you later, girlfriend," she hollered as she drove away.

Trudy waved.

CHAPTER 20

The next morning Trudy was out of bed by six, jogging her usual four blocks after one of the best night's sleep she'd had for a long time. When she did wake up, her mind was no longer filled with the usual doubt and uncertainty over what she should do once Kenny arrived home. She was dreaming up plans to make his welcome even better.

Wanting him to know how serious she was about mending their marriage, she had moved his clothes from the guest bedroom closet and drawers back down to their bedroom late last night. She couldn't help but feel a little apprehensive after what Jan had said earlier. 'What if he comes home and wants out of the marriage?' She had no reason to think that would happen but couldn't block it from her mind.

She hoped he would be pleased with the house she had rented for them at Smith Mountain Lake and pleasantly surprised about the realtor she had scheduled to show them lake properties for sale. She was going to offer a third of her monthly pension income to him to help pay for a house if it was what he wanted. Surely he would notice the effort she was making to mend their marriage.

Ending up in front of her house after jogging, she pulled the newspaper from the box and went inside. She hit the coffee-maker button on her way to the shower.

Twenty minutes later while primping in the bathroom and planning a day of rest, the telephone rang. She glanced outside the door at the end table phone and reached for it once she saw it was from the Foundation office.

"Hello."

"I'm sorry to bother you," Jennifer, her secretary apologized. "I know you wanted to be left alone this week if possible."

"It's okay, Jennifer. What is it?"

"The State's Educational Commissioner will be in Lynchburg Wednesday considering grant requests for some of the colleges here in Lynchburg. Mrs. Winkler invited him to come over and talk to the Foundation about how to apply for available grant monies. He wants to meet with some of the board members to review the guidelines. He asked to meet with you personally at eight o'clock since she named you as the contact."

Trudy did a turn in the kitchen. *She knew I had planned this week off and purposely set this up. But if I can get some money it would most definitely help. Oh well.* "Call Dr. Waleski and one of the other board members to see if they can come and sit in on the meeting with me. Hopefully, it won't take too long."

"Who else would you want me to call?"

"It doesn't matter. I'm sure Mrs. Winkler will think I've handled it wrong if she's not in on it." Trudy rolled her eyes. "Give her a call and see if she'll come, since it was her idea."

"Certainly, and I apologize for intruding on your time off."

"I understand. It comes with the job." Trudy remembered Jennifer scheduling time off also. "I thought you were taking a couple of personal leave days this week."

"I had planned to, but Mrs. Winkler insisted that I work since you wouldn't be in the office."

"But I gave you permission to be off. She has no right to second-guess my decisions. Just hang a sign on the door telling everyone that we'll re-open on Thursday."

There was silence, until Jennifer responded, "I'm okay with it. I can take time off later."

Trudy fretted, knowing Mrs. Winkler was once again overriding her authority. She also knew Jennifer was trying to keep the friction down between them. "Okay," Trudy said reluctantly. "I'll see you in the morning at eight...and thanks, Jennifer. I appreciate what you're doing. I'll make it up to you later. Bye."

"Who was that on the phone?" April asked, entering the kitchen.

"Jennifer called and said I'm needed at the office Wednesday morning. It shouldn't take long, though."

"I thought you had planned this week off."

"I did. This should only take a couple of hours." She reached inside the fridge. "Want a yogurt and some wheat toast with your mother?"

"Sure."

"Blueberry or plain?"

"Blueberry." She poured their coffee.

"Trudy got the toaster out and dropped a couple pieces of wheat bread in it. She reached for her cup of coffee, leaned against the counter and took a sip. She noticed April staring.

"What's on your mind?"

"I was wondering what made you decide to work things out with Dad. You hadn't said much about him lately and I wasn't sure." She glanced away.

Knowing she needed to be honest with her daughter, she waited until her glance met her eyes. "I've known your dad for twenty-six years and been married to him for twenty-four. Sure, we've had problems for the past two or so years but we've also had a wonderful life together. If you get right down to what happened between us, it was both our faults. We let everything and everyone else in our lives become a priority. We owe ourselves a second chance."

The toaster popped up. Trudy reached for the toast and April handed her a couple of small plates. Trudy carried the toast to the table with a jar of apple butter. April followed with yogurt, silverware and napkins.

"You do know your father will have to want this marriage to work too," Trudy reminded her, spreading apple butter on her toast.

"He mentioned you a lot in the letters I got from him."

"He did?"

"He's really looking forward to coming home." She spooned her yogurt. "I don't think he ever quit loving you, Mom. Not ever," she spoke softly.

"Maybe you never stop loving someone after you loved them for a quarter century, I guess. No matter what happens." Her thoughts turned to Richard.

They sat silent for a moment, eating. Finally, April broke the silence as if reading her mother's mind.

"What was Richard like?"

The question surprised Trudy.

"Grandmother showed me a picture of him when I helped her put photos in her album. You and Richard were sitting on a tractor together."

"She didn't put it in the album, I hope."

"No, only family."

Trudy hesitated before responding. "Richard and I grew up together, kind of like you and Matthew did. Even though we only spent summers together, the letters back and forth during the year gave us a chance to really know each other. We came from different cultures and different parts of the world, but our feelings for each other were sincere. Regretfully, it didn't work out. Maybe your grandmother said it best. Destiny kept us apart."

"Did you love Dad the same way?"

"It was seven years later before I allowed myself to love someone again. That's when your father came along and swept me off my feet. In no time I wanted to be with him every minute of the day." She sat back in her chair and sipped her coffee. "Of course, it was different with your father. I was more mature but it felt wonderful to have my heart awakened again by someone who appreciated me."

"Have you ever regretted marrying Dad?" April asked more pointedly.

Trudy chose her words prudently, knowing her daughter was getting ready to make a life-long commitment to the boy she loved. "I love your father more today than I did twenty-five years ago."

April looked puzzled.

Trudy spoke honestly. "Young love is mesmerizing. Knowing you're marrying the cutest guy in town and finding yourself wanting to be with him every minute of the day is wonderful. Eventually, though, it changes. You become best friends, soul mates, parents, and all those other new experiences that come with maturity. You look beyond the present and know this is the man you want to spend the rest of your life with." She reached over and patted April's hand. "That's when you know you married the right guy."

"Has anything changed while you and Dad were separated?"

"April, most people who stay married will eventually have a bump in their life. When they choose to work it out, it doesn't mean they'll love each other any less. It'll bond their commitment to each other even stronger. That's what love is about, going through the good and bad times together, just like your father and I have."

April finished eating and sat back. "Thanks for making an effort to work things out with Dad. It means a lot to Matthew and me."

"I wouldn't have wanted it any other way." She smiled. "And I want this engagement party to be special for you. Something you'll remember the rest of your life."

"I'm sure I will." April glanced at her watch. "I've got to go meet Matthew."

"What are you two doing today?"

"We're going to look at furniture for our condo. He wants to move in next month if we can get a couple of rooms furnished."

"I can remember when...." Trudy smiled, getting up and carrying her plate to the sink.

"Is there anything I can help with before leaving?"

"No. You go do what young people in love do. I will finish cleaning up, then I'm going to finish reading a novel I started a couple weeks ago."

"Matthew and I are taking Grandmother out for dinner this evening. She gave us a lot of her keepsakes. We figured she could tell us the stories about them. We'd love to have you go, too."

"You're in for a treat. I think I'll decline because I need some quiet time to get my thoughts together and get ready to meet your dad tomorrow. I've got a lot to think about."

"If you change your mind, call me."

"I will."

April stepped closer and hugged her.

"Love you, Mom."

"Love you, too." Trudy watched April walk away, happy that everything had worked out so well for her, and for herself.

The day passed quickly for Trudy as she busied herself with chores and reading and talking to the realtor about which lake houses she wanted to tour.

Every once in awhile her mind drifted back to Richard and she wondered how he reacted after reading her note and leaving without saying goodbye. Even though he had turned out very different than the boy she once knew, she still held fond memories of him. *I'm glad he didn't call me. I'm not sure how I would deal with it if he did. I wish we could've met and parted on different terms. It's over. I need to move on.*

Trudy was glad when night came. She had sat and stared at a movie she didn't even remember. April, Matthew and her mother had gotten home and she listened to their chatter for a while, responding only when spoken to. Finally, mentally exhausted, she excused herself and left to go to bed. She heard April say as she walked away, "Mom isn't acting right."

Her mother chuckled. "I think she's a little nervous about meeting your father tomorrow."

Trudy grinned, stepping inside her bedroom. *She's right. How right, she is.*

CHAPTER 21

Trudy got out of bed determined she wasn't going to let anything distract her today. She turned the television on and listened to News 13 talk about the Reservists coming home. They were keeping the public informed hourly on their journey to Lynchburg and urged the city to turn out to welcome them home.

Knowing Kenny loved her homemade bread, she made a couple of strawberry bread loaves and a blackberry cobbler, his favorite dessert. She went over to the mall and picked up four Ralph Lauren shirts, his favorites to wear, and hung them in the closet with his clothes. She made sure there were raw peanuts, popcorn, salsa and Michelob Light, his favorite beer, in the fridge. She restocked the bathroom drawers with Irish Spring soap, shaving foam and all of his usual toiletries. She wanted him to know she had planned for him to come home and stay permanently. Finally, News 13 said the Reservists would be arriving at five o'clock.

Trudy stood in front of the bathroom mirror primping more than usual, wondering if Kenny would approve of her shortened hair. She stood in her closet, searching racks of clothing, trying to make up her mind about what to wear. She wanted to look great since she would be there with women a lot younger than herself, waiting for their husbands. She settled on a cream-colored silk top and a light-blue skirt that showed off her shapely legs and curvy figure. She put on a pair of small hoop gold earrings and a double braided gold chain around her neck. After one last pause in front of the mirror she went downstairs, nervous as a schoolgirl on her first date.

She glanced at the microwave clock and it was four-fifteen. "You want to ride with me and your grandmother to meet your dad or are you driving?" she asked April who was sitting patiently waiting on her.

"I'll ride over with you. Matthew is meeting me there."

Later, April, Matthew, Trudy and her mother stood in a roped-off area at the airport, under a cloudless sky, waiting for the military plane to arrive. Several hundred people stood behind the restricted area to welcome the Reservists home. A high school band in uniform played patriotic songs while the local ROTC stood at attention, bearing the nation's flag. The local media were busy filming, taking pictures and getting interviews, while a flurry of men and women dressed in military uniforms mingled with the crowd.

As she overheard some of the young wives and fiancées giggle and talk about their husbands and loved ones coming home, Trudy felt anxious waiting for Kenny. She remembered waiting for her father's return home from tours that took him away for a year or more at times. She remembered how sweaty her mother's hands often became as they waited and her mom constantly massaged her small hand. Knowing now what her mother had to endure and why she always made her father's return special, she glanced back at her mother. She stood several feet behind them with an intense look on her face. Trudy knew that waiting for Kenny was bringing back memories. When she saw Trudy looking at her, she forced a smile to let her know that she was okay.

Suddenly a military plane approached the airport runway. A cheer erupted from the crowd of bystanders. The band started playing the national anthem as children, wives, and other relatives inched their way closer to the front of the enclosed area.

A large camouflaged military plane finally came to a halt about a hundred feet away. The crowd became quiet. Trudy felt her mouth getting dry and her hands becoming sweaty. Anticipating how Kenny would react to seeing her after a year apart made her nervous. Would he still want to pursue the new beginning they'd talked about or would their time apart have taken a toll on their marriage? She anxiously waited.

The ROTC, along with several branches of the military, marched up to the plane's ramp and stood at attention. The door opened and young men and women in their army fatigues began disembarking. Military officers saluted them at the bottom of the ramp. When someone in the crowd saw their spouse or friend, they broke into a run to meet them.

After almost all of the troops had departed the plane, Trudy had yet to spot Kenny. She glanced around to see if maybe she'd missed seeing him, but all she saw was everyone hugging, kissing, and crying as they reunited with their loved ones.

Turning her attention back to the plane's ramp, she finally spotted him among the last to come off the plane. Most of the other soldiers had scattered to unite with their families. She stood by herself between the crowd and plane.

He looked tanned and appeared to be about twenty or so pounds lighter. She noticed how handsome he looked in his army fatigues, even with his unshaven face. Their gazes met. Trudy held her breath momentarily, unsure as to what she should do.

Kenny paused and stared at her, too, as if he were making sure she was his wife. Trudy knew it was her short hair he wasn't sure of. She stood rigid, her hands clasped in front of her, smiling as if she were waiting for his approval. Kenny's lips tightened, his eyes narrowed, then he gave her his half-lip smile that always drove her crazy. Unsure of how to greet him,

Trudy decided not to hold back. She ducked under the rope, ran to him and threw herself into his arms.

Without saying a word, he picked her up and sailed her around with her feet dangling in the air. Trudy felt embarrassed, but when her feet were back on the ground, he kissed her and she returned it passionately.

"I didn't expect a welcome home like this," Kenneth finally said, with a big grin on his face. "You must have missed me."

"Every day," she responded enthusiastically.

"What's this about?" he asked, running his fingers through her hair.

"Do you like it?"

"You've never looked better." He held her face in his hands and gazed into her eyes. "I've thought about you every hour of every day and missed you so much. I hope we never go through this again."

"I've missed you, too." Trudy took his hand. "Come on. The rest of the family is here."

They walked over to April, Matthew and her mother standing behind the rope.

April rushed into her father's arms. "I'm so glad you're home."

"I hear that I'm going to lose you," he said with a grin.

"No, you're gaining a son," she reminded him.

He turned to Matthew, who stood wide-eyed, wearing a big smile.

"And I think he's going to be a darn good one, too."

Matthew laughed, extending his hand. "Welcome home, Mr. Quinn."

Kenneth, with his hands on his hips, stared at him and said, "Matthew Simpson. We have a rule here that you'd better get used to if you're going to be a part of this family. You shake hands with strangers." He glanced around at all the other people hugging each other. "Do you see anyone shaking hands here, Matthew?"

"No, sir," Matthew responded.

"I didn't hear you, Son!" Kenneth shouted.

"No, sir. I don't!" he shouted back.

Kenneth grabbed him and gave him a bear hug.

"Son, welcome to the family. I'm so thankful you're the one who's won my daughter's heart."

"It took me awhile, but I pulled it off," he responded, eyeing April. "She was definitely worth the effort."

Mrs. Meyers caught his gaze with a solemn look on her face so Kenneth reached for her and hugged her tightly. Neither said a word.

Trudy watched as she remembered how worried her mother had been when she learned that Kenny was going to Iraq. She knew her mother was overwhelmed with relief that he had returned home.

Kenneth stepped back and held her hands. "Thanks for praying for me every day."

"I didn't miss a single day."

"I know. I felt them." He squeezed her hands tightly before letting go.

Trudy stood beside Kenny, holding his hand during the brief welcoming home ceremony. His fingers caressed her hand continuously, and he glanced her way often. She felt warmed by his affection and remembered their last conversations before he left. Maybe they were already rekindling the passion that once wove their lives together.

Finally, after April and Matthew left to take her mother home, Trudy and Kenny got in her car to head for home. She had been looking forward to having the house alone with Kenny, even though she hadn't admitted it earlier.

"When was the last time you ate something?" she asked him.

"I don't remember, and I'm not sure it was even food." He chuckled.

"You want to stop and get something? Or I can fix anything you want when we get home. I've got a couple of steaks we can grill."

"Let's get something on the way in. I'm tired and would rather eat light before I turn in tonight."

"You choose. My treat."

"I would like to find the largest burger that I can bite into. In fact, I don't think I've had a decent burger since I left the States."

"Then a burger it is." Trudy pulled into the local curbside diner. "Would you rather go inside or sit out here?"

"Out here's fine. I'm not ready for the crowd scene yet. I've been traveling nonstop for the last couple of days, and I want to get a shower and some real sleep before I get around folks. They might like me better."

They ordered burgers and Kenneth tuned the radio to an XM 70 station playing seventies music. They were playing "Leave Yesterday Behind" by The Carpenters.

Listening to the music, Trudy wondered when it would be a good time to tell Kenny about the letter and her meeting with Richard. Once they got home, she decided they could have a glass of wine on the back porch, where they usually talked easily to each other about things on their mind. She wanted to make sure he knew about it and had every word rehearsed as to how she would tell him.

"A penny for your thoughts," said Kenny, tilting his head toward her.

"It's nothing." She jumped when he spoke. "I was thinking about your party, I mean the engagement party for April this weekend," she stammered.

"Are you sure?"

Trudy quickly thought about the realtor she had lined up to show them lake property. "Well... maybe that and the surprise I have planned for you tomorrow."

"Coming home and finding my wife happy to see me is enough for me. I don't think it could get any better."

"Well, there's one more tomorrow. I hope you'll approve of what I'm doing."

"Anything I can help with?"

"We'll talk about it tomorrow." She reached over and stroked his bristled face. "I just want you to rest up so we can start spending the rest of our lives together."

"I've been waiting a year to hear you say that," he sighed heavily. "You just don't know how hard it was for me to leave a year ago, especially after what I had put us through."

"It was both our faults and it's behind us now. I love you, Kenneth Quinn."

"I love you, too, Trudy Quinn," he said, breaking into a wide smile.

They leaned over and kissed. Their kiss lingered.

"The cost is $11.23," the young waitress said, tapping on the car door, smiling at them.

Embarrassed, Trudy fumbled in her purse for money while Kenny laughed.

CHAPTER 22

Trudy took out a bottle of wine she'd chilled in the fridge. Holding up a couple of wineglasses, she asked, "Want to have a sip before you shower?"

"Sure. I haven't had a taste of wine for more than a year." He rubbed his hands together. "What else are you planning to domesticate me with that I've been denied for the past year?"

"The night's still young," she replied, suggestively. "Follow me."

On the back porch, Trudy leaned against a column and gazed into the yard while Kenny stood beside her, his arm around her waist.

"What was Iraq like?" she asked, after sipping her wine.

Kenny was silent.

Trudy turned toward him. "You don't have to talk about it if you don't want to."

"That's all right. There are a lot of good people over there that are hurting. They just don't have the same opportunities we do. For them it's a struggle to survive one day at a time. They never know what they might have to face tomorrow." He frowned. "They become your friends, show you their children's pictures, eat with you, and sleep in the barracks beside you." He paused. "But you always have to wonder if they're going to be the one to show up the next morning wearing a suicide vest to take you out."

Trudy put her arms around him, with her head against his chest. "I'm sorry. I shouldn't have asked you to talk about it."

"It's over and I'm home. Let's just pray all of our troops can be home soon." Kenneth lifted his wineglass. "Okay, it's time for a toast."

Trudy stepped back and her eyes lit up. "Okay." She lifted her glass.

"Let's put the past where it belongs. Behind us." He tilted her chin up. "You remember the conversation we had before I left?"

"Yes," she smiled, pleased that he remembered.

"I've thought about us a lot this past year and want you to know I meant every word of it."

"I've thought about us, too."

"I don't know when or how it went wrong for us but one thing I'm sure of. I never want to go through another crisis like we had before I left. If you'll trust me and give us a chance... then somehow and some way, I promise to make it up to you."

"You already have," Trudy beamed. "You came home."

"Then let our new beginning begin here tonight, this moment," Kenny pledged, lifting his glass.

They clinked glasses and drank.

Kenneth glanced around the yard. "I really do like the landscaping you've started."

"I want to add more plants and flowers this summer, especially back here near the porch. We need more color when we're out here, but I didn't want to finish until you knew what I was doing."

"You're the one who has the green thumb. Whatever you want is fine with me."

"I guess it stuck with me while working at the flower farm when I was a teenager. I loved to coordinate colors of plants and flowers." She thought about Richard and figured it was a good time to broach the subject of the lost letter.

She set her wine down on a table on the porch. "Kenneth, there's something I need to talk to you about."

His eyes narrowed. "Is something wrong?"

"No, not at all," she answered quickly. "It's just that last week, I received a letter from my teenage sweetheart."

"Why is he sending you letters now?"

"He didn't. I mean it was a letter mailed to me thirty-five years ago, but was never delivered until now."

Kenneth chuckled. "Did the post office make you pay the difference for today's postage rate?"

"No," she giggled.

"Who is or was this guy?"

"He's a Dutch boy I met when I was working on his grandfather's farm in the seventies."

"You never told me about him."

"There was no need. Our time together happened long before you and I ever met. It's kind of one of those teenage love and lost stories."

"Sounds like it might be interesting."

"Well, it's kind of gotten interesting. The Postal Service released a story about the letter, and now it's all over the national news. They're making a big deal about trying to figure out who the mystery woman named Trudy is and what the letter was about."

"Are you going to tell them?" He finished his wine and set his glass down.

"Actually, I granted an interview to Courtney Emerson, one of the staff writers who works with April. I think she turned it in for publication today and it might be in tomorrow's paper. It'll be carried by all the major media outlets. April is so excited." Trudy felt comfortable about how Kenny was reacting.

"I had no idea my family had become celebrities while I was away."

"I wouldn't say that." She responded. "You want another glass of wine? I want you to read the letter and then I need to tell you more about this guy who sent it."

"Let me shower first. I'm not going to last much longer." He yawned. "I think sleep is calling me."

"I've got all your clothes back in our bedroom so go in there and shower."

He grinned.

"Go shower and then we'll talk more," Trudy assured him.

Trudy sat, wondering how Kenny would react once he found out she'd actually met Richard. So far he hadn't taken anything she said seriously. After all, she only had dinner and conversation with Richard. She'd done nothing to feel ashamed of. But would Kenny feel intimidated once he knew the man she'd met was the famous businessman, Richard Vanderveer? No. She knew Kenny better than that. Besides, she needed to get this behind her before Courtney's article was published.

Trudy went to the bedroom to check on Kenny to make sure she'd put a towel out for him. He was already in the shower when she stepped into the bathroom. Seeing no towel, she pulled one from the bathroom closet. As she hung it on the wall hook beside the shower door, his profile in the steamed shower stall caught her attention. He was standing, letting the shower spray his face, his hands against the wall and eyes closed while savoring the water on his tanned body. Trudy's stare lingered until she realized how much she longed to be close to him.

Feeling aroused, she began to undress. Without shifting her gaze from Kenny, she dropped her clothing, one piece at a time until it all lay on the floor. Opening the shower door, a gush of heat engulfed her already flushed body. She savored the warmth of the steam. Stepping into the shower stall behind him, she molded her body against his back with her arms encircling his chest.

He turned around slowly, reaching for her with both hands as he gazed into her eyes. Then he kissed her passionately.

Following the long kiss, she reached for the soap and began lathering his body. Afterwards, he did the same for her. Minutes later they were on the bed letting the passion between them unfold.

Tenderly exploring each other's body, they kissed as their breathing became heavier in their quest to please. Trudy responded to Kenny's advance, not wanting this moment of ecstasy between them to end. His lovemaking was intense but gentle, and she yielded to his every touch and movement, remembering this was the way they used to make love a long time ago. Their effort to please each other went on and on until their passion subsided and they lay still.

Afterwards, Trudy lay at his side with her head on his shoulder, listening to him breathe while his fingers stroked her neck. Finally, his hand lay still. When she looked up at him, she discovered he had fallen asleep.

She went to the kitchen, locked the doors, and turned out the lights. After pulling the covers over Kenny, she eased into the bed beside him.

Subconsciously, he rolled to his side, cuddling her and reached for her hand, weaving her fingers into his. Cradled in his arms, Trudy listened to him breathe until she fell asleep.

CHAPTER 23

Awakening, Trudy realized that she'd slept soundly all night without waking. Kenny had rolled to his side of the bed. Waking up to find him sleeping beside her made her feel warm all over. She wanted to slip over and cuddle with him all day.

Suddenly, she thought about the meeting at the Foundation scheduled for that morning. She glanced at the clock. It was ten minutes before seven. She hurriedly eased out of bed and went to the shower.

An hour later, she stood looking in the mirror to make sure her makeup was okay and her hair was in place. Dressed in a gray pantsuit and white blouse she grabbed her gray slippers and headed for the door. Kenny had begun to stir but hadn't awakened completely. She eased the bedroom door shut so she wouldn't wake him when she pulled the car from the garage.

At the kitchen counter she left him a note.

Kenny,

Do not go anywhere this morning. I have to go to work for a while. I will tell you about the surprise I have planned for you when I get home.

I'm sorry I'm not here to fix breakfast. I have bacon and eggs in the fridge and a fresh strawberry bread loaf in the plastic container on the counter. Looking forward to our day together.

Love, Trudy

Before driving her car into the street, Trudy stopped to get the newspaper, curious to see if Courtney had published her interview. It hadn't been delivered. Since the interview was just a toned down version about her and Richard in the seventies, she figured it would make no difference if Kenny read it before she told him about their rendezvous anyway. Glancing at the time, she knew she'd be late for her meeting so she called Jennifer on her cell phone.

"Good morning. Thank you for calling The FEW Foundation, Jennifer speaking."

"Good morning, Jennifer. I'm running five to ten minutes late. Has Mr. Lawrence arrived?"

"Yes. He's already in the board room waiting for you."

"Please ask Dr. Waleski to start the meeting. I'll be there in five minutes."

"Certainly."

"Did Mrs. Winkler come in or are we privileged to have someone else?"

Jennifer giggled. "No. She's here."

"Oh, well. I'll see you in five minutes."

Trudy thought about the brief presentation she was prepared to give about the Foundation. She had no idea how much money the state was considering for their scholarship requests or what kind of restrictions there might be. Perhaps having Dr. Waleski from the largest area university on her board would encourage them to be generous.

When she arrived at the office building, Trudy parked her car, grabbed her briefcase, and made a dash for the front door. Inside, she was greeted by Jennifer, who rose from her desk to follow her down the hallway.

"Kenny came home yesterday and I forgot to set the clock," Trudy explained, hastily walking toward the conference room.

"That's good. Have you seen the paper this morning?" Jennifer interjected with a note of alarm in her tone.

"No. It hadn't been delivered when I left home."

"Do you know about the article in it about you and the lost letter?"

"Yes, I was expecting it today." She stopped at the conference room door. "Don't let anyone bother us for any reason," she told Jennifer before closing the door.

She apologized for being late and took a seat beside Dr. Waleski and Mrs. Winkler, who was dressed in a black suit as if she had come prepared for mourning. When Trudy glanced at her, an image of sour grapes came to mind. Trudy thought *I must really be on her bad side this morning.*

Mr. Lawrence, a short, bald man, wearing large rimmed glasses, introduced himself in a squeaky voice as the State Commissioner Program Director overseeing the state's expenditures for educational grants. He wore a brown pinstriped suit, befitting his apparent personality.

Trudy pulled out notes she'd prepared for her presentation and put her iPhone on silence, laid it on the table, and spoke.

"Mr. Lawrence, thank you for considering our request for a grant to help fund our scholarship program."

"We want to help if we can. But, as you know, any government funding assistance comes with restrictions," he answered. "We're able to fund only certain scholastic programs where money has been allotted by the assembly. Hopefully, you'll have students who will qualify."

"Would you like me to give you an overview of how we operate?" Trudy asked. "Perhaps that will assure you how thorough we are in qualifying the students we choose."

"There's no need for that. Instead, let me give you the criteria for qualifying for funding first, and then we can have a discussion."

"Very well, Mr. Lawrence. Enlighten us, please."

Trudy listened intensely, but for some reason she knew that she didn't like this man. His presentation was definitely preprogrammed and it was obvious he knew he held the state's purse strings. Hopes of receiving enough money to make a difference for her students faded as she listened to him drone on and on.

Trudy noticed her cell phone messaging, but no one could hear it since she'd silenced it. When she saw that Jan and April both were trying to call her, she thought about leaving the room so she could speak to them, but Mr. Lawrence was in the middle of his bureaucratic summary and she figured he would be insulted if she excused herself.

A text message from Jan appeared on her phone. She discreetly read it, trying hard not to seem distracted.

Urgent! Call me. Read newspaper!

Knowing it had to be important, Trudy decided to give Mr. Lawrence two more minutes, before excusing herself to call and find out what was so urgent.

Suddenly, a confrontation could be heard outside in the hallway. Jennifer was arguing with someone.

Everyone in the room looked toward the door when the voices grew louder. "You can't go in there!" Jennifer shouted.

"Like hell I can't," a man's voice responded.

Trudy stood as the door burst open and Kenneth walked in holding a rolled-up newspaper. Jennifer followed with a panic stricken face. His eyes were squinted, his face distorted by anger, and his lips pressed tight as if he were holding something in his jaw that was straining to burst out.

Trudy had never seen Kenneth so enraged by anything and knew something dreadful must have happened.

"What's wrong?" she blurted out, forgetting where she was.

Everyone at the conference table sat upright and very still.

"I got your surprise this morning," Kenny shouted, holding the paper up in the air. "I found out what's been going on for the past year while I was away. When were you going to tell me or were you simply waiting to find some way to let me down easy?" He sneered as he waited for her reaction.

Trudy didn't know what Kenny was talking about and felt embarrassed. "Kenny, please!" she pleaded. "Stop acting like this. I have no idea what you're talking about!"

He slammed the paper down in front of her. "Couldn't you have just sent me a Dear John letter while I was in Iraq? I would've been man enough to handle it!" He pointed his finger at her. "Or was it too convenient for you to have me out of the way while you enjoyed this...this fantasy."

Trudy glanced at the paper and turned pale when she saw the picture. On the front page was a picture of her and Richard standing in the hallway at *The Greenbrier* in house robes. She was on her toes in his embrace. Both were grinning from ear to ear.

"Kenny, I can explain," she pleaded as panic gripped her.

"No need to waste your breath explaining. You already have. I think it goes something like a picture is worth a thousand words."

"But it's not what you think," Trudy insisted, almost in tears. "Let me explain."

"I'm going to be a man about this, Trudy," he yelled, pointing a finger at her again. "You can have this poor excuse of a man. At least he's got money." Gritting his teeth, he continued, "Is that what this is about?"

"No! No, Kenny! Not at all," she choked up.

With his voice cracking, Kenny replied, "You just couldn't wait and give us a chance, could you?" He glanced around at all the faces in the room staring at him and then focused his anger back at Trudy. "I'm out of here...I'm out of your life."

He turned and walked toward the door. Everyone's eyes followed him, as he stopped and looked back at Trudy with tears welling in his eyes. His voice trembled as he spoke softer, almost pleading. "Would you mind telling me one thing? I really need to know."

Trudy stared at him, too emotional to even speak as tears rolled down her cheeks.

"What was last night about?" He bowed his head and stomped out.

Dazed, Trudy swept her eyes across everyone in the room. Mrs. Winkler's stare was filled with self-satisfaction, but she didn't care.

The others sat motionless, glancing nervously at each other. Trudy's body quivered and her legs felt weak. "I...I..." She tried to apologize, but the words wouldn't come out. She glanced down and read the headline above the picture in the newspaper. It read: *Lost Letter Mystery Solved. Richard Vanderveer and Trudy Quinn rendezvous at Greenbrier.*

She collapsed in her seat. Jennifer rushed over to her as Dr. Waleski tried to regain control of the meeting.

"Maybe we need to give Trudy some privacy and we can further discuss this over at my office, if that's okay with you, Mr. Lawrence," he suggested.

"Su...Sure," Mr. Lawrence nervously agreed in his squeaky voice.

CHAPTER 24

Clutching a handful of tissues, Trudy sat on the sofa in her private office with Jan and April trying to console her.

"I had no idea this was going to happen," she said as she stared at the newspaper on the coffee table in front of them. "I didn't know this picture was taken."

Then she remembered the young man who had walked past them a couple of times in the hallway talking on his cell phone and realized that he must have taken the picture.

"What were you doing?" April asked incredulously.

"We'd just come back from riding a Harley and had gotten drenched in a downpour. We came in through the service entrance and changed clothes in the bathrooms down there." She shrugged. "We were just standing in the hallway picking at each other when this young guy walked past us a couple of times. He must have taken our picture."

"Wouldn't you like to get ahold of him?" Jan grimaced angrily.

"Why didn't they tell you they were going to print this?" Trudy questioned April. "They knew you were my daughter."

"My editor called and apologized this morning. That's when I found out about it." She frowned. "Apparently Courtney told him she might have the interview ready last night, but it would be late. He told the night shift editor to watch for it and rush it to press if it came in, giving it priority status." She paused. "Courtney didn't get it to them, and when the blogger's story came over the news wire service, he assumed it was okay to print the story, since it was getting so much national attention. I am so sorry, Mom." She sniffled noticeably.

"It's not your fault. I guess this blows the story for Courtney."

"It doesn't matter. I just want you and Dad to get this worked out." April sniffled, teary-eyed, her voice quivering.

Trudy glanced at Jan. "I should get Mother and tell her what's happened before she hears about it otherwise. Hopefully it won't be on the television news, too."

"I'll go get her," April suggested. "Why don't you go home and talk to Dad?"

"Yes...Yes, you're right," Trudy swallowed hard. "The sooner I tell him everything, the better off we'll be."

"Leave your car here," Jan suggested. "You're not in any shape to drive right now." She took Trudy's hand. "Your hands are still shaking. I'll take you home."

Jennifer walked into the room looking uncomfortable. "Trudy, I had no idea you didn't know."

"It wasn't your fault, Jennifer. You tried to tell me, and I ignored you."

"What can I do now?"

Trudy thought for a moment before responding. "Call Dr. Waleski and see how the meeting ended. I can only imagine what he thinks about me. And who knows what Mrs. Winkler will try to do."

Jan glanced over at Trudy as they drove home. She sat quietly clutching a handful of tissues in her fist, staring out the window with a blank expression on her face.

"Do you think Kenneth has calmed down by now?"

"I don't know. I've never seen him this angry before."

"Do you think he's mad enough to maybe try to hurt you?"

"No. He would never do anything like that." Trudy continued to stare out the window. "I hurt him. I hurt him really bad," she repeated, sniffling.

"You both are hurting." Jan reached over and laid her hand on Trudy's shoulder. "We're going to get this straightened out for you. Don't worry."

"I hope so," she murmured, choking back a sob.

As Jan pulled into the driveway, Trudy noticed that Kenneth's pickup truck wasn't parked there.

Briskly walking into the house, she looked around and then went into their bedroom. A couple of empty drawers were pulled out of the dresser. Her heart palpitated at the thought that he might have left her. When she looked in their walk-in closet and found most of his clothes gone, panic engulfed her. Feeling faint, she sat down in the bedroom chair, burying her face in her hands.

Jan came to check on her.

Trudy glanced up, her face wrenched in fear and spoke nervously, "He's left me."

"Maybe it's just for today while he thinks things over."

"No. He's packed almost everything." Frantic, she raved, "What have I done? Oh, what have I done?" She began sobbing.

The telephone rang. Jan left to answer it. "This is the Quinn's residence. May I help you?"

"May I speak to Mrs. Trudy Quinn, please?"

"She's not available. May I take a message?" She picked up a pen to write on a notepad.

"I'm a writer for the *National Bloggers Website*. I've been following the story about the lost letter. Now that we know Mrs. Quinn is the recipient of the letter that was sent to her by Richard Vanderveer, we want to talk to her about it. We're willing to compensate her well for an exclusive."

"I'll pass the information to her. Goodbye." Jan put the phone down quickly.

April and her grandmother walked through the front door.

"Where's Mom?" April asked.

"She's in the bedroom." Jan pointed with her chin. "Your dad packed and left. She's not taking it well."

April walked toward the bedroom.

"I was afraid something like this might happen," Trudy's mother said, as she took a seat at the kitchen table. "I should've tried to talk her out of going to see him."

"We all might have done something differently if we'd known this was going to happen," Jan echoed, sitting down beside Mrs. Meyers. "Let's not forget, your daughter didn't do anything wrong. All of this is happening because some blogger wanted his few minutes of glory through the media."

The telephone rang again. Jan took the call. After speaking for a few minutes, she hung up, irritated. "Another national news service wants the story. This phone is probably going to ring all day."

April and Trudy walked into the kitchen. Trudy's mother stood and hugged her.

"I'm sorry, Mother. I should've listened," Trudy said.

"You haven't done anything wrong; I know Kenneth well enough that once he knows what happened, he'll understand."

"I hope so. I just don't know what to do or where to start looking for him. I really need to talk to him."

The telephone rang again.

Jan checked the caller ID and said, "Don't answer that. It's probably another news service." Then she asked, "Does Kenneth have a cell phone?"

"No." Trudy shook her head. "I haven't reactivated it yet. I was going to do it today."

"Do you think he's going to stay with his family or friends?" Jan asked.

"I'm not sure. I have no idea where he might go."

"Maybe we should call around and see if anyone has heard from him," Mrs. Meyers suggested. "At least have them call us if they see or hear from him."

"That's a good idea. I just can't believe this is happening," Trudy sighed heavily, burying her face in her hands.

"Why don't you three start calling your family and close friends?" Jan suggested. "I'll fix something for us to drink."

April, Trudy and her mother got on the phone and their cell phones and began making calls. Everyone had seen the morning's newspaper so they talked around it the best they could. Everyone promised to call if they heard anything.

Finally, two hours later, exhausted from talking to so many people, they figured they'd covered everyone they knew to call. The three of them met on the back porch, sipped tea, and tried to figure out what their next plan of action should be.

Trudy watched April closely and could see the anxiety on her daughter's face. Even though she hadn't mentioned it, Trudy knew that her engagement party, just four days away, weighed heavily on her daughter's mind. Knowing she'd let April down, she had no idea how to make her and Kenny's falling out mend itself. What should have been a celebration of her daughter's engagement was now a chaotic family crisis brought on by her own self-serving interest. She felt emotionally distraught. Would she ever be able to convince Kenny that meeting Richard was harmless? Would April ever forgive her for what she had done to embarrass her?

"Trudy...Trudy...Trudy!" Jan interrupted her thoughts.

Trudy snapped back to attention. "I'm sorry. My mind was wandering."

"This is what we've decided to do. Your phone is probably going to ring off the hook with everyone in the media trying to get to you."

"No." Trudy interjected. "They couldn't care less about me. It's Richard they want to get something on. They know they don't have a chance to get any information from him, so they're trying to use me to get to him."

Her defensive remarks caught everyone by surprise.

"How do you feel about that?" Jan asked.

"I would never say anything to smear his reputation." Then she added, "I guess my actions have done enough damage already."

The phone rang again. April glanced at it. "It's another 800 number."

"As I was trying to say," Jan quipped, "why don't you come home with me for the night? April and Matthew can stay here to see if Kenneth comes by or calls. That way you can think this through and get some rest."

Trudy paused. "Maybe you're right. I need to leave. I'll go pack a few things."

"I can't believe this is happening," April said furiously as she stood and walked off the porch into the yard.

Mrs. Meyers watched her and said to Jan, "This is going to be as hard on April as it is on Trudy."

"If it were anyone other than some wealthy CEO, the papers would've never mentioned it," Jan speculated. "They're going to rant about this for a month now, knowing it'll sell more papers for them. Maybe Trudy's right. It's their way to smear Richard."

"I hope you're wrong," Mrs. Meyers said, shaking her head. "Kenny and Trudy will never be able to work this out if they do."

Trudy returned to the porch carrying an overnight bag. "I'm ready."

She looked around for April and saw her near the border of the lawn picking at the foliage.

"Give me a minute," Trudy requested, putting her bag down.

Walking up behind April, she spoke sadly, "I am so sorry."

April spun around, a frantic look on her face. "What's going to happen to you and Dad?"

Trudy knew she needed to give her daughter hope, "None of this looks good right now, but I love your father. Do you think I'm going to let him get away from me this easily?" she said, forcing a smile. "Once he calms down I'm going to tell him everything so he will understand why I went to see Richard."

"But what if he doesn't believe you?"

"I'm not giving up. I don't care how long it takes. I'm going to win him back," she responded convincingly.

"I hope you're right. But what if Dad doesn't come to my, our, party?"

Trudy embraced April's shoulders. "Your father would never do you like that. He's going to be there for you just like I will. He would never let our differences stop him from being a part of one of the most beautiful days of your life. Besides, he's got to make the engagement announcement for you."

"But, what if...?"

Trudy put a finger to her lips to quiet her. "Look, April. I know I've screwed up and have no earthly idea how I'm going to fix things. I also know your father well enough that when he finally learns the truth about this whole story we're going to be fine. In the meantime, I just don't know when that will happen." She tilted her head so April would look directly at her and forced a smile. "I just want my little girl to be happy and thinking of nothing but one of the most beautiful days of your life that is about to happen." She leaned closer and kissed April on the forehead. "Will you do that for me?"

April nodded and wiped at tears collecting in her eyes.

"Will you be okay if I leave?"

"I called Matthew. He's coming over."

"You're so lucky to have a young man like Matthew."

"I know," she answered, choking back tears.

"I'll call you in the morning. We'll go to Isabella's and pick out the colors for the bridesmaids' gowns. Okay?"

Trudy hugged April and walked away, her heart aching because of the undeserved anxiety she had brought on her daughter.

CHAPTER 25

Trudy sat on Jan's back porch and watched waters rise in the James River resulting from heavy rains in the mountains that swept through the Lynchburg Valley. The house sat high on a knoll in the city with a perfect view of the river. Her thoughts were on how insecure and depressed Jan had been during her divorce three years ago. She had sat with her for hours offering her encouragement. Now she was the one emotionally distraught and Jan was consoling her. Chills shivered up and down her spine as she imagined what going through a divorce would be like.

The thought of losing Kenny burdened her greatly. A year ago, she had doubts about their marriage, but now all she felt was panic and remorse over her misguided actions. She couldn't believe how naïve she'd been, thinking that meeting Richard wouldn't have consequences. How was she going to convince Kenny that her rendezvous with Richard was innocent? Would Kenny ever trust her again?

She heard the patio door slide open and Jan asked, "You ready for a cup of coffee, maybe some breakfast?"

"Coffee sounds great," Trudy agreed. "I'd thought about slipping out so I wouldn't bother you, but then I realized I didn't have my car."

"And since when did you become a bother?" Jan asked.

"I've been awake for hours. I couldn't sleep and I've got so much on my mind." She looked toward the river. "I feel like I need to go off somewhere by myself and start screaming."

"Well, before you start screaming, come in and let me fix you a bite to eat. The coffee's on, and I have an idea I want to share with you."

Following Jan into the house, Trudy smelled the freshly brewed coffee. "Ideas are welcome, but I think I need a miracle at this point."

Jan poured two cups of coffee and handed one to Trudy over the kitchen island.

"You said something last night that got me to thinking." Looking over her cup after taking a sip she continued, "You said the only reason the media is pursuing this story is because of Richard."

"Of course," Trudy agreed. "Richard's a very private person and won't give interviews. By keeping the story in the news, they think they can force something out of him. They couldn't care less about me, unless..." she paused as a frown crept over her face, "unless they think I would give them something on Richard with which to taunt him."

Jan leaned forward on the island counter. "What if Richard said something to the media about the picture and that you two were just friends having dinner to reminisce about old times? He could explain the picture in the hall, the bike ride and getting wet."

Trudy stared into the distance, frowned, and turned her gaze back. "Don't you remember? I left him a Dear John note that pretty much told him to stay out of my life. And I left without even saying goodbye."

"Yes, but surely he wouldn't mind helping you out if he knew what you were going through with Kenneth because of meeting him." Jan watched Trudy closely to gauge her reaction. "Don't you think it's at least worth a try?"

"I don't know if it would be a good idea or not. What if Kenny found out I spoke with him again. Why would he even believe anything Richard said?" She breathed deeply. "I've screwed up and my only hope is that Kenny will believe me when I get a chance to explain everything."

"Okay." Jan relented. "What would you like for breakfast?"

"If you have to do something, then wheat toast and one egg will suit me."

"Coming right up." Jan pointed to the kitchen table. "There's this morning's paper if you want to read it."

Trudy reluctantly looked at it.

"You're safe. You're not in it."

———

While Trudy rode with Jan to pick up her car, she called April to see if she'd heard anything from Kenny.

"Morning, Mom," she answered, her voice revealing a hint of displeasure.

"Good morning, Sweetie. Did you and Grandmother rest well last night?"

"We had fourteen more calls from newspapers and talk radio hosts. They were still calling at ten-thirty. I finally cut the phone off after Dad called."

"He called?" Trudy asked expectantly.

"He called me on my cell phone late last night. I thought about calling you but figured you might have gone to sleep."

"There was little sleep for me last night." Trudy was almost afraid to ask, but she did. "What did he say?"

"He apologized that so much has happened but promised he would come to the engagement party. He asked me to make sure he didn't have to be around you anymore than he had to. And he wanted to leave as soon as he could."

"See, I told you that you don't have to worry about him not coming."

"But the party is a surprise for Dad, too. All of his friends and our neighbors are going to be there. What are we going to do?" April anxiously reminded her.

"I don't know, April." Trudy bowed her head. "I just don't know how I'm going to fix this right now. Please know I'm going to do everything I can to smooth it out." Her voice broke as she continued. "I'm sorry you're caught in the middle of this."

"Are you okay?" April asked.

"Yes, I'll be fine." She forced herself to speak calmer. "Jan is driving me over to the office to pick up my car. How is Matthew dealing with all of this?"

"He called his parents last night. They had a long conversation and want to know if they can help in any way."

"They're good people. You're so lucky to have Matthew."

"I know. He's just as upset as...." April's voice trailed off.

"I understand," Trudy interjected. Wanting to change the subject, she asked, "When do you want to go to Isabella's?"

"I thought about going this morning."

"Then give me about thirty minutes. I'll meet you there."

"Oh, I almost forgot. Jennifer called and wants you to call her as soon as possible. She said it was urgent."

"We're pulling into the office parking lot right now, so I'll speak to her."

"Then I'll see you later. Love you, Mom."

"Love you, too," Trudy replied.

"Is everything okay?" Jan asked, as she parked the car.

"April heard from Kenny, thank goodness. He said he didn't want to have anything to do with me during the party."

"Are you okay with that?"

"I have no choice." She opened her door to step out and paused. "I certainly can't blame him. I'm the one frolicking with another man with our picture plastered in every newspaper in the country."

"Maybe you two will have a chance to talk before Saturday and get this straightened out."

"I doubt if that's possible. We have only three days. I just hate this for April."

They crossed the parking lot in silence and entered the office building.

"Good morning, Jennifer. April said you called."

Jennifer looked up from her desk. "Good morning, Trudy… Jan. Are you okay?" she asked wryly.

"What's wrong?" Trudy reacted to Jennifer's expression, knowing that bad news was coming.

"Mrs. Winkler came by this morning. She made several phone calls earlier to all of the board members. She doesn't know I overheard her or that I've called you."

"I wouldn't expect anything less of her. What is it about?" Trudy braced herself for whatever was coming next.

Jan stood listening attentively while watching Trudy grow increasingly tense.

"She's trying to convince the board to ask you to take a leave of absence. Something about the media coverage, public perception and all that stuff hurting contributions."

Trudy, now irritated, paused before responding.

Jan moved a little closer.

"Thanks for letting me know. I'll be prepared for the call," Trudy said nonchalantly. She checked her watch. "I've got to run. April is meeting me at Isabella's. I just came by to get my car."

"Let me know what I can do to help."

"You already have. See you." Trudy smiled to hide the anger she felt brewing inside of her.

Following her out the door, Jan commented, "I can't believe they would ask you to take a leave of absence."

"The leave of absence is just the beginning," Trudy stated, walking faster, her insides knotting up. "Next they'll ask me to voluntarily resign."

"After all the years you worked for them as a volunteer," Jan blurted out. "You've helped thousands of kids go to college.

You've done more for students than the rest of them put together."

Trudy stopped at her car and spoke sarcastically. "Well, now I'm a liability. I guess if you're going to screw up your life, you might as well do it right." She opened the car door and flung her handbag in.

"Trudy, this isn't your fault! You need to take this seriously," Jan insisted.

"Seriously! What am I supposed to do?" Trudy raised her voice to match Jan's intensity. "I've lost my husband, screwed up what should've been one of the happiest days of my daughter's life, and just lost my job." They faced each other through an awkward silence until Trudy spoke. "I just want to be left alone, go somewhere and scream and not have to apologize to everyone I know. I'm tired, Jan. I'm just tired."

"Trudy, I'm sorry. I didn't mean to upset you. I'm on your side, remember."

"You didn't. I'm pretty dang good at doing it to myself," she quipped as she slid into the car seat.

"Do you want me to go with you?" Jan asked.

"No," Trudy quickly replied. "You've done enough. I've got to figure this out myself." She cranked the car.

"You know where I am if you need me," Jan spoke softly.

"Thanks. I'm sorry I blew up. I'll call you later," she said, looking straight ahead before speeding away.

At the parking lot exit, Trudy glanced in her rearview mirror and saw Jan leaning against her car, with her arms folded, looking in her direction. Feeling badly about sounding off her frustration to her friend, who was only trying to help, she became even angrier with herself. She hesitated and then pressed the accelerator, burning rubber, as she sped into the street.

CHAPTER 26

Walking into Isabella's, Trudy glanced around, looking for Mrs. Ferguson. Toward the back of the shop, she recognized April's wedding gown covered with plastic wrap hanging on a rack. Stopping to look at it, she imagined how beautiful April would look at the wedding.

A voice broke her reverie. "Good morning, Mrs. Quinn." Trudy turned to find Mrs. Ferguson behind her.

"Good morning."

"April is going to look beautiful in this," Mrs. Ferguson said, touching the gown.

"I have to agree. But then, I know I'm a little partial," she smiled.

"You just missed your husband by five minutes."

Trudy was surprised, but did her best not to show it.

"As scheduled, he came by to get sized for his tux."

"Forgive me. My mind hasn't been with it lately," she said, realizing it was highly likely Mrs. Ferguson knew about her situation.

"No need to apologize. I can only imagine what you're going through. I mean..." she fumbled for an explanation. "A couple of the bridesmaids were in here yesterday getting sized for their gowns and, regretfully, my employees were freely expressing their ideas about what happened. Please know that I think this matter is solely between you and your husband. I made sure they all understood that yesterday."

"Thank you." Trudy felt relieved. "I hope to get it resolved soon."

"I'm sure you will. Remember, our hearts are unique. They often resolve things for us that our minds could never accomplish."

"I hope you're right because my mind is definitely taking me in the wrong direction," Trudy responded. "Let me go ahead and pay you for April's dress," she added, wanting to change the subject.

"Mr. Quinn paid for it."

"Then I'll pay for all of the other accessories."

"He's covered it all," Mrs. Ferguson assured her. "I told him it was okay to pay later once the alterations were done and you picked up the dress, but he insisted."

"Hi, Mom." The familiar voice caught Trudy's attention.

She turned and saw April approaching.

"What do you think?" Trudy asked, as she turned the gown to face her daughter.

"It's beautiful!" she exclaimed, reaching out to touch it. "Do you think my daughter would want to wear this dress when she gets married some day?"

Trudy and Mrs. Ferguson laughed.

"For what this dress is costing, I expect to see several generations of daughters wearing it," Trudy jokingly suggested. April smiled.

"I have several styles of gowns and colors for bridesmaids hanging in the dressing room for you to see," Mrs. Ferguson suggested.

For the next hour Trudy and April brainstormed about colors and styles that would complement the décor of the wedding and her gown. Finally, agreeing upon multicolored floor-length silk gowns with single shoulder straps, they were pleased with their choices and agreed to go home and have lunch together on the back porch.

While following April home, Trudy thought about how she'd blown up at Jan earlier and began to feel remorseful. Thinking about calling her and apologizing, she wanted to do something special to make it up to her friend. She could cook her special dish, baked chicken Parmesan, and invite her to spend a night at the lake with her since she had already rented a house. It would give her a chance to get away from everyone, and maybe she could think more clearly about how to deal with the crisis she had brought upon herself.

—

Sitting on the back porch, Trudy and April sat quietly eating a tomato and chicken salad lunch, both absorbed in the crisis at hand. Finally, April broke the silence.

"Have you thought about what we're going to do at the party with Dad's friends coming? They're going to know about the picture in the paper and notice the friction between you two."

"I'm still trying to sort it out, April."

"I hope this doesn't end your chances of working things out with Dad. He was so happy to see you."

"I know. Somehow, I've got to sit down with him and make him listen to me. What did your father say when you spoke with him last night?"

"He just said he would do whatever I needed him to do." She paused and dropped her eyes. "But, as I told you, he asked me to make sure he didn't have to be around you anymore than he had to. And he wanted to leave as soon as he could."

Trudy squirmed in her seat. "Oh."

"I tried to tell him what you told me about Richard."

"What did he say?"

"He said you had told me only what you wanted me to know and if there was nothing to hide you would've told him about Richard."

"I tried," Trudy quickly replied, remembering their encounter in the shower. "But we kind of got distracted."

"How are you going to convince him that you met only as friends and nothing more?"

"I don't know yet." Trudy admitted, knowing she needed to give her daughter hope. "I know I did wrong by putting myself in a compromising position, and I have no one to blame but myself. I'm hoping in a couple of days your dad will calm down and give me a chance to explain everything. I don't know what else to do."

"Maybe your friend Richard could call and talk to Dad, if you ask him," April suggested.

"I wish he could, April." She frowned and sat back, flustered. "But it's complicated now, and I don't think that's a good idea."

⁓

Jan parked her car at *The Greenbrier Resort*. She was determined to see Richard Vanderveer. After making several calls, trying to speak to him and getting put off by the resort desk clerk or passed off to his assistant who sounded like some foreign guy, she figured the only way she was going to speak to Richard was to meet him face to face. She just hadn't yet figured out how to make that happen.

Walking through the white columns and doors at the front entrance, she had forgotten just how elegant *The Greenbrier* was. It had been at least five years since she'd enjoyed the amenities of this elegant hotel even though she had wanted to visit the recently renovated resort that included an underground casino and outside ice skating rink.

She stood in the center of the lobby, trying to figure out how best to meet Richard. Dressed in a blue silk dress that snugly held her figure, and a colorful cream tinted silk scarf wrapped loosely around her neck, she held her beaded brocade fabric evening bag and stood high in her blue Valentine heels. She hoped her appearance would get his attention long enough for her say what she wanted him to know about Trudy. She looked around the room for a house phone.

Making her way to a server by the wall, she picked up the receiver and dialed the front desk.

"Front desk, can I assist you?" the attendant responded.

"Would you give me the room number of Mr. Vanderveer, please? I'm a guest here and need to meet him, but I lost the note that had his room number on it."

"I'm sorry. We aren't allowed to give out room numbers. But, if you wish, I could forward your call to his room and, let me see...you said Mr. Vanderveer," she paused. "It looks like we have three Vanderveers here. A Patrick, a Raymond and a Richard. Do you know which one?"

"It's Richard."

"Very well, I'll connect you."

Jan heard several rings then a pre-recorded hotel message came on. She hung up the phone knowing she had to get face to face with Richard if she expected to speak with him. *Now, how do I find out which room he's in?*

She went to the concierge desk and asked for paper, pen, and an envelope. Taking a seat on a sofa, she thumped the pen on her chin until she decided what to write.

To Richard,

I'm a friend of Trudy Quinn. She needs your help badly. I'm here in the hotel lobby and need to speak with you about her. Call me on my cell. 434-555-3684

Thank you.

Jan Hensley

She wrote on the envelope, *To Richard Vanderveer.* On the left corner she scribbled, *Confidential and Urgent.* Sealing the envelope, she went to the concierge's desk and gave instructions to an attendant.

"I have an urgent message I need to get to Richard Vanderveer. Do you have someone available who can take this to his room immediately?" She handed the attendant a ten-dollar bill.

"Yes, ma'am. I'll get this right up to his room for you."

Jan stood in the elevator corridor where she could see who walked away from the front desk with the envelope. She would simply get on the elevator and follow them to the floor where they got off, so she could see where her note was delivered.

Finally, she saw the front desk clerk call the attention of a small man dressed in a dark gray uniform. He took the envelope and walked toward her. Trudy turned away. When he walked by, she followed him down the hallway.

A crowd of people was waiting at the elevator. Jan knew there was no way everyone could ride up on one elevator. She edged closer to the uniformed man, obviously a foreigner, and was determined to get on the elevator if he did.

The door opened and after several people exited from the elevator, the crowd pushed forward to enter. Standing close to him, Jan waited anxiously to see if he stepped on so she could quickly ease her way on. Finally, everyone had gotten on except them, leaving only a small space for one more person to ride.

He turned toward her, gestured with his hand, and said, "Ma'am, would you like to take this spot?"

"No. I'll wait," she replied, figuring he would wait for the next elevator. Her heart sank when he suddenly stepped on, leaving her standing in the corridor by herself. When the door started closing, a bell went off and the door re-opened, as the elevator was loaded beyond capacity. Trudy breathed a sigh of relief when he stepped off.

"You're not from around here, are you?" Jan asked, figuring conversation would be good, since they were alone waiting for the next elevator.

"My home is Korea," he replied with a slight smile.

"Do you like working here?" she asked.

"No, no," he shook his head. "I don't work here. I work for Mr. Vanderveer."

"Would that be Richard Vanderveer?" Jan asked, curiously.

"Yes, ma'am," he replied.

Bingo, Jan said to herself as the elevator door opened.

"What floor for you?" he asked, glancing back at her, ready to push a button.

"Uh…Uh, I'm not sure," she stammered. She started digging in her purse. "I'll look at my key. You go ahead and get your floor."

He pulled a key out and slid it in a slot that read private suites and pushed the top floor button. He looked back at her with a questionable expression.

"That's the floor I need, too." Jan felt relieved that her effort was finally paying off.

On the top floor the door opened and Jan followed the Korean man. When they stepped off the elevator, two tall, husky men dressed in business suits stepped over to greet them. The Korean man reached in his pocket and pulled out what looked like a pass, flashed it at them, and walked by. Trudy followed, but they cut her off.

"Do you have a pass to be on this floor?" one of them asked, eyeing her closely.

"I wasn't aware I needed a pass," Jan replied, unsure of what they were talking about.

"Yes, ma'am, you do."

"Why?" Jan blurted out, watching the Korean man turn the hallway corner and walk out of sight.

"They should've told you at the front desk." The two men separated and stood on each side of her. "We have an official government meeting going on up here and unless you've been cleared by our security team downstairs, this is as far as you get."

Jan huffed a sigh of discontent, shrugged her shoulders and said, "I guess I need to go down and get securitized then. I certainly wouldn't want to upset the Washington elite."

"Sorry, ma'am," he replied, pushing the elevator button.

They stood close to her until she was back on the elevator.

I cannot believe this is happening, Jan thought to herself as she rode the elevator down. *What do I do next?* She exited the elevator, walked across the room, and sat on the sofa, frustrated. *Maybe he'll read my note and call. I have no choice but to sit here and wait. There's nothing else I can do now.*

CHAPTER 27

Two hours later, Jan was startled when her cell phone rang. Seeing that it wasn't Richard Vanderveer calling, she was disappointed. Then, seeing Trudy's number appear, she felt relieved. She'd been concerned about her all day after seeing her melt down earlier.

"Hello," Jan answered in her most pleasant voice, hoping Trudy was in a better mood.

"Hi. What are you doing?"

"I'm… I drove over to Roanoke today to look at some antique furniture I want to put in the guest bedroom." Telling Trudy a little white lie was better than telling her she was sitting in *The Greenbrier* waiting to talk to Richard. After all, she had passed an antique store in Roanoke on her way up and thought about stopping on the way home.

"First of all, I want to apologize for being a jerk this morning. I guess I needed to unload on someone. I've felt awful about it all day."

"Apology accepted. I'm sure I nailed you a few times when you stuck by me while I was going through my troubles. Not that I'm insinuating you're going through a divorce," Jan quickly added.

"I guess time will tell," Trudy said, pensively.

"What've you been doing today?" Jan asked, keeping her eye on the hotel elevator.

"Actually, my day got better, thank goodness. April and I went to Isabella's and picked out colors for the bridesmaids' gowns and had lunch together. I can tell she's almost as emotionally distraught as I am."

"You two have always been close. I think you've become her best friend now that she's leaving the nest."

"I don't know. I'm just hoping she won't hate me for the rest of her life after what I've done to embarrass her."

"Trudy, you've got to get beyond beating yourself up. It's going to work itself out," Jan assured her, trying to sound convincing.

"Well, the reason I called, beyond apologizing, of course, is I've got to get away from here tonight. This phone keeps ringing off the hook with reporters and talk show hosts leaving messages. They want me to tell my side of the story."

"Great. You can stay with me tonight."

"I really thought about the two of us going to the lake. I've already paid for a week's rental at Smith Mountain and I might as well use it some. At least I won't have to listen to the phone ring all night. April is going out with some of her friends for dinner and will be staying with Mother tonight at her house."

"That sounds fine, but I'm not sure when I'll be back in Lynchburg," Jan said.

"I'm in no hurry. I'll put some food together. I thought about fixing baked chicken Parmesan for us tonight."

"You don't have to cook. We can grab something light on the way to the lake."

"No, I need to stay busy. Maybe it'll help keep me from self-destructing again. Besides, I know it's one of your favorites."

"Okay. But I'll get the wine."

"Great. Call me when you get home."

Jan was relieved that Trudy's day had gone better and she had gotten over being angry with herself. She knew her friend would continue to have mood swings until she got things worked out with Kenneth one way or another.

Checking the time, Jan realized she had been waiting for Richard's call for two hours. She'd closely watched Richard's assistant at the concierge stand, knowing he would probably move toward him if he came down to the lobby. Then she would know who Richard was and would seize the opportunity. She just had no clue how to approach him yet.

Suddenly, the Korean man walked briskly toward the elevator corridor. The door opened and a gray-haired, elderly man, followed by a much younger, neatly dressed man, stepped out into the lobby. Immediately, several men approached them from different directions with cameras flashing and shouting questions over each other.

Jan rose from the sofa, somewhat surprised by the attention the two men garnered. She figured it was Richard, who looked younger than she pictured him, accompanied by his father. But she had no idea how to get close enough to get his attention, much less speak with him over all the competing chatter directed toward them by the stalking reporters.

As they crossed the lobby, she stepped in behind the reporters when they started down a long hallway. Two of the hotel concierges stepped in front of the mob of reporters and stopped them at the hallway entrance.

"Okay, that's enough," one of them commanded, holding up both of his hands.

"You can't harass our guests. If the Vanderveers wish to speak with you, that's fine. But it's obvious they don't want to be bothered. So keep your distance or you'll have to leave the premises immediately."

The mob of reporters turned away, mumbling among themselves.

Jan knew this was her last chance to get face to face with Richard. Once the reporters cleared the hallway entrance, she hastily walked with her head high as the concierges glanced her way and let her walk by without incident.

The men had already turned the corner in the long hallway and were out of sight. She kicked off her heels, picked them up and ran.

She turned the corner and met a young man and woman whose kids were skipping all over the hallway. She veered to her far right past them and kept her stride.

Suddenly, someone stepped into her path from the outside patio. Jan collided with a man talking on his cell phone, knocking him to the floor, tumbling over him, her heels flying through the air. What seemed like an eternity lasted only seconds as both sat up, dazed.

With her hands behind her, supporting her, Jan glanced over at the man who hadn't yet said a word.

"Are you okay?" she finally managed to ask.

"Yes, I think so," he replied, pushing himself up slowly.

Jan turned her head and noticed her dress was heaped up around her hips. She yanked the dress down as the neatly dressed stranger extended his hand to help her up. Jan couldn't help but notice how handsome he looked in his black sports jacket, white turtleneck and gray trousers.

"I am so sorry," she offered, regaining her footing, and brushing the wrinkles from her dress.

"No. It's my fault for walking through the door with my cell phone glued to my ear," he said, looking around on the floor to find it.

"Well, I was running, trying to catch up with someone," Jan replied, gathering up her heels. "I should've known better."

"If a hallway cop comes by, we'll just tell him it was both our faults. Maybe we won't get tickets," he suggested, smiling and reaching for his phone.

Jan leaned against the hallway wall while stroking her hair back in place.

The stranger stepped closer. "Are you okay? You look a bit winded."

"I think so," she replied. "Don't let me hold you up. I'm fine and will be on my way as soon as I catch my breath."

He reached for the patio door and opened it. "Come outside and get a breath of fresh air. I'll wait with you for a minute." He held the door open for her.

She yielded, thinking, *Not only is he good-looking but he's also a gentleman.*

Out on the patio, he asked, "Where was this person going that you were trying to catch? I'll go get them for you."

"I'm not sure. I was trying to follow him to see where he was going. It's a long story." She realized that she was not making any sense.

"Anything I can help with?"

"Probably not," she said, shaking her head. "You might have heard about the lost letter story in the news."

His eyes squinted and he smiled a bit. "Just vaguely. What about it?"

"This weekend my friend met a guy up here whom she hadn't seen for thirty-five years." She quickly added, "But only as friends, though. Some Internet blogger snapped a picture of her and this man in a compromising position and her husband, who just came home from Iraq, went ballistic when he saw it in the paper. He left her their daughter is having an engagement party in three days that's possibly going to turn into a big embarrassment for her and she's going to lose her job over it." Catching her breath, she glanced away. "I'm trying to meet this man to see if maybe I can convince him to make a statement to the media about the whole incident in hopes of helping my friend."

She glanced back at the stranger and froze once she recognized who he was. She'd been so convinced that the man she saw earlier was Richard that she had failed to see the resemblance of this stranger and the picture in the paper.

"You must be Jan," he said, scrutinizing her closely.

"And you're Richard!" She felt awkward and unsure of what else to say. "Why didn't you call me?" she blurted out.

"Why didn't Trudy call me if she needed my help? She's got my private number," he snapped back.

"She doesn't know I'm here and..." Jan clenched her hands together, unsure of what she should share with Richard. "She wasn't sure if it would be a good idea to have further contact with you."

"Why? Does she have a reason to feel guilty about seeing me again?"

"No, of course not. Why should she?" Jan responded defensively.

"Maybe it's because she came up here with some motive of leading me on and pretending not to know what happened to us thirty-five years ago," he argued, shifting his stance.

"What do you mean?"

"Well, for starters," Richard spoke harshly, "the whole time she was here, she pretended to know nothing about a check my father gave her mother. She went to her room with the pretense of calling home, left without so much as a goodbye and gave Kwan, my assistant, the old check to give to me without any explanation. And that was after she'd told me how greedy and selfish I was. I think her trip up here to see me was some vindictive way of getting even with me for who knows what reason."

"That's not what happened," Jan began to explain. "She went to her room to call home and an envelope her mother had put in her handbag fell out. That's when she found the check and a note from her mother. She told me she broke down and cried once she realized that the check never had anything to do with you two not having a life together. It was the lost letter that kept you two apart. Nothing more."

"And giving the check back to me was supposed to accomplish what?" he spoke defiantly.

"The check was never intended for you." Jan declared, trying to make Richard understand. "She wrote a note to you, but must've given the check to you by mistake."

"She could've come down and told me about it," Richard snapped back, pointing his thumb back at himself. "I thought we'd done just fine dealing with everything together. What did she have to hide?"

Jan hesitated. She wasn't sure if sharing what Trudy had told her about Richard was the right thing to do. She felt her body tensing and knew that if she couldn't make Richard understand, there was no way he would try to help Trudy. In a frantic voice, she spoke firmly.

"She left because she loves you, Richard, just like you fell for her. Or have you already forgotten? Knowing she could no longer trust herself with you, she was afraid of where her feelings for you might lead. She figured it was best to leave and left you the note explaining why."

"Then, where's the note?" he asked.

"I...I don't know." Jan heard footsteps approaching behind her. Turning around, she saw the elderly man she had tried to catch up with earlier standing behind her. She assumed it was Richard's father.

Richard put his hands in his pockets, and looked out onto the lawn, ignoring her. His father stood quietly on the far side of the patio watching them.

Jan had gotten beyond angry. She wanted to set the record straight for her friend. Nothing else had worked so she figured she had nothing to lose. She took a few steps closer to Richard and spoke.

"Maybe coming up here to see you wasn't the smartest thing for Trudy to do. All she wanted was to try to make things right for herself and a boy she once loved." She moved herself into a position forcing Richard to look directly at her. "She never planned to lead you on or to get emotionally involved again. Her hope was only to meet you, clear up the past, and maybe be friends with you. Regretfully, it turned out differently after she met you. So she had no choice but to leave the way she did."

"Leaving and not telling me why wasn't much of a choice. And what turned out differently after she met me?" Richard asked, staring intently at her.

"Because Trudy had to choose..." she paused, her eyes narrowing, "she chose her family...I'm sorry, Richard." She dropped her gaze and walked away.

Emotionally distraught, Jan couldn't leave fast enough. Their meeting had gone nothing like she'd imagined. She obviously hadn't gotten through to him and she couldn't believe the contempt he held for Trudy. He definitely wasn't the man Trudy described to her. She wondered what Trudy saw in him. When she reached her car, she got in, slammed the door, and sped away.

—

"I didn't mean to intrude on you, Son," Richard's father said, walking over to him.

"No...no, you didn't; it's just a misunderstanding between Trudy and me. She's the girl who...." he hesitated.

His father interrupted. "I know who you're talking about. Hearing that woman speak to you reminded me that I have something that belongs to you." He began checking his coat pockets. Finally, he pulled out an envelope. "I meant to give this to you first thing when we met yesterday, but it slipped my mind." He handed Richard the envelope. "You know my mind just isn't what it used to be."

Richard took the envelope and opened it. Without saying a word, he unfolded the paper, stepped away from his father and began reading.

Richard,

You will always be the boy I once loved with everything in me. Our three summers together are etched on my heart forever.

I know destiny has dealt a devastating blow to us. If it were possible to change time and make things right for us, I surely would. But to give up what I now have, my husband and daughter, is a sacrifice I could never make.

I wish only the best for you and hope someday you'll again have a significant other in your life who will bring you what dreams are made of, as Kenny has done for me.

Kenny is my soul mate, best friend, and lover. I could never imagine my life without him and can only hope to be as good a wife for him as he has been a husband to me. Even though we've been challenged recently, I know in my heart he's the man I want to spend the rest of my life and grow old with.

My wish for you is that you can be as lucky as I and find that special person to spend the rest of your life with.

Forgive me for not saying goodbye. I never was good at it anyway.

Always, Trudy

Richard looked up and saw his father leaning and staring over the patio wall with his hands clasped. He now realized that Trudy had intended to give the check to his father.

"At first I didn't know what the woman who gave me that letter was talking about. She gave the letter to me when I walked into the lobby Monday night and rambled something about how she didn't need my money. She said no amount of money could ever buy her love from anyone." He dropped his eyes. "I think I know what it all means now…I'm sorry, Son."

Richard walked to the edge of the patio, wiped his eyes, and sniffed a couple of times. He stood silent for a moment, staring out at the lawn. Finally, he broke the silence. "Why did you do it?"

His father moved beside him with his hands in his pockets. "To please your grandfather, I had asked her mother to keep her away from the farm. He threatened to cut you out of the family inheritance if you married someone outside the Dutch community. I didn't agree with him, but I wanted to make sure you got your share of the family wealth." He looked at Richard with a sorrowful expression. "I was wrong for doing that. You don't know the torment I went through after you left school and I didn't know where you were for two years."

"But why did you give Mrs. Meyers money to keep Trudy away from me?" Richard asked. His face twisted with emotion.

"Who told you I gave money to keep Trudy away from you?" he asked with a glare.

"Raymond told me."

"Raymond was a ten-year-old-kid and didn't understand what I had done. I gave her mother a check to help fund Trudy's education. When she started working for us at the farm, she'd told me she was going to save the money she earned for college." He shrugged. "I was so impressed with this outgoing and determined young girl and the fact that she was a darn good worker, that I simply gave her money to help with her schooling. She worked for us for three summers and I had already planned to give her scholarship money. I gave money to a lot of kids who worked at the farm. At least to the ones that I thought would amount to something someday. You knew that."

"I forgot about that," Richard admitted. "I think I do remember hearing you and Grandfather talk about it a couple of times."

"Your grandfather was set in his ways, sure enough. But he was always generous and encouraged me to share our wealth with those less fortunate. Whenever I told him some things I did, he was pleased."

"Then the check was never meant to...."

"No," Patrick interrupted, shaking his head vehemently. "I would never have done something like that. I guess I failed to make myself clear when I gave it to her mother."

"Then why didn't you just tell me about all of this?" Richard asked.

"Richard, you didn't speak a word to me for five years. Remember? Besides, I never knew the check was even an issue until now."

Richard was silent for a moment and then he spoke. "Father, I've held this inside of me all my life thinking that you actually paid money to keep Trudy away from me."

"Well, you thought wrong, Son."

Richard stared at his father in silence for a moment. "I can't believe this. I never should've put you through what I did. Can you ever forgive me?"

Patrick laid his hand on Richard's shoulder and with a broken voice said, "Son, I forgave you a long time ago."

Richard hugged his father. They embraced for a moment, patted each other's back and then stepped back.

"Sounds like this Trudy may have herself in a mess."

"Yes, she does and it's my fault."

"Is there anything we can do to help her?"

"I'm not sure. Her husband's left her, and she's got a daughter announcing her engagement in three days. And according to her friend, Jan, she's losing her job, all because I invited her up to see me."

"She probably would like to know you're on her side. Should you get in touch with her?"

"I don't know. I need to do something to help her but I just don't know what. Some of the reporters have been hounding me about us since the photo came out. Maybe I can say something to them to help."

"Well, give it a try, Son," he patted him on the shoulder. "Because of us, she's had more than her share of disappointment in life. Let me know if I can help."

CHAPTER 28

"I wondered where you two were," said Raymond, as he joined Richard and his father on the patio.

"Richard and I kind of got sidetracked and have been out here talking," Patrick explained.

"Did you tell Richard about our plans for the family business?"

"No, Son. It's your decision. You need to tell him."

"Tell me what?" Richard asked, looking curiously at Raymond.

"Father and I are putting the family businesses into a trust with us maintaining control as long as we're able to manage them. We can pass everything down to the next generation if we choose without a lot of tax liabilities."

"That's a good idea."

"Tell him the rest of it," his father urged.

"The trust is going to be set up with both of us, you and I, having equal shares," Raymond added, smiling.

"Why?" Richard asked, surprised. "I've done nothing to help you with the businesses. You've done all the work and have been doing a darn good job at it, I must say."

"Father and I have talked it over. We know you kind of went your own way, but you're family and half of the estate is yours. I think it's the right thing to do."

Richard considered his vast wealth compared to theirs and couldn't believe they thought he was due anything. "I don't deserve any part of it," he declared.

His father stepped between them. "Enough arguing, boys. You can spend the rest of your lives working it out." He patted them both on the back. "Who wants to have dinner with a tired old man?"

"You two go get a table for us," Raymond suggested. "I need to pick up something at the front desk, and I'll catch up."

"Why would Raymond agree to my getting anything from the family estate?" Richard questioned his father after Raymond walked away. "After all, Grandfather cut me out of the inheritance long ago."

They began walking down the hallway toward the dining room. "Your grandfather was born and raised in the old country and lived his life as many before him had done generation after generation. I didn't always agree with him but respected him because he was my father. When he disinherited you, I made up my mind that once the family wealth was in my control, I would make sure you got your share."

"But you and Raymond did all the work," Richard responded.

"I know. And believe it or not, the idea came from Raymond. You've always been his hero. Even today he watches and reads everything about you that he can get his hands on. I'm proud of both of you," Patrick said, with obvious pride.

"But I don't need the money. I've got a fortune many times over."

"Money has nothing to do with it. It's Raymond's way of telling you he wants to be a part of his brother's life." He held his palms up. "It's up to you now, though. He's made the gesture. I hope you'll think about it."

"Of course I'll do it. But why don't you take my share of the inheritance and do with it as you see fit?"

"I'm a tired old man," he chuckled. "All I want to do is complain about what politicians are doing to destroy this world. That and spoil my grandkids." He stopped walking as he entered the restaurant entrance. "Accumulating more wealth means nothing to me anymore. In fact, when I look back at what I've accomplished, the things that mean the most are the ones I chose to give away. And I'm not talking about just money. When I'm dead and gone I'd like to know that people remember me for more than just boxes of plaques and trophies I've accumulated, which won't mean a damn thing to anyone."

They were escorted to a table, and Patrick picked up where he left off. "A man needs to have a purpose in life, Son. For me, it's finding some small way to help others, hoping that it might leave a lasting impression on this old world. Giving is a gift I've come to appreciate even more as I've gotten older and wiser. I guess it was an unspoken lesson your grandfather passed on to me. I hope you'll understand too someday." He smiled as he picked up the menu. "Don't wait until you're an old man like me before you do."

Richard put his hand on his father's arm. He already understood.

CHAPTER 29

Pulling the baked Parmesan chicken from the oven, Trudy said to Jan, "You've been quiet this evening. Is something bothering you?"

"No. I'm just listening to you and glad to see you rebounding. I was really worried about you this morning," Jan responded, raising her eyebrows. She stood at the kitchen counter, folding a napkin for each of them.

"I can't believe I got so upset with you this morning. You're possibly the only friend I'm going to have after this is over," Trudy replied, sticking a fork in the chicken to see if it was done.

"I know what you're going through. I'm here for the duration."

"Pass the plates over and I'll cut a portion for us."

"What did you see in Richard or what made you fall in love with him?" Jan asked.

"Oh, I don't know. A combination of things, I suppose."

"There must've been that one special time or event that bonded you two," Jan stated, as she filled their wineglasses from a bottle of Chalk Hill.

Trudy sucked the sauce off her thumb. "Well, what makes any seventeen-year-old fall in love? For starters, he was really cute, so I'm sure I lusted after him." She snickered. "And I think it was because he was so different from other boys. I don't mean because of his accent or that he was from the Netherlands. He was an outsider, like me. I often found myself the new kid in town because Dad moved Mother and me all over the world to different military bases. That and the fact Richard always talked about his future and was so confident he could become anything he wanted to be." She sat at the table with Jan and continued. "The last summer we spent together, all he talked about was our future and the things we would do and have. It never even bothered him that his father might not like me."

"Did it bother you?" Jan asked.

"Yes, it did, at least a little," she responded with a grimace. "I used to worry about what would happen between Richard and his father if he didn't agree to our getting married. I guess the very thing I was afraid might happen did, and I never knew about it."

"But that wasn't your fault," Jan quickly interjected.

"That's what I keep telling myself." Then, tired of talking about the subject, she said, "Come on. Let's eat before the chicken gets cold."

For the next hour, Jan purposely talked about everything she could think of, trying to keep her friend's mind so busy she wouldn't dwell on her present misfortune. After their meal, Jan began to clean up.

Trudy stood at the window gazing down at the lake reflecting the setting sun on its smooth, glassy surface.

"Why don't you walk down to the lake? I'll finish cleaning up," Jan suggested.

"No. I'll help."

"You did the cooking. I'll do the cleaning," Jan insisted.

"Okay," Trudy agreed. "But come out as soon as you can."

She grabbed an afghan to ward off the cool evening air and walked down to a knoll that overlooked the docks. A few birds flew by and she heard the honking of geese in the background, but no one was in sight. She sat on the grassy knoll with the afghan around her, staring across the lake, thinking of Kenny and how she might convince him that meeting Richard was innocent.

It saddened her to know her already strained marriage would probably end. What kind of work would she look for now, since it seemed inevitable she would lose her job with the Foundation? She watched the sun drop behind the tree-lined ridges as a dark shadow crept across the lake.

Hearing footsteps, Trudy turned. Jan approached with a blanket in hand.

"Want some company?"

"Sure."

"It's beautiful out here," Jan exclaimed, sitting down beside her.

"Yes, it really is."

"Trying to sort it out?" Jan asked, tentatively.

"Yes," Trudy spoke softly.

"Trudy, I know there's little I can say to make you feel better right now. But know I'm going to help you get through this."

Trudy sighed heavily. "I know you are. I just need to get the next couple of days behind me so I can figure out what Kenny is going to do."

"Once Kenneth knows the whole story, he will come around," Jan encouraged her.

"I hope so. But with all the trouble we had before he left, I doubt he'll ever trust me again."

A shadowy dusk had darkened the ridges across the lake that now looked like black silhouettes against a fading sky. Trudy wiped at tears welling in her eyes.

"You okay?" Jan asked.

Knowing Jan was struggling to find some way to comfort her, she swallowed hard and spoke. "I can't believe this is happening. I've spent a year questioning whether Kenny and I might be able to work things out. Now that I'm sure I actually want our marriage to last, this has happened. I'm scared, Jan. I'm scared."

Jan put her arm around Trudy.

227

CHAPTER 30

A spring breeze blew cold air across the water and over the rolling knolls at Smith Mountain Lake. Having had a restless night, Trudy figured a jog would help calm her nerves before going home to face reality. Dressed in her light gray and white workout sweats, she casually jogged along the houses that lined the lakeshore. Focused on nothing but her problems and how she was going to handle April's engagement party, Trudy was unaware that she had broken into a full-fledged sprint. Step after step, her feet pounded the pavement as she circled the development and neared the knoll where she had started jogging.

At a distance she saw a boat sailing on the lake. It broke her concentration, causing her to stop running. Out of breath she almost collapsed. For several moments she strolled around the knoll catching her breath, listening to rippling waves stroke the shoreline and thinking of her and Kenny's plan to live on the lake someday. Now because of her carelessness, it all seemed lost. What could she possibly say or do to win his trust again. She had to find a way. He had to let her explain. But how? Determined, she ran toward the house.

She practically ran in the door of the lake house, startling Jan.

"What's wrong?"

"Do you mind if we leave now to go back to Lynchburg?"

"No, not at all. Are you okay?"

"I've got to find Kenny. One way or another he's going to listen to what I have to say."

"Go shower and dress. I'll pack the car."

Thirty minutes later they were on their way back toward Lynchburg. Jan drove while Trudy dialed April on her cell phone.

"Hello," April answered.

"April. Do you know where your father is staying?"

"He told me he's staying at a cabin on the river. At a Mr. Tucker's place, I think. His son used to work with Dad on some of his fire and rescue training."

"I know him and think I remember how to find his place. Your dad and I went up for a cookout years ago when they were training together."

"Is something wrong?" April asked, concerned.

"No, I just want to find him and talk with him."

There was silence on the phone.

"April...you still there?"

"Do you think it's a good idea to go and find Dad without him knowing you're coming?"

"Maybe I won't have to. Do you have his phone number?"

"I've got the number he called me from."

"Give it to me and I'll try." She fumbled in the glove compartment for paper and a pen. "Okay, I'm ready."

April gave her the number. "Mom, please don't say anything that will cause another argument," she pleaded.

"I'm not calling to start an argument. I'm going to try to convince him to come over to the house and sit down with me so we can have a civil conversation about what happened."

"Do you think he will?"

"I've got to try. Once I let him read Richard's letter, I think he'll at least listen to what I have to say."

"Is there anything I can do?"

"Probably not. Maybe if he comes over you can ride out with Grandmother and give us some time alone to talk."

"We can do that."

"I'll let you know. Thank you, Sweetie."

"Love you, Mom."

"Love you, too."

"Sounds like you might have a plan," Jan readily interjected.

"I've got to get this resolved one way or another. Their party is tomorrow and I want to know where I stand with Kenny. At least I can prepare myself mentally and deal with it, I hope."

"Now this is the Trudy I know. Not letting this get you down and meeting it head on. And knowing you," she smiled, "you'll have this resolved by tonight."

"I can only hope so." She breathed a heavy sigh. "Here goes." She dialed Kenny's number.

"This is Kenny. I'm not available to take your call. Please leave a message."

Trudy hung up. "He didn't answer."

"Maybe he doesn't have his phone with him."

"Maybe he saw my number come up and didn't answer," Trudy added. She stared out the window in silence.

—

Entering Lynchburg, she saw a grocery store.

"Stop here at Kroger's. I need to pick up some dip mixes and sauces for the party tomorrow. It'll save me a trip later."

They parked and went into Kroger's together.

Jan motioned to Trudy. "I'm going over to the bakery to pick up a couple of items. I'll meet you up front."

"I'll be in aisle four. It shouldn't take but a couple of minutes."

Trudy started up the aisle but stopped when she saw Mrs. Winkler in front of her, pushing a buggy. *I don't need to deal with her right now. I'll slip back and maybe she won't see me.* Trudy stepped back to the end of the aisle and ducked behind the end cap, peeking to make sure Mrs. Winkler didn't turn around.

"Well, Trudy Quinn, how are you?"

The voice startled Trudy. She turned around and found Pam Shively, a teacher she'd taught with at Lynchburg Middle School.

"Hello, Pam," she answered, reluctantly.

"How have you been? I don't think I've seen you since you retired."

"I've been busy with the Foundation and working with some of the other non-profits. Doing what most retired people do, I guess." She shrugged.

"You look great. How are Kenneth and that beautiful daughter of yours?"

"Kenny just got back from Iraq and April is getting engaged." Trudy could imagine how much she had been talked about in her circle of used-to-be friends since the photo of her and Richard was plastered on the front page of the paper. She wanted nothing more than to escape the conversation. "I would love to chat but I've got someone waiting on me."

"Oh, don't let me hold you up. But please come by the school and visit sometime."

"I can't wait. Bye." Trudy exclaimed, walking away, relieved.

She went to the mixes and picked up a couple pouches of dry Hidden Valley Ranch and Italian Dressing. She saw that Knorr's had a spinach dip and turned it over to read the directions.

Mrs. Winkler's voice caught her attention from the aisle over. Then she heard Pam chime in on the conversation. She ignored them until she heard her name mentioned.

"I just saw Trudy Quinn a minute ago in front of the store," Pam spoke.

"I don't know how she has the nerve to show her face in public," Mrs. Winkler said. "After what she did to her husband.

And the scene she caused at one of our Foundation meetings. Oh! It was so embarrassing."

"I heard Kenneth left her."

"Do you blame him?"

Trudy tensed up.

"How long do you think this had been going on?"

"Probably ever since Kenneth's been away. And there's no telling how many flings she's had with other men while he was gone. He was lucky to find out about this one."

Trudy bit her lip and clenched her fist to keep from losing control.

"You really think there were more affairs?"

"Oh. Let me tell you. You work with Trudy for a while and you'll find out just how cunning that woman can be," Mrs. Winkler boasted. "I bet she could write a handbook on how to skip out on your husband."

Pam laughed. "It would become a best seller, I'm sure."

That did it! Trudy was going over to give them a piece of her mind. She started around the corner. Suddenly, she felt someone tugging at her arm.

"I just saw Kenneth checking out up front and leaving!" Jan whispered excitedly.

"Hold these." Trudy practically threw the mixes at Jan. She sprinted toward the front, but Kenneth had left the store. She ran outside and looked around. She didn't see him so she walked into the parking lot looking for his truck.

She spotted it pulling out into the traffic. She ran toward it waving her arms, but he kept going. She watched him drive into the street and stood there wondering if he had seen her but refused to stop. Frustrated, she went back into the store and met Jan.

"No luck, huh?" Jan was standing in the express lane.

"He was already pulling out before I got close. I'm not sure whether he saw me or not."

Trudy stepped up to the cashier to pay.

"The total is $8.43."

Trudy dug in her purse and handed her a ten-dollar bill. When she glanced up, she saw Pam and Mrs. Winkler in the lane over, gawking at her. She had forgotten about them.

"What are you going to do this evening?" Jan asked.

"I'm going to start writing a book I've been thinking about," she said, intentionally loud.

"Really. What's it about."

"It's going to be a step-by-step handbook on how to become a cunning woman so she can have every man eating out of her hand." She was amused at how quickly Pam and Mrs. Winkler turned away.

Leaving the store, Jan asked. "What was that about?"

"I'll tell you on the way home."

CHAPTER 31

As soon as Trudy got home, she sat down with Jan, April, and her mother at the kitchen table to finalize their plans for the party the next day. She tried focusing on festive details, but thoughts of Kenneth distracted her. Finally, she gave up when she started repeating herself while everyone stared silently.

She had an idea.

"April, I need to borrow your phone."

"Sure. But what's wrong with the wall phone here in the kitchen?"

"Kenny wouldn't answer when I tried calling him on my cell earlier. He probably won't answer seeing the number of our house phone either."

April pulled her cell phone from her purse and handed it to Trudy. "Mom, please be nice if he answers."

"Believe me," she said shaking her head, "starting a confrontation is the last thing on my mind. I think if I can get him to listen, just for a minute, I can convince him to come over and talk to me."

She looked at the phone and glanced back up at everyone silently watching. "I'm going out to the porch to make the call." She rose from her chair, stepped toward the door then glanced back. "Wish me luck."

She sat on the porch for a moment gathering her thoughts. All morning she'd rehearsed what she would say to him if she got a chance. Hesitantly, she dialed his number.

"Hello, April," he answered.

"Kenneth…this is Trudy."

There was silence.

"Please don't hang up on me," she quickly said, her voice breaking.

Still, there was silence.

"I want to…really need to talk to you…. I feel so bad about what happened." She sniffled, getting choked up. "Please listen to what I have to say. Give me a chance." Talking to him was more difficult than she'd anticipated.

Finally, he spoke gently, "How are you?"

"Miserable…and missing you."

"Trudy. Why?"

"I had every intention of telling you about Richard, our meeting and everything."

"Why didn't you?"

She cleared her throat and spoke easier. "Remember I told you I wanted you to read the letter and then I wanted to tell you more about Richard? You went to the shower and I came in and… and you fell asleep. I thought it could wait till later. I had no idea that picture had ever been taken."

She could hear his heavy sigh over the phone.

"Trudy, that picture wasn't two friends posing for a reunion shot."

"Kenny. I know how bad it looked. All I'm asking is that you give me a chance to explain. If you won't do it for me, then do it for April. Her heart is breaking, and she's counting on us tomorrow."

"Is this Vanderveer guy still in the picture?"

"No, I'll never see him again. Seeing him was a mistake and we didn't exactly part on good terms. It was nothing more than dinner and a few hours together, anyway. If you'll come over and read the letter and let me explain, I think you'll understand."

There was silence. Trudy glanced up and saw April standing, listening.

"Give me the phone," April pleaded.

Trudy handed it to her.

"Dad, why won't you give Mom a chance to explain what happened between her and this Vanderveer guy? she asked.

"April?"

"You're never going to have a chance to work this out unless you two sit down together," she emphasized firmly, and "talk about it."

"April!" He spoke angrily. "Coming home after being away for a year and finding out my wife, your mother, had slipped off to see an old boyfriend is just more than I want to deal with now."

"She didn't slip off!" April responded angrily. "She told me and grandmother about him before she left to meet with him. If it hadn't been for that lost letter showing up and making national news, we wouldn't be having this conversation."

"April, I'm sorry you had to get caught up in the middle of all of this."

"Dad, I'm your daughter. Remember? I'm supposed to e in the middle of it. And I would really like to know my mother and father were at least making an effort to work this out before my engagement party." She glanced over at her mother staring solemnly. "Is that asking too much?"

She could hear her dad sighing.

"Dad, at least Mom's making an effort, you're not."

"Well, let me think about it…and tell your mother I might drop by later this evening."

"Thank you for making an effort. That's all I'm asking for."

"I'm not promising anything though."

"I understand. But I know you're trying."

"Okay," he added and hung up.

Aril looked at her mother. "Dad's coming over after awhile."

Trudy stared at her daughter, amazed. April had been able to take charge and accomplished something she hadn't been able to do. To talk her dad into listening to what she had to say. She definitely took after her grandmother, Trudy thought.

April looked at her mother wryly. "Mom, will you be okay?"

"I think so."

"What are you going to tell Dad when he comes?"

"The truth."

"What if he doesn't believe what you tell him about Richard?"

"Then I don't know what else to do," she nodded.

"It may take awhile for him to get over this"

"I don't care how long it takes. If he gives me a chance, I'm going to win him back."

"You really want things to work out with Dad now, don't you?"

"Yes, April, I do," she said firmly. "I love your father and if he loves me, then we will get through this somehow."

Jan came out to the porch." Didn't you say we needed to pick up the cakes at the bakery after three today?"

"Yes. What time is it?" Trudy asked.

"Two-thirty."

"I guess I need to go."

"Let us go do it," April volunteered. "I promised to take Grandmother over to her house this evening. She packed up all her whatnots to take back home. You know her. When she's ready to do something she's not going to rest until it's done. We can stop by the bakery on the way back."

"And it will give you some time to think about what you want to say to Kenneth," Jan agreed. "He may come by while we're gone and you two can have time alone."

"I...I guess I should." She thought about changing clothes and looking her best for Kenny if he came over. "Okay."

Trudy watched them drive away and was relieved to have time alone for a while. She went upstairs to her bedroom closet and looked through her clothes. She pulled out a short, summer white and flowery Lily Pulitzer dress, one of Kenneth's favorites that showed off her legs and shapely figure. Whenever she wore it, he always whistled and complimented her on how sexy she looked. She put on a pair of sailboat earrings and a multicolored stone necklace he had given her, and ended with a light blush to her face. Gazing in the mirror, she was pleased with the way she looked and tried to hide the anxiety written all over her face.

She busied herself doing mindless chores around the house until she got tired of glancing at the clock that now read three-thirty. Feeling antsy, she picked up a *Southern Living* magazine and went to the back porch to read, hoping it would calm her nerves.

—

Kenneth sat on the back porch of the cabin watching and listening to the river stream over the rock formations. Whenever his mind was burdened or he had a lot to think about or just needed some quiet time, sitting and looking out over a lake or watching the river flow calmed his mind. Maybe that was why he loved the lake so much.

Ever since Trudy had called, he'd been thinking about her, about them. What would life mean without her? He couldn't sleep, he didn't want to be around anyone, and the thought of losing her forever haunted him. The three months they'd been separated before he went to Iraq were the most miserable he had ever lived through and now he dealt with those same insecure feelings again. The year in Iraq had been taxing but at least he had hoped they would reconcile once he returned home. Now he sat aimlessly, trying to block out his thoughts of losing her permanently and he couldn't comprehend it. He had to do something.

Maybe he did jump to conclusions about the picture and should have given her a chance to explain. After all, she had tried before they got distracted and fell asleep. One thing was certain: He didn't want to return to the same hopeless lifestyle he'd lived while they were separated.

Guilt overtook his thoughts. He was troubled over how he had acted and treated Trudy. Yearning to see her, he wanted to tell her he was sorry for ever doubting her. He would go and ask her for forgiveness and promise he would never raise his voice at her again. Maybe they could have the new beginning they sought.

Kenneth checked his watch. It was three-thirty. He jumped up, went inside for a quick shower and put on a pair of gray casual dress slacks instead of his usual jeans. He found the new light-green silk Ralph Lauren shirt Trudy had bought him, instead of his usual cotton shirt with the sleeves rolled up. He dashed on a spray of Ralph Lauren aftershave, Trudy's favorite. He rushed out to his truck and sped off with one thing on his mind. To win back the heart of the woman he loved.

Stopping by Doyle's Florist on the way, he picked up a dozen roses, wrote her a message on a small card and placed it in the roses.

⁓

Just as Trudy sat down on the back porch the doorbell rang. She sprang to her feet and walked through the house, stopping briefly on her way to the front door to glance in the mirror in the off-kitchen bathroom to make sure she still looked okay. When she opened it, she froze. Her heart palpitated at the sight of him standing on the porch, his hands in his pockets and a slight grin on his face.

Trudy tried to speak but couldn't. Her stare met his gaze. She glanced away, feeling awkward and unsure of what to say.

Finally, Richard broke the silence. "I was passing through and realized I never got a chance to tell you goodbye."

"I...I guess I owe you an apology," Trudy finally stammered, meeting his gaze in what seemed like a moment of eternity.

"No. It was me. I'm sorry I acted the way I did. I didn't realize how much I had upset you."

"No. That's not what it was," she added, shifting to a casual stance. "When I went to the room, I found a note my mother had put in my handbag." She wasn't sure if she should tell him about the check she found. "I got emotional and fell apart and figured maybe I shouldn't see you again."

"I understand all that now. And you would think by now we could figure out how to get a letter to each other."

"What do you mean?"

"You gave Kwan the check to give to me, and the note you wrote you gave to my father." A smile crept across his face.

Trudy's eyes popped wide as she put her hands to her face. "I can't believe I did that. No wonder your father looked so confused."

"If I had gotten that note from you, I would've followed you all the way to Lynchburg that night. Now when I think about where we were headed, you did the right thing."

Trudy felt awkward standing in the doorway. "Maybe you can come in or we can go to the back porch and talk."

"I would like to if you have a few minutes."

She glanced down the street and saw Kwan standing beside a black Town Car. "What about Kwan?"

"He's fine. I only have a few minutes and need to catch a flight shortly."

They walked through the house to the back porch and sat in chairs opposite each other. Richard glanced around at the huge back yard accentuated with bushes and clusters of flowers blooming and the landscaped patio Trudy had groomed picture perfect.

"You have a cozy place here."

"It's home," Trudy replied, imagining the mansions he owned. She relaxed once her curiosity prevailed. "When did you find out about the mix-up?"

"Not until your friend came up yesterday."

"Who came up?" Trudy asked, surprised.

"Jan came up to see me. But I was angry and refused to meet her. For some unknown reason, we managed to collide in a hallway. She told me what she was trying to do for you."

"I can't believe she didn't tell me."

"Oh, believe me, it wasn't pleasant at all. I told her off and she kind of let me have it, too," he snickered. "She is one heck of a friend. I hope she'll accept my apology."

"She will once she knows what happened, I'm sure."

"My father overheard us and remembered the note you had given him. When I read it I understood why you left."

"I'm so sorry, Richard."

"Neither of us did anything to be sorry about," he adamantly responded. "I found out it never was about the check my father gave your mother anyway. Turns out that Father was so impressed with you when you worked on the farm, he simply gave you scholarship money. He did it for a lot of the young people who worked for them on the farm back then and I had forgotten about it. Raymond simply didn't understand when he heard father talking about giving money to your mother."

Trudy stared and listened in awe.

"Father wants you to know he's sorry about the misunderstanding with the check and what he did and if there's anything he can do to help now, let him know."

"I appreciate his concern, but it's behind us. I guess we just need to let it go."

"If I hadn't been so independent and the renegade son back then, leaving school and going into hiding, maybe I would've found out what happened. It could have been different for us."

She could hear resentment in his voice.

"No. Don't go there. You weren't to blame for what happened. I think my mother put it best. It was destiny that kept us apart." She held back tears. "That and a lost letter."

"I asked Father to forgive me once I found out what had happened. I've lived my whole life holding something against him that never happened. There's probably a lot I missed by not letting him be a part of my life."

"You still have time, don't you?"

"Maybe you're right."

"Trudy," Richard's tone turned serious. "I came down to see what I could do to help. I'm leaving the country shortly but wanted to know if there's anything I can do to help straighten this out for you before I leave. Jan mentioned Kenneth has left you and it's possible you're going to lose your job over this."

"It doesn't look good on the job thing. But Kenny is coming over later and I hope we can talk about what happened." Trudy stared out in the distance as she spoke. "Richard, I don't know what you could possibly say or do to make a difference. I don't think there's anything anybody can do." She glanced back. "It's got to be settled between Kenny and me."

Kenneth drove up and noticed the Town Car parked on the street in front of his house. Thinking nothing of it, he parked across the street and with a dozen roses in his hand walked up the driveway to his house. The door was slightly open so he walked in and through the house looking for Trudy, wanting to surprise her. The kitchen door was open and he heard voices coming from the back porch. He walked through the kitchen, intending to step outside but stopped when he heard a man's voice. He stood silent and listened.

"Trudy, I want you to know your coming to see me has changed my life. Because of you, I have a whole new purpose and outlook on life."

"It's meant a lot to me, too." Trudy replied.

"I wish we could've found each other years earlier."

"I do, too."

"Have you ever told Kenneth about us?"

"No. I never told him. There was no reason to, until now."

Kenneth stared through the window and saw Trudy dressed in her favorite summer dress, the one he had told her made her look sexy. She wore the earrings and necklace he had given her. Richard's back was to him.

"How do you think he will take it?" Richard went on.

"I'm not sure. The only thing I can do is tell him the truth. He's been hurt over this and I don't want him dealing with it anymore. Hopefully, he'll understand and forgive me."

"Do you want me to tell him about us? Man to man makes it easier to understand sometimes."

"No, it might make things worse. He needs to hear it from me. I need to tell him in my own way."

Kenneth tensed up; listening to their words infuriated him. He wrestled with his thoughts about what he should do. He wanted to go outside and confront them and tear this man apart for stealing his wife but thought better of it. She wasn't worth the trouble he would bring on himself, he reasoned, knowing it would solve nothing.

She must have planned for him to be here. She's even got herself all dressed up for him. And she just told me that she would never see him again. They planned this, hoping I would come by.

I'm not going to fall into this trap. I'm not going to give her the pleasure of playing me into whatever little scheme they have. To hell with her, I deserve better!

His insides knotted up and his stomach churned. He felt nauseated. Quickly, he walked out of the kitchen, down the hallway and out the front door clutching the roses in his fist so hard the stems snapped and roses fell, trailing across the porch, the sidewalk, and lawn as he made his way to the street. Walking faster, ignoring the short man leaning on the Town Car, he crossed the street, threw what was left of the roses in the gutter and got into his truck. He wiped tears welling in his eyes and paused momentarily. *Why is Trudy doing this to me? No man deserves to be treated this way. Was it her way of getting even with me for the way I'd treated her at work? Why couldn't she have been honest with me and told me when I'd first gotten home? I could've handled it. I would've been a man about it and moved on.*

Anguished and raging inside, he turned the ignition and gunned the engine.

April had noticed her dad sitting in his truck on the street as she drove into the driveway with Jan and her grandmother. She waved but he never looked her way as his truck sped off, tires squealing, leaving a trail of smoke.

April jumped out of her car, assuming his meeting with her mother must not have gone well. She sprinted toward the house with Jan and her grandmother close behind and burst through the door yelling. "Mom...Mom!"

Trudy met her in the kitchen. "What's wrong?" she asked, looking bewildered.

"What happened between you and Dad?"

"Nothing. I haven't seen your dad!"

"He was sitting in his truck in front of the house when I drove up. He looked upset and sped off."

Jan walked into the kitchen holding several broken rose buds in her hand. "These were strewn all over the porch, sidewalk and yard."

Trudy stood aghast, lifting her hands to her face and turning pale. "Oh, God, he was here!"

"What's wrong?" April dreaded asking.

All fell quiet when Richard walked in from the back porch.

CHAPTER 32

Richard introduced himself, since Trudy was too emotional to speak. He explained that he had only come down to mend his feelings with Trudy since they'd parted on what he thought were unfriendly terms and to see if there was anything he could do to help her mend her relationship with Kenneth. He apologized over and over to Jan for how he'd treated her at The Greenbrier.

April called and called her dad on her cell phone but couldn't get an answer. Finally, April and Jan decided to drive over to the cabin where Kenneth was staying. Trudy struggled through giving them directions. Mrs. Meyers went to the back porch and sat quietly.

A few minutes later after everything calmed down, Richard checked the time. "I have to leave if I'm going to catch a flight out tonight." He strolled over to Trudy, who now stood quietly at the kitchen counter, staring out through the window at nothing. "I had no idea, Trudy. My timing was incredibly bad. All I've been is a bad omen to you."

"It's not your fault. We were having problems before," she tried to sound convincing.

"I never would have invited you to come see me if I had known this would happen."

"It was my choice, not yours. It will work itself out one way or another. Please don't feel guilty." She glanced down. "Maybe it was supposed to happen this way."

"But if I can help…."

"There's nothing you can do, Richard," she quickly but adamantly responded.

"Then I guess I should leave."

She walked with him out of the house and strolled down to his car, where Kwan stood waiting. Richard turned to her.

"This is not the time to be bringing this up again. But what I said at The Greenbrier that night, I meant every word of it. The offer was sincere then, now, and later if need be."

Trudy forced a smile. "Oh, Richard, what am I going to do with you? I'll always love the boy I once knew, played with, and grew up with. But you and I could never make it. You know that. Besides, Kenny is the man for me and I love him. I guess we just have too much vested in each other." She frowned, knowing Richard would understand that. "If it doesn't happen then I'll…" she choked back a sniffle. She was about to burst out crying so she reached up and hugged Richard without saying another word.

Richard must have seen how emotional she was, because he didn't press her. "Maybe I'll call sometime and check on you."

She only nodded and pressed her lips together while tears streamed down her face.

Richard got into the car. He and Trudy stared at each other through the window as Kwan drove away.

When Trudy turned around she spotted a small envelope at her feet. She picked it up and saw her name on it. She pulled the card from it and read.

Trudy,

Words could never say how sorry I am for acting the way I have. I should never have doubted the most beautiful woman I've ever known. If you will forgive me and give us another chance, I will love you more and more every day. I promise.

Love, Kenny.

Trudy broke down and began sobbing.

~

Richard had ridden a couple of blocks away.

"Kwan, stop the car."

"We won't make the flight, Mr. Vanderveer."

"It doesn't matter. We're not going anywhere."

~

April and Jan returned home to report they'd had no luck. Jan eventually left and everyone purposely stayed out of each other's way. Trudy went to her bedroom, shut the door and cried her heart out. Finally, glancing at the clock two hours later, she came out knowing she had to talk to April and her mother.

April was sitting at her desk working when she walked into her room. Trudy sat on the edge of her bed, searching April's eyes and saw that she had been crying, too.

"I'm sorry," was all Trudy could manage to say.

"We need to call off the party tomorrow," April stated firmly. "There's no way you or Dad will be in any shape to entertain anyone."

Trudy nodded. "Maybe you're right. But you have a lot of Matthew's family coming over for the first time. Some of them have already traveled from out of town. I don't want to spoil the day for you and Matthew because of...." she paused.

April returned a hard stare.

"I had no idea Richard was coming down. If I had known, I would've never allowed it." Trudy had to make her daughter believe her.

"What did Dad hear you two talking about to get so angry?"

"I'm not sure. We were just talking casually about what had happened and you came in. Richard was only trying to help. Nothing more."

"What do we need to do about tomorrow?"

"I've been thinking about that," Trudy sighed. "Before we cancel the party, call your dad. If he doesn't answer, leave him a message. Tell him he's got to let you know whether he's coming to the party or not because, if he isn't, we need to call a lot of people first thing in the morning and call it off."

— ⁓ —

Trudy found her mother sitting on the back porch in the dark.

"Mother, are you okay?" she asked, taking a seat across from her. Once her eyes adjusted to the darkness she made out the handful of tissues her mother held.

"Trudy, I am so sorry," she murmured.

"Mother, you've done nothing to be sorry for."

"If I had told you what happened thirty-five years ago, none of this would've ever happened."

"You don't know that." Trudy tried to sound convincing. "What could you or I have done differently back then that would have changed anything?"

"It just hurts me to see you hurting all over again," her mother replied, wiping at her cheek with a tissue.

Trudy moved over to a chair beside her mother and placed her hand over her mother's hand. "Mom, listen to me. Neither you nor I did anything wrong thirty-five years ago or now. I'll admit the timing of that letter getting to me...and Richard being in the country...and Kenny and I having problems...." she hesitated.

"Oh, Trudy. What are we going to do?" her mother sniffled.

Hearing her mother cry reminded Trudy of the nights she'd lain awake listening to her cry years ago. "I don't know. This evening I thought I had it worked out...Now I'm not sure." Her heart aching at the thought of how upset everyone was, she began to cry.

CHAPTER 33

The alarm went off. Trudy rolled over to glance at the clock through burning eyes. Seven o'clock. She remembered glancing at the clock at one-thirty last night and hadn't slept since. Her eyes were dry and the lashes stuck together from crying so much.

She eased out of bed once she smelled the aroma of coffee and cinnamon rolls. Putting her hands over her face she thought about all she'd have to face today and beyond. Her marriage was over and there was nothing she could do about it.

Would Kenneth still come to the party or would she and April have to spend hours on the phones calling and canceling with everyone. April had acted and spoke defensively with her last night. Would her relationship with her daughter be forever strained because of what had happened? Her life had fallen apart in less than two weeks and she had no one to blame but herself. She wanted to curl up in bed and stay there all day but knew she had to face the consequences.

She strolled downstairs and found her mother and April seated at the kitchen table. They watched her come into the room but said nothing. She poured a cup of coffee, turned around and took a sip, her eyes studying them over the rim.

"Sleep well?" April broke the silence.

"No, not really."

"Dad left me a voice mail this morning at four o'clock."

"I guess he didn't sleep either...What did he say about the party?"

"He said..." April hesitated, as if rethinking her words, "he's going to come to the party but doesn't want to stay any longer than he has to." She dropped her gaze. "He said he would come over around three o'clock."

"I understand." It was all Trudy could think to say. "Since your dad thinks this is just your engagement party maybe we ought to forget the welcome home thing. Maybe call his friends outside of our immediate families and tell them the welcome-home party is off."

"No!" April snapped back. "I planned this party for us to try to be a family and I'm not going to change it."

"I'm not trying to change your mind. I just don't know what to expect."

"Maybe if you keep your boyfriend away, it might be okay!" April shot back. She got up and briskly walked away.

"That's not fair!" Trudy shouted. "You don't talk to me that way. You have no idea what happened!"

"Let her go," Mrs. Meyers said, softly.

Trudy turned and stared.

"She has a right to be upset. You both need some time to calm down."

Trudy sat down, flustered.

"I wish we didn't have to go through this, Trudy. But it's been to us, so let's make the best of it and do what we have to do. What can I help do?"

"Jan's coming over in about an hour and we'll start decorating. We'll prep the fresh foods this afternoon. The caterers will set up the tables and chairs on the back lawn for the barbeque and be ready to serve by four."

For the rest of the morning, Trudy helped Jan and April decorate the house. The front had a welcome home theme for Kenneth, with a banner placed above the porch that read

Welcome Home Kenneth. Yellow balloons were tied to all the porch posts, trees and bushes in the yard.

The back lawn had a wedding theme. White tablecloths covered two tables that held flower arrangements and hors d'oeuvres. On another table were April's and Matthew's pictures from the time they were babies until now. Some of them were pictures of them taken together several years ago as friends long before their romance began. And a small banner lettered in silver read *The Journey.* Trudy tried to stay helpful and not do anything more to antagonize April. Knowing their relationship would likely suffer for a long time bothered her.

Finally, after all was done, Mrs. Meyers had prepared a quick lunch for them. They sat on the back porch nibbling fresh-cut veggies and a pasta salad. After lunch and an hour of calm and casual conversation, everyone went to the kitchen to prep the fresh vegetables and dips.

April worked beside her mother mixing dips. Trudy took a spoon and dipped it into the spinach dip and held it for her to sample.

"Hmm, that's good."

"I never tried it before. Thought it would be something different."

April turned to her mother. "I want to apologize for what I said this morning. I know it hurt you."

"We're all under a lot of pressure now. I understand, Sweetie."

"Maybe so but that was a low blow."

"We're all guilty of saying things we shouldn't at times. I just want you to remember one thing today for me. This day is about you. Regardless of what goes on between your dad and me, we both love you and want this to be a celebration you'll remember forever. We're not going to let anybody steal this moment in time from you."

Trudy glanced over at Jan and saw her smiling.

The time was now two o'clock and they had an hour before guests would arrive. The caterers were already busy setting up tables and chairs for the barbeque. Everyone decided to get dressed for the parties.

Trudy looked through her closet for several minutes and couldn't decide what to wear. Finally, she settled on a long, sleeveless pale-blue dress and flat shoes since she would be outside. Her nerves were getting the best of her. She went downstairs and sat on the sofa, trying to convince herself that everything would be okay. It was three o'clock and guests should start arriving any minute. She had counted on Kenny being here.

———

Kenny had been so upset the night before that he had driven over to his mother and dad's home in Boones Mill, Virginia. He had to talk to someone—anyone who would listen. They insisted he spend the night with them because he was so upset. He talked while they listened without commenting. His mother suggested he still go to the party for April's sake and urged him to find some time afterwards to talk to Trudy alone. His father said he had trouble believing Trudy would do something so out of character.

Kenneth left Boones Mill at one o'clock and arrived in Lynchburg an hour later. He knew he would be running close but needed a change of clothes before going over to the party, so he drove up to the cabin. The black Town Car was sitting in the driveway. He swore, thought about driving off again, then parked and stepped out.

The doors on the Town Car opened and out stepped the short uniformed man and a man whose face was familiar from dozens of newspaper articles.

Richard stepped around the car toward him. "Mr. Quinn, my name is Richard Vanderveer. I would like a word with you, please."

Kenneth's temper flared. "I know who you are. I have nothing to say to you and don't intend to waste my time listening to anything you have to say. You know where the road is. Find it!"

"I didn't come here to upset you, or start anything. But I insist you hear the truth about what went on between Trudy and me."

Kenneth stepped toward him with his fists balled. "What is it you can't understand about leaving, Mister?"

Kwan stepped between them. "Mr. Quinn. You don't want to go there," he warned, standing tense.

Kenneth scowled at the little man but backed up. Whether or not the man was some kind of martial arts expert, he didn't want to fight a stranger.

Richard put up both hands. "Give me ten minutes of your time. If you still feel the same way, I'll call Kwan off and you can beat me to a pulp."

Kenneth paused for a moment. Maybe it wouldn't hurt to hear his side of the story. I would like to know what kind of spin he puts on it. "Come on," he motioned. "We'll go to the back porch. I only have a few minutes, so make it quick."

Richard sat in a rocker and leaned forward, his elbows resting on his knees and hands clasped. Looking out over the river he reminisced and started speaking. "It was the summer of 1973 when I first met Trudy. My father and grandfather hired her at the request of one of our neighbors. In fact, I think she was the only girl they ever hired. My brother, Raymond, and I lived in The Netherlands but came to the States every summer to work and learn about one of the family businesses my grandfather and his brother had started over here.

"Being shy and not used to the customs of folks here in the Shenandoah Valley, Raymond and I kind of kept our distance from the other kids. One day some of the young guys my age started picking on us over the way we dressed and made fun of our accents. Being outsiders and naïve, we just stood there and took it. Trudy overheard them and told them off. She called them rednecks," he snickered. "I thought Raymond and I were going to have to fight our way out of that one, but Trudy stood her ground and backed all of them down. She was one spirited young lady…. Gosh, she was beautiful," he nodded, not losing his train of thought.

Mesmerized, Kenneth relaxed and listened as Richard continued his narrative.

—

Trudy glanced at her watch. It was three-fifty and Kenneth hadn't shown up yet. In the past thirty minutes almost a hundred people had arrived. It seemed everyone she'd invited was coming. Was it to honestly celebrate with the family? Or because she was now the most gossiped about celebrity in Lynchburg? She tried to put that thought out of her mind.

Jan walked up with a glass of wine. "You doing okay?"

"After three more of those," Trudy pointed, "I'll let you know."

Jan handed the wine to her. "Everyone is settling in and finding some way to entertain themselves."

"They're probably waiting for the grand finale."

"Trudy, you need to relax. You're getting yourself worked up."

Trudy glanced at her watch again. "It's four o'clock. Kenny was supposed to be here an hour ago." She saw Kenneth's mother and father drive up. "Let me go see if they know where he is. I hope they're not bringing bad news." She walked away.

Jan went over to the table of pictures where April and Matthew stood talking to guests. Once they were alone, she asked, "You don't think your dad would skip out on the party do you?"

"No," April said. "If he wasn't coming he would have called me by now."

"Help me keep an eye on your mother. She's really getting stressed."

"This is not like Dad. Something must have happened."

"Maybe you should call and see where he is?"

April went inside the house and called. No one answered. She tried again but got the same response. Worried, she went looking for her mother.

Jan saw April come out of the house in a hurry walking toward her mother. She followed.

"I just spoke to Kenneth's mom and dad," Trudy told them. "They said he spent the night with them and left their house around one today planning to come to the party. He's had plenty of time to get here."

"It's four-fifteen now," April reminded her.

They looked around at the hundred plus people standing around, waiting for the food to be served and the celebration to formally start.

"What should we do?" Jan asked, frowning. "The caterer has the barbeque ready to serve."

Trudy downed what was left of her wine and handed the glass to Jan. She looked at April, whose color had drained from her face. "April, I'm sorry. Your father and I both have let you down. I have to say something because it's obvious your dad isn't coming. I'll try not to make a complete ass out of myself."

Trudy walked to the middle of the guests, composed herself, and spoke loudly. "May I have your attention, please?" Standing tense with her hands clasped tightly, she waited for all the chatter to stop. "First, I would like to thank all of you for coming today—whether for Kenny's welcome home party or April's special announcement, which we will share with you later, or just for some of the best barbeque south of the Mason-Dixon Line."

Everyone chuckled.

She took a deep breath, dreading what she had to say next. "Kenneth was supposed to be here earlier and apparently he's been delayed." She cleared her voice and continued. "As most of you are aware, Kenny and I were having problems and were separated before he went to Iraq. When he got back, we…" she felt someone tugging at her arm, and turned to see Jan.

"You need to go to the front yard. Your mother said Richard just drove up. He's standing in the yard."

Trudy's eyes widened. She felt a lump swell in her throat and a wave of panic breaking over her. "Oh no," she breathed. "No." She gasped for breath. If she ignored Richard, he might come back here and she couldn't deal with that scene.

"Excuse me for a minute please. I…I'll be right back," she stammered.

She ran around the house through the side yard and found Richard and Kwan leaning on the Town Car in front of her house.

Suddenly, Kenneth drove into the driveway, fast, skidding to a halt. He jumped out of his truck and briskly walked toward her.

"Oh Lord," she whispered. This was her worst nightmare.

Unsure of how to react, her heart fluttering, body tense, she suddenly realized she stood between the two men in her life. She glanced back toward the house and saw Jan and April staring at the three of them, aghast at what they, too, must have assumed would be a violent confrontation. Trudy braced herself while adrenaline fed her panic.

She glanced at Richard, hoping for some kind of explanation, but his expression remained unreadable. Watching Kenneth approach her, she tried to read his mood. Her insides knotted as he walked the last few steps toward her. Unsure of his intentions, she raised her hands between them. He reached out to gently place his hands on her arms. Unsure of how to react and unable to speak, she gazed into his eyes for any clue of his intention.

"I am so sorry. Will you ever forgive me?" Kenny calmly asked.

Trudy stood silent and motionless, staring at him. What was going on?

"I understand now," Kenneth said, speaking soothingly. "I know what happened and why you went to see him. It's all right."

She opened her mouth to speak but words eluded her. Overwhelmed, she still couldn't comprehend what he expected of her.

Kenny reached up and held her face with his fingers. "I should never have doubted you and put you through this. Please forgive me," he repeated, gazing into her eyes then kissing her on the forehead. "I love you, Trudy Quinn."

"What...what changed your mind?" Trudy finally managed.

Kenneth looked toward Richard. "He did. When I went back to the cabin this afternoon to get ready to come over, he was sitting in the driveway waiting for me. Apparently, he slept in his car last night waiting for me and had driven back and forth today trying to catch me at home. That's why I'm late. Richard told me all about you two in the seventies. I was skeptical at first, but he told me everything. I now understand why you two needed to see each other again."

"I never meant to hide anything from you. All I did was meet him for dinner and we...." her voice trailed off.

"It's okay," Kenny assured her. "He told me everything about you two meeting and showed me the letter."

Trudy glanced over at Richard and then back to Kenny. "I don't understand. I have the letter. It's thirty-five years old. What could it possibly say to change your mind?"

"No." He shook his head. "He showed me the note you wrote and left him. It said it all. I never gave you a chance to explain. Can you ever forgive me?" He waited for her response.

Reaching up and clasping his neck, Trudy's eyes teared up. Overwhelmed with relief, she stepped closer and his arms engulfed her. When she glanced up he kissed her.

Suddenly, loud clapping and cheering broke their concentration. Trudy stepped back. The guests had all followed her around the house and stood quietly observing them from a distance. She felt embarrassed but stood holding onto Kenneth, smiling.

Jan looked over at April and grinned. "April, I hate to tell you this... but I think your mother just stole your party."

"Isn't it wonderful?" April gasped, wiping at her eyes, holding onto Matthew.

"I probably need to say something," Kenneth suggested. "Let's see if we can get this party back on track."

Holding Trudy's hand, Kenneth held up his other to quiet the now lively crowd. Once he had their attention, he began. "I realize I'm late and you're doubtless hungry so I'll make this brief. While I was away this past year a lot has happened and I've had a lot of time to think. As most of you were aware, Trudy and I were separated when I left to go to Iraq. That was a mistake I've had to live with for more than a year." He squeezed her hand. "When I came home she made every attempt to welcome me back, with open arms and open heart so we could be a family again. Instead of welcoming the chance she offered, I acted like a jerk and chose not to trust her over what some blogger had posted about her in a newspaper." He looked at Trudy. "I have made so many mistakes and don't know where to start. But one thing is certain; I have missed you every hour of every day and never want to go through that again. If you'll give us another chance, I'll try to be the man you want and deserve. Trudy, I want to love you and spend the rest of my life with you, if you'll have me back."

Teary-eyed, Trudy stepped closer and hugged him tightly.

Everyone clapped again as some of the guys in the crowd whistled and hooted.

"Also, I would like for you to meet Richard Vanderveer," he turned and pointed, "my friend and Trudy's pen pal from the seventies who decided they should meet when the lost letter story made news. I'm sure everyone saw the picture in the paper and I want you to rest assured that it was nothing more than two friends taking a bike ride at the worst possible time, getting caught in a downpour and having to get out of their wet clothes before going to their rooms. Now that I've put most of this to rest, I smell barbeque. Let's eat."

"Thank you," Trudy whispered to him. While everyone walked away she suggested, "I should speak to Richard."

Kenneth agreed. "I invited him to come over after I saw how serious he was, wanting me and you to work things out. Invite him and his driver to stay and eat with us. I'll go mingle with the crowd and get them started. Come around when you're ready."

Trudy walked down to the car where Richard stood with a slight grin on his face. Kwan stood at his side but walked away as she approached. Standing with her hands clasped, she wasn't sure what to say.

"I assume everything is back to normal?" Richard opted for her.

"I never expected this or for you to go find Kenneth."

"When I left yesterday and saw how badly you were hurting, it tore my heart apart. There was no way I was going to leave the States until I had this resolved. As you know by now, I'm pretty persistent when I want something." He grinned. "I remembered the address you gave April so I wrote it down and found him."

"He said you slept in your car last night waiting for him."

He chuckled. "The things I do for you, Trudy. Thirty-five years ago I lived in a homeless shelter for weeks, and now you have me sleeping in the back of a car all night."

"I'm sorry."

"I would do it over and over again for you and you know it."

Trudy glanced away, then looked back at him. "You're going to stay and eat with us, aren't you?"

"I would like to, but I look a bit rough. I haven't had a shower or shave, and my clothes are wrinkled and...."

She cut him off. "And that's no excuse. You and Kwan go wash up in the bathrooms and change clothes if you want to. You're having dinner with us."

"Okay, I am a bit hungry."

For the next hour everyone ate barbeque or nibbled on hors d'oeuvres and congratulated Matthew and April. Kenneth captivated an audience by telling war stories, and Richard cornered the caterers and tried to convince them to start a chain of barbeque restaurants. He was giving them step-by-step instructions on how to do it. Trudy mingled with the other women for a while. When she finally got a break, she came over and sat beside Jan.

"I now know what it was that held you and Kenneth together," Jan acknowledged.

Trudy looked at her.

"You two never quit loving each other. It's that simple. When you separated, you didn't do it for yourselves. It was a sacrifice you made for each other. You did it because you both were hurting and wanted to give each other room to find out what the other wanted."

"You know, Jan, I think you could be on to something."

"I don't know many marriages that would have ever lasted through this. You and Kenneth have something special. One in a million, I'd say."

Kenneth came over. "I think a toast to Matthew and April would be appropriate."

"Go ahead," Trudy agreed.

"No, from both of us. I'll do one for Matthew and you do one for April."

"I wouldn't know what to say."

"You'll do fine. Just follow your heart is what I think your mother would say."

Kenneth took a fork and tapped his glass until all fell quiet. "Trudy and I would like to propose a toast to our engaged couple."

Everyone reached for a beverage.

"First Matthew. I want you to know how proud we are knowing you'll soon be our son, too. April, you chose well. I do intend, of course, to have a few man-to-man talks with you, Matthew, before you take my daughter's hand. So be ready."

Everyone chuckled.

"Also, a bit of advice, knowing you probably won't need it until the honeymoon wears off twenty years or so later." Kenneth grinned. "Always listen to her. No matter how small or uneventful it seems, listen to every word she says. If it's important enough for her to talk about, it's important enough for you to listen." Kenneth dropped his gaze to Trudy. "And when you get a chance to go with her on a weekend excursion, to a convention or somewhere she has to be to cover a story that means absolutely nothing to you, go with her anyway. Be a part of her journey. Because, at the end of the day when you two are alone, dining in a restaurant in some far away place you've never been before, nothing else will matter. Just look across the table and you'll see this most beautiful woman who chose to be your wife. Remember love works both ways. Do your part and it will last forever."

Kenneth sat down and Trudy rose. How could she ever say anything as wonderful as that? She cleared her voice and spoke.

"April. Every mother wants her princess to marry a prince. You did well. But more importantly, every mother wants her daughter to marry someone she loves and can love forever.

"My advice is, if you ever get a chance to sit in the back of a boat, in the middle of a lake at midnight, wrapped in a blanket and drinking coffee to stay warm because Matthew asks you to go fishing with him, do it." She dropped her gaze down to Kenneth. "Let him know that you want to be a part of his life, and what's important to him is also important to you. Seek to experience the things he likes to do and share with him the things you like. And every chance you get to spend time together away from work and chores that you've gotten acclimated to, do it. Be spontaneous and plan new adventures and go to new places often. And at the end of the day when you're cuddled, you'll realize nothing else matters but being with the prince who won your heart, loving him because you know he loves you."

Everyone stood and clapped, and one person shouted, "Great advice!"

Once the crowd settled down, Trudy glanced around for Richard but didn't see him.

Jan leaned over and whispered, "He got up and left while you were talking."

Trudy turned to Kenneth. "I'll be back," and left hurriedly.

She sprinted to the front of the house just as Richard was getting into the car. She hollered. He hesitated while she walked toward the car.

"You're leaving without saying goodbye?"

He frowned. "You and I were never good with goodbyes, were we?"

"Maybe we need to get beyond that."

"Trudy," he spoke softly. "Did we bridge those thirty-five years just to say goodbye?"

"I hope not," she replied.

An expression of bewilderment crept across his face.

"I mean," she began in a somber voice, "for thirty-five years I've held onto a memory of the boy I first loved. Every time I read something about you or saw your name mentioned in the news, it made me think back to our time together. But it always left me with a question. What happened? I've finally found the answer, Richard." She paused. "Now when I hear or read about you, I will have nothing but wonderful thoughts about…the boy I loved."

"And you'll always be a part of me, too, Trudy. I just wish we could have put that time in a bottle and kept it forever."

"Our time together was special, but we both have a lot of special moments in our lives with other people. You had your time with Iona and now your daughters. My time is still with Kenny and a wonderful daughter."

"Yes, I can see you and Kenneth have something special. It reminded me of a girl I loved a long time ago."

"I would like to know if I could see or hear from you again sometime?"

Richard nodded. "I guess at this time in our lives, being friends makes more sense."

"I would like that."

"Trudy, you were always good for me, you know," Richard said with a hint of nostalgia.

She nodded, feeling the emotions beginning to rise within her again.

Richard stepped away from the car and she reached out and hugged him. Without saying another word, he got into the car. Trudy stood and watched until the Town Car was driven out of sight.

"Where's Richard?"

"He had to leave," Trudy answered, turning around to face Kenneth.

"Was something wrong?"

"No… it was time for him to go." *And for me to let go.*

"Is everything okay?" Kenneth asked, noticing her eyes.

"Everything's fine now," she responded, leaning into him.

CHAPTER 34

After finishing up her two-mile walk on the treadmill, Trudy checked the time. It was eight-thirty. She was looking forward to leaving Lynchburg and going back to the lake for a couple of days, a much-needed respite after the turbulent week she'd had. The parties had gone well but she was exhausted.

Stopping by the laundry room, Trudy grabbed an armful of towels. As soon as she stepped into the kitchen, the telephone rang.

"Good morning, Jan," she answered, holding the towels.

"Do you have your television on?" Jan blurted out.

"No, I've been on the treadmill."

"Quick! Turn it on. They're getting ready to talk about Richard this morning. I'll call you later."

Trudy picked up the remote. She started to turn the television on but hesitated when Kenny walked in. He took the remote from her hand, planted a kiss on the side of her face, and pressed the remote button on.

One of the two news anchors was speaking. Kenny nuzzled up to Trudy but stopped when Richard's name was mentioned.

They both listened as the news commentators continued.

"Over the weekend, Vanderveer Enterprise and the Winchester Fruit Company came to an agreement over the hostile offer Vanderveer had previously made for the company," the commentator said. *"It appears that instead of an outright buyout, Vanderveer Enterprise will take only a 10 percent stake in Winchester. In return, Vanderveer*

has agreed to use their domestic and international marketing efforts to enhance sales opportunities for both companies."

"On a separate note," the other commentator began, *"Richard Vanderveer has purchased the business assets of his father and brother, Raymond, and merged them into Vanderveer Enterprise, the company he started from scratch in the seventies. He also announced that he would step down as president and his brother would replace him.*

"When asked why he was stepping aside, Richard explained that Raymond would bring fresh talent and new ideas to Vanderveer Enterprise and that he wanted to spend time with his aging father and find new purposes and challenges for his life.

"Also, a question was raised about a photo that has been hyped in the news lately of him and a lady named Trudy Quinn taken at The Greenbrier Resort. He said they met while working on his grandfather's farm in the Shenandoah Valley back in the seventies and remained pen pals for a while after he went back home to The Netherlands. After the lost letter made the news, he contacted her and they met for old time's sake. A blogger's photo of them after they were caught in a downpour sent rumors flying, although they are no more than friends. He reports that Mrs. Quinn and her husband had a great laugh about it."

"Wow! This guy never ceases to amaze me," the commentator added. *"One of the wealthiest men in the world, and he's just going to walk away from his empire at fifty-four years old. Wouldn't you like to know what drives him?"*

Kenny started nuzzling up to her again.

"I need to put these towels in the closet so we can go to the lake and meet the realtor." She slid from his grasp. "Or, we can go get in the shower."

Kenneth grinned and, as he was about to answer, the telephone rang.

Trudy reached for it when she saw her office number on it.

"Good morning, Trudy," Jennifer answered sheepishly.

"What's wrong?" Trudy asked, almost afraid to know.

"Mrs. Winkler and Dr. Waleski wanted me to call and see if you were at home today and, if so, could you come by the office for a few minutes this morning?"

"Why?"

"The board has a called meeting for this morning."

"Did Mrs. Winkler have something to do with this?" Trudy asked.

"Yes," she replied.

"I...I guess I could. I'm headed out of town for a couple of days, but I'll stop on the way out if that works." Trudy had a bad feeling about this. "Is the whole board there?"

"Yes. I'll tell them you'll stop by shortly," Jennifer quickly replied.

Trudy knew that Jennifer must not have been alone in her office due to the formal response she got. She also knew no board meetings were scheduled this week. If a special meeting had been called, it was to deal with the publicity she had stirred up.

She handed the towels to Kenneth, looked up at him, and asked, "Can you put these away so I can get showered and dressed? I need to stop by the office on our way so I can get fired."

An hour later, they drove into the parking lot at her office. Trudy had listened to Kenneth apologize over and over about the scene he had caused at her office until she felt he had endured enough. She wanted to put his mind at ease.

"Kenny, it's not your fault. I'm the one who put myself in a compromising position, and now I have to pay for it." She wanted to put a positive spin on everything. "Besides, we're back together and April is happy. Two out of three isn't bad."

She hurriedly walked to the door, thinking how she was going to gracefully handle losing her job. After all, she agreed with what Jan had said days ago. She'd done more to get scholarship money for students to go to college than all the other board members combined. Knowing that she would no longer be able to interact with and seek help for them bothered her as she walked into the office. However, she knew Mrs. Winkler looked forward to seeing her leave. She would surely be nominated as the new president and program director.

Inside the office, she received a nod and a sobering look from Jennifer. She returned the nod as she walked by, letting her know that she knew what to expect. In the conference room she found Mrs. Winkler and Dr. Waleski, along with four other board members seated at the long, hardwood table.

Everyone was cordial and spoke to her. Mrs. Winkler sat motionless, except for her eyes stalking Trudy's every move like a cat about to pounce on its prey.

Trudy took the seat at the middle of the table opposite Mrs. Winkler. She braced herself for what was about to happen. *They must have already voted me out and Mrs. Winkler in as president. Getting fired is bad enough, but why did they elect to let Mrs. Winkler have the privilege of doing it? They know there's always been friction between us.*

Glaring at her, Mrs. Winkler began. "Trudy, as you know, as members of this board, we have always held ourselves to the highest standard of conduct."

Trudy felt a knot gnawing at her insides.

"Protecting our board's integrity and trust has to be of utmost importance. Therefore, we find it necessary that a change...."

A knock at the door interrupted her. Everyone looked up as Jennifer stepped in with the FedEx deliveryman. "Excuse me, but there's a priority package with special instructions for Dr. Waleski," she said, apologetically.

"Can it not wait?" Mrs. Winkler barked, clearly annoyed by the intrusion.

"No, ma'am, it can't," the deliveryman replied. "I have instructions to witness you opening and reading it, and the papers need to be signed and returned immediately. If you don't comply, I have instructions to take the package back and have it locked in our safe."

"The safe," Dr. Waleski replied, turning around. "Uh... then I suppose we need to read it."

Taking the parcel and ripping the tab, Dr. Waleski pulled out the contents. There was a silver folder with several pages and a small envelope in it. He began to read as the others sat quietly watching his expression change as he mumbled to himself. Finally, he turned to the deliveryman and said, "I guess I need to sign documents for you to return."

The deliveryman gave him several sheets of paper to sign and excused himself as Jennifer ushered him out.

Mrs. Winkler quickly began where she left off, almost as if she had frozen in time. "About the change we were discussing this board has unanimously agreed and voted this morning...."

Dr. Waleski elbowed her abruptly, causing her to pause and look at him sharply. Pushing a letter in front of her, he uttered, "Read this."

"What Mrs. Winkler is saying, Trudy," Dr. Waleski interjected, "is our board understands what you've had to deal with personally and want you to know that we stand with you whole-heartedly as you deal with your personal matters and wish only the best outcome for you and your family." He glanced around at all the other board members who looked stunned. "And I guess I need to read to you this letter we just received." Mrs. Winkler leaned back in her chair, a scornful look on her face, her thin lips pressed together. He took the letter from her, cleared his throat, and read.

To the Board Members of the FEW Foundation:

This morning I have escrowed and am ready to deposit into the Further Education for Women Foundation bank account a check for two million dollars as a contribution to help students further their education and to cover any other expenses deemed necessary by Mrs.

Trudy Quinn. This contribution becomes valid only if Mrs. Trudy Quinn remains president and program director of the Foundation and has sole discretion over how this monetary gift is to be appropriated. If the board is able to comply with my wishes, then simply sign the enclosed documents and the monetary gift will be deposited immediately. You may call your bank and find this gift ready to be placed into your account without further stipulation if the board is compliant with my stated wishes.

Anonymous Giver

Dr. Waleski pushed across the table toward Trudy an envelope that had come inside the parcel with the letter. It was addressed to Trudy and marked confidential. "Maybe this will clear it up, at least for you." He glanced around the room. "I move that we adjourn this meeting and everything we discussed and voted on this morning be stricken from the record."

"I second," someone quickly added.

Everyone except Mrs. Winkler wished Trudy the best. She had made a beeline for the door without speaking to anyone.

Alone, Trudy sat reflecting on what had just happened. This has to have been Richard's doing. But did he give the Foundation the gift out of genuine concern to help students, or was it just another gesture to manipulate the board with his money to save her job? He knew what it meant to her. After hearing the news anchors talk about him that morning, she genuinely felt that he was changing his priorities to become a better person. She opened the envelope, pulled a note out, and began to read.

Trudy,

I'm sorry I didn't recognize you when I met you in the hotel lobby. I was confused and it took me awhile to put it all together and, with the help of your friend, I finally did.

What I did to separate you and Richard was wrong. I know that I set in motion the events that changed your lives and futures forever. I humbly ask for your forgiveness.

I lost my son for years and even though we eventually reunited and tolerated each other, it wasn't until we spoke recently that everything came to light and was finally cleared up between us. Richard and I will be spending a lot of my remaining years together, all because of you.

I never meant for the money I gave your mother to be anything more than a scholarship for one of the hardest working young people I ever had the privilege to know. I guess I didn't relate that to your mother well enough.

One of my fondest pastimes as an old man is to see how many lives I can touch and help before I leave this world. My hope is that you will be able to help hundreds of students with this gift, and I wish I could watch every one of them progress along the way. Maybe you can do it for me.

I recently told both of my sons how proud I am of them. I am equally proud of you for your accomplishments in life, many of which I have recently learned. If ever you need help with anything, please call upon me. It would be a privilege to work with you.

Because of you, Richard is a better man, and I now have my son back. Words will never be enough to thank you for what you've done for my family. Please accept my gift to your Foundation as a small token of my appreciation.

Sincerely,
Patrick Vanderveer

Trudy wiped at tears streaming from her eyes. Hearing a sound, she glanced up and saw Jennifer and Kenny staring intently from the doorway.

"Are you okay?" Kenneth asked.

She walked to the door as Kenneth and Jennifer watched anxiously.

She smiled at them and gushed, "I keep my job."

They all smiled and shared a group hug.

"And, Jennifer…" Trudy turned toward her, "before I come back to work on Wednesday, pick out a chair and desk that you like, wallpaper or paint for the office and decide whether you want wood or tile for the floor here in the foyer."

"Won't the expenditures have to be approved by the board first?" Jennifer cautiously asked.

"They already have been. Now, close the office and take a couple of days off with pay. You deserve it. Just put a sign on the door that says, 'Closed until Thursday as approved by Trudy Quinn.' And that isn't open for discussion." She punctuated her order with a smile.

⁓

Kenneth drove their Dodge Ram pickup along US 29 south of Lynchburg toward Smith Mountain Lake. Trudy's cell phone rang. Glancing at it, she saw that April was calling. Knowing that she and Matthew were in Florida spending time with his grandparents to tell them of their engagement plans, she thought something must be wrong and answered quickly.

"Hello, April. What's wrong?"

"Nothing's wrong," she excitedly said. "I just got a call from *The Business Journal International* wanting me to do an exclusive interview with someone for them."

"Why are they calling you? You're on vacation, for heaven's sake. How did they even get your cell number?"

"They called the news office and spoke to my editor. When they told him what they wanted, he thought it was important enough for them to call me."

"And who would be that important?" Trudy asked.

"It's Richard. He's agreed to give an exclusive interview about his life's story and how he succeeded in business," she shouted. "It's going to get world-wide distribution and be written in five different languages."

"And there's no need for me to guess to whom he has chosen to give the interview," Trudy said, rolling her eyes and laughing.

"Yes. It's me!" April screamed.

"I'm happy for you," Trudy replied. "But remember where you are and who you're with. There'll be plenty of time for gloating when you get home."

"Mom, I can't wait to get started."

"April, you need to forget about work. Do fun stuff while you're in Orlando and get to know Matthew's grandparents. There's plenty of time for work when you get home."

"I will, Mother. But I know I won't be able to sleep until I'm home and can get started."

"I love you, Sweetie. Remember what I said."

Trudy hung up the phone and noticed Kenny snickering.

"Just what do you find funny?"

"She kind of takes after her mother, doesn't she?"

"What do you mean?" Trudy asked, narrowing her eyes at him.

"She's on vacation with the boy she's going to marry and already she can't wait to get back home and go to work. Poor Matthew," Kenny said, shaking his head at the thought.

"That's not fair." Trudy tapped him on the shoulder. "She's just excited and wanted to share some good news with her mother."

Turning onto Route 40 at Gretna, Kenneth asked, "How many houses are we looking at today?"

"There are five I've chosen for us to see."

"I can't wait."

"Have you put some thought into the new boat you want to buy?"

"I've been thinking that maybe we would buy a used pontoon boat instead of a new one."

"Why would you want to do that?"

"Then maybe we could buy a used bass boat, too. There's a lot of good fishing in that lake, you know."

"We could. But with the money we would save, we could build a backyard patio with an outdoor stone grill with lots of landscaping. The pictures of those houses I looked at have great backyard views of the lake."

"Sounds like we've got to compromise here," Kenneth replied.

"Great. Which boat do you want to give up?"

"Well, that's not quite the kind of compromising I had in mind."

"Then, what do you have in mind?" Trudy asked, shifting her eyes at him.

"Oh...I thought about dinner over candlelight, a little wine and maybe a couple of slow dances to start with." He grinned.

"Hmm...I think I could get into that. You aren't trying to persuade me to give in on the boat idea are you?"

"What makes you think I would do something like that?"

Trudy reached over and laid her hand in his. "Kenneth," she spoke softly.

Calling him by his first name, Kenneth knew Trudy was serious. He glanced over at her staring solemnly at him.

"I'm glad you didn't give up on me. I really want this to work out for us."

"No, Trudy...We didn't give up." He squeezed her hand. "We didn't give up on us. And we are going to find a way to make this work out...together"

ACKNOWLEDGMENTS

Over the past year as I wrote this 80,000 word love story, I could only imagine how the book would look in final print, bound gracefully by a beautiful cover. Then I realized that to my supportive team of friends the finished book would prove to be just as exciting for them as the journey was for me. I must share some of my thoughts and sincere thanks to them for their help and belief in me.

To Jackie, my wife, for your encouragement and patience while I crafted this story by stealing minutes and sometimes hours from our busy lives to bring this story to life.

To my author friend, C. Shea Lamone. I loved the emails I received from you every couple of days while you were reading and editing my first draft of *The Lost Letter*. Not only were they motivating, but your sincere encouragement could only have come from a true friend.

To Susan Elzy, friend and author. You always challenged me with your thoughts and willingness to share ideas on how to make a good story great. I know you were always trying to bring out the best in me. Your friendship and encouragement are invaluable.

To Katherine Johnson, author. Your editing and suggestions to make *The Lost Letter* a tighter and more meaningful read is just what the story needed.

To Madison Turner for so graciously allowing me to use your photo to give *The Lost Letter* a more meaningful beginning. It brings the cover and my words to life. Kudos!

To Joyce Maddox and Amy Moore of Warwick House Publishing. Thank you for your steadfast patience as I fumbled through several revisions of this story before bringing it to the final version. Your efforts to dot my i's and cross t's to make my words flow smoother is much appreciated. You have made yet another dream come true for me. The beautiful cover you created is just what this novel needed for completion. I can't thank you enough!

To Greenbrier Resort, a favorite destination for Jackie and me, which inspired the setting where much of this love story unfolds.

OTHER NOVELS
BY
DONNIE STEVENS

Old Man Missing

Sara Williams, a career nurse and single parent, finds her life turned upside down when her aging widowed father turns up missing. A drama unfolds as the local sheriff leads a rescue effort, knowing that every passing hour lessens the chance of survival for her father in the rugged Blue Ridge Mountains of Floyd County, Virginia.

Inn In Abingdon

Spencer Aubreys finds more than inspiration when visiting this most famous inn in Abingdon, Virginia. Captivated by a young girl he meets (Katherine Broadwater), Spencer believes her to be from the local theater because of her old-fashioned dress, southern dialect, and a story she weaves about herself and a boy named Sam that took place during the Civil War when the inn was used as a hospital for wounded soldiers.

Available on Amazon

Made in the USA
Charleston, SC
24 October 2013